The Team That Wouldn'
Everything seems to be
They lose every game
and Alex rally together
of the team but things seem to go from bad to worse. It looks as if United may be relegated from the Sunday Junior League. But nobody can say Darton United aren't keen. At last the three friends have an idea which gives the team a break.

Mascot
When Damian Tennant is chosen by his local Football League club to be their mascot, it's the happiest day of his life. But his selection causes jealousy among his team-mates and threatens his captaincy of Sunday League side Darton United. He must prove to them he's the leader they need. But how?

Soccer Special
Miles likes football more than anything else in the world – he'd rather be an international centre-forward than become the editor of the *Daily Express*. But there's no chance of that. Miles is forbidden to play and contents himself with writing and producing his own newspaper, *Soccer Special*. That is, until he takes a chance and plays goalie in a school match and survives the challenge of an assault course against his rival, Geoff Leyland. Surely this must prove that he's fit enough to play football now . . .

Also by Michael Hardcastle

Football Stories
Away From Home
The Away Team
Free Kick
Half a Team
In the Net
Mascot
Soccer Special
The Team That Wouldn't Give In
United!

Motocross Stories
Fast From the Gate
The Green Machine
Roar to Victory
Tiger of the Track

Riding Stories
The Saturday Horse
The Switch Horse

Advantage Miss Jackson (A Tennis Story)

Michael Hardcastle regularly visits schools and libraries around the country. If you would like to meet him, please ask your teacher or librarian to write to the address below:

MAMMOTH Press Office
38 Hans Crescent
London SW1X 0LZ

MICHAEL HARDCASTLE

MASCOT

THE TEAM THAT WOULDN'T GIVE IN

MASCOT

SOCCER SPECIAL

MAMMOTH

First published in Great Britain as three separate volumes:

The Team That Wouldn't Give In
First published in 1984 by Methuen Children's Books Ltd
Magnet paperback edition published 1985
Published 1990 by Mammoth

Mascot
First published in 1987 by Methuen Children's Books Ltd
Magnet paperback edition published 1989
Published 1991 by Mammoth

Soccer Special
First published in 1978 by Methuen Children's Books Ltd
Magnet paperback edition published 1978
Published 1990 by Mammoth

This omnibus edition published 1992
by Mammoth, an imprint of Reed Consumer Books Ltd
Michelin House, 81 Fulham Road, London SW3 6RB
and Auckland, Melbourne, Singapore and Toronto

ISBN 0 7497 1317 8

A CIP catalogue record for this title
is available from the British Library

Printed in Great Britain
by Cox & Wyman Ltd, Reading, Berkshire

Contents

THE TEAM THAT WOULDN'T GIVE IN

One

Damian Tennant watched glumly as the opposition's centre-forward danced back to the centre circle in triumph after scoring his side's seventh goal. He ought, he knew, to feel anger at the way the goal had been given away by feeble defensive work. Instead, he simply felt numb. Behind Damian the goalkeeper, Davey Scott, fished the ball out of the net and punted it towards the middle. He exchanged shrugs with one of his full-backs but neither of them bothered to say anything. With another big defeat looming for Darton United there really was nothing to say that hadn't been said before, many times.

Almost reluctantly, Damian made his way back to his midfield position for the kick-off. There were times when he wished he'd never heard of Darton United or pulled on the team's green shirt and yellow shorts. This was definitely one of those times. With only ten minutes of normal time remaining there was no way in which United were going to salvage anything from this Sunday League match. Admittedly, a couple of goals from their strikers would help to improve the score-line; but, from the way they were playing, it was obvious that the forwards were in no better form than the defenders. So far Burnwood's goalkeeper hadn't had a real shot to save. It was no wonder that, at one point, a supporter had given him an anorak to help keep out the cold.

When the ball was pushed back to him, Damian decided to try a solo run. Probably he wouldn't get very far but at least it was a *positive* move and he would get some satisfaction out of it. He was supposed to remain in midfield to help try and stem the red tide of Burnwood attackers. However, he'd heard a top professional say on television that the best way to defend was to start an attack. Now Damian was about to put that theory to the test.

With the ball at his feet he suddenly surged forward and over the halfway line, taking two opponents completely by surprise because so far they'd seen him only as a central defender. Damian cleverly changed pace to outwit a Burnwood midfielder and the ease with which he made progress was an inspiration. Neil Dallimore, United's gangling striker, galloped ahead of him with renewed purpose and then called for a pass.

In United's three previous attacks – and there had been only three in the entire game – Neil had contrived to miss an open goal when a defender miskicked and then almost sprain an ankle when he clumsily trod on the ball. United could well do without another Dallimore disaster. So Damian ignored his team-mate and swerved towards the touch-line, thus surprising friend and foe alike. Nobody had the foggiest idea what he would do next, Damian included. On the other hand, he was still in possession of the ball and by now well into Burnwood's half of the field. At long last, he felt, Darton United were putting the opposition under real pressure.

Apart from Neil, no other Darton player had moved up in support of his run, as Damian quickly realised. That wasn't surprising. He and his team-mates were accustomed to spending the majority of their time penned in their own half with only the occasional fierce clearance to relieve the pressure on them. Fortunately, though, the Burnwood side were as baffled as everyone else by Damian's move and so no one tried very hard to tackle him. The nearest players simply stood off, waiting to see what he might try next.

The game appeared to have come to a halt. Then, losing patience, the Burnwood skipper rushed across, determined to get the ball. Skilfully, Damian dragged the ball to one side and out of anyone else's reach before darting forward again. As another opponent lumbered across his path, Damian deliberately flicked the ball against the boy's legs and then collected the rebound. The trick that he'd long wanted to try had worked beautifully. Suddenly, he was on the edge of the penalty area.

'It's a one-two, Neil!' he yelled to the willowy centre-forward as he drove the ball across to him and prayed for the instant return pass.

For once Dallimore played to instructions and the ball came back into Damian's stride. After so much inactivity the goalkeeper couldn't make up his mind whether to come out or stay on his line. It didn't matter to Damian what the goalie did. With the net in his sights he hit the ball with all the power he could muster.

Unhappily for him and United, his foot was under the ball rather than over it at the moment of contact. So his shot was still rising as it zoomed over the crossbar. The goalie's anxious expression switched to a smile.

'That was a really good move and a good run of yours, son,' murmured the referee as he came alongside Damian while running backwards to the halfway line. 'Next time just try to keep your shot down and then you'll really hit the net.'

Those were the most encouraging words about his football that Damian had heard for a very long time. He could sense that the referee wasn't just speaking out of sympathy for Darton's present plight.

For a few moments the United players responded to Damian's enterprise by tackling and kicking with zest. Billy Sandford, their skipper, actually began to yell enthusiastically to drive them on to new heights. For once he delivered a splendid pass for Neil to run on to – and Neil, still glowing from his successful exchange with Damian, tried to repeat that feat. This time, however, a Burnwood ball-winner felled Damian instantly with a crunching tackle.

That tackle was from behind and while the offender's name went into the referee's notebook the victim painfully got to his feet. It was one of those moments when Damian wished they had a trainer with a magic sponge (or, at the very least, a pain-killing spray). But even Mr Sandford, who liked to describe himself as United's manager, wasn't present at this match. Ruefully Damian rolled down his sock and rubbed at the scraped skin above the ankle. Undoubtedly he'd have a champion bruise there in the morning.

The game had to go on and he hurried to take up a good position for the free kick on the edge of the box. Billy, trying to assume a professional air as he realised the importance of this kick, flighted the ball well.

Although not very tall, Damian had strong legs and could jump to an impressive height. With his back to the goal, he met the ball perfectly with his forehead and glanced it down and sideways. Dallimore was in just the right position to take advantage of such skill. But instead of picking his spot and coolly slotting the ball into the net he lunged at it

- and inevitably ballooned it over the bar to the delight of the stationary Burnwood defenders.

After that rare burst of excitement among the attacking force, the United team were unable to achieve any more near-triumphs before the final whistle shrilled. In fact, with thirty seconds to go they conceded another goal when Davey Scott fumbled a hopeful long shot from a Burnwood player who was simply trying his luck. Davey immediately explained to his pal, the full-back, that he'd let the shot in only because his hands were so cold because he hadn't touched the ball for a long time! 'Rotten luck, Davey,' said the full-back, and meant it.

Nonetheless, several of the team appeared quite cheerful as they trooped off the field and Billy Sandford was one of them.

'Well, not too bad this week, lads,' he announced to all who would listen to him. 'Kept the opposition down to single figures, didn't we? So we must have played twice as well as we did last week against Warton. Pity Dad wasn't here to watch us in this form.'

'Away scouting for some new players, was he?' asked Davey Scott with a perfectly straight face. 'I mean, we could do with one or two, couldn't we?'

'Like a new goalkeeper, for instance,' suggested Neil Dallimore, grinning at his own humour.

'Look, you weren't so good when you were the goalie, Dally-a-lot,' Davey snapped back at him. 'You were in goal when we had that record defeat

and so you were the one that let in 28 goals. That's twice as bad as I've ever done. So you have no room at all to talk.'

By the time they reached the dressing-room the argument between the pair of them was still going strong. Davey was repeatedly pointing out that if the so-called strikers would score a few then he, as goalkeeper, wouldn't be under so much pressure throughout the match – and, also, the score-line would look a lot better. Anyway, he concluded forcefully, it would soon be his turn to figure in the forward line and he would show them all how to find the net.

'I think we should stop changing our goalkeeper at regular intervals,' Damian announced as he sat on the bench to remove his boots and socks. He leaned his back against the wooden wall and looked around at his team-mates to see what effect his words were having on each of them. 'You can't take any pride in a job if you know it's not going to last very long. In this team I don't think we've got enough pride - and we ought to have *lots* of pride.'

'You're only saying that because it'll soon be your turn to go in goal,' Davey said quickly, his eyes narrowing with worry. 'Anyway, why should *you* miss out on the toughest job in the team?'

'I'm not trying to miss out on anything,' was the mild reply. 'But, in any case, I'm not really tall enough to be in goal, so – '

'Height doesn't really matter,' Davey cut in anxiously. 'It's all about being willing to throw yourself around and dive in among the flying boots where it hurts. That's what counts. My dad's mate is a goalie and that's what he says and he should know, shouldn't he? Oh, and he's not tall, either.'

'All I'm saying, really, is that we should stop switching around and try to become *specialists* in whatever positions we play,' Damian explained. 'We're bound to become better players if we concentrate on our own skills. If we improve as individuals we're bound to improve as a team. I mean, that's totally logical, isn't it?'

'My dad says all soccer players should be versatile and that's why he wants us to play in different positions,' Billy Sandford pointed out heavily. 'He's the manager so what he says goes. O.K.? You're not the captain, Damian, so I think you should shut up about tactics. You wouldn't be talking like that if dad was here in this dressing-room now.'

'So where is our manager today, then?' inquired Paul Merchant, who used to be a winger but had been converted into the team's sweeper by Mr Sandford. 'He was supposed to be telling me after this match whether I could go back to being a forward. He knows I'm not happy at the back. Come on, Billy, tell us why he isn't here.'

'Er, he, er, he just couldn't get away,' was the hasty answer as Billy thrust one leg after the other into his jeans. 'You see, er, well, it was the only day he could do a full check on the car. The engine's been making some weird noises lately and he wants to find out if, er, well, if it's safe to go on driving it without . . . without. . . .'

His voice tailed away as he ran out of ideas. He wished somebody would help him out but no one spoke. To cover his embarrassment he bent down and began a search under the bench for his socks.

'I think Mr Sandford has gone out shooting rabbits,' announced Ian Venn, emerging suddenly from the showers where the streaming water had darkened his straw-coloured hair. 'When my dad went into the gunshop the other day Mr Sandford was just buying himself a rifle and telling the manager he was going to have a change of sport at weekends. I don't think he noticed my dad had come in because he didn't speak to him. Or maybe he just didn't want to admit he was so fed up with our team he was abandoning us.'

For a moment or two no one could think of an appropriate comment on that astonishing bit of news. Billy, now distinctly pink with embarrassment, continued to scrabble under the bench for the elusive socks. Ian himself, pausing only to see the effect of his words on his team-mates, returned to the hot water to complete his ablutions. One of the smallest but most determined players in the squad, he normally didn't say much at any time. Accordingly, when he made a pronouncement it was taken to be the truth.

'Maybe,' said Neil Dallimore very slowly, 'maybe we can find another manager, somebody with lots of ideas and, er, lots of faith in us.'

'Nobody will want to take us on, not with our sort of record,' Paul Merchant admitted. 'Anyway, managers who are any good at all always go to the best teams. They don't identify with failure.'

This time everybody tried not to look at Billy Sandford. Billy stayed where he was, still searching. He knew how fragile was his hold on the captaincy of Darton United. Desperately, though, he wanted to retain it.

'I suppose we could try and join other teams –

you know, those that haven't got a full squad,' Davey Scott murmured in a voice that couldn't disguise his doubts.

'No chance!' was Damian's crisp rejoinder to that. 'You should know the rules, Scottie. The League doesn't allow transfers in the middle of a season unless there's an emergency. That wouldn't apply to us just because our manager had packed it in.'

'Maybe *we* should pack it in ourselves and then we can have some *fun* on Sundays,' someone else suggested gloomily.

'No! We've got to stick together and help each other to get better,' said Ian, stepping out of the showers again and this time reaching for a towel. 'We can do it if we really, really try hard to improve.'

Vigorously he rubbed his hair dry and then glanced down at the United's skipper.

'By the way, Billy,' he said casually, 'your socks are where you always put 'em – stuck in your jacket pocket.'

Two

As he scraped the last spoonful of yogurt from the carton Damian studied the Redbourne Sunday League tables on the sports page of the *Echo*. Although it was the most depressing sight imaginable, and he really did want to read something else to cheer him up, his eyes kept straying back to the table that included the name of Darton United. Nobody would have to look hard to spot it. United were bottom of the table.

What was even worse, they so far hadn't won a single point, let alone a match. All ten games played had resulted in defeats, ranging from those that could simply be described as heavy to others that were more like burials. On average they'd conceded more than twelve goals per game ... and scored exactly one goal every other game. To take the analysis one stage further, those five goals credited to Darton United included two penalties and one own goal. So, looked at from the bleakest possible viewpoint, that meant that United had managed to score only two goals themselves from open play in more than ten hours of playing time.

Damian shuddered and pushed the yogurt carton to one side. He didn't like yogurt, anyway, and ate it only because it was an energy food. Reaching for the jar of clover honey, he spread some thickly on a slice of wholemeal toast. One bite of that and he began to feel better: only fractionally better but, still, better. Soon he might even start to enjoy his breakfast. He could, for instance, take some comfort from the fact that the team directly above United in the table, French Hill Eagles, were only one point better off.

True, the Eagles also had a superior record in the goals for and against columns; but if United could defeat them when they met the following month then there was a distinct possibility that Darton would start to climb up the table at last. What was needed was a new team spirit and all-out determination to overcome all the odds that seemed forever to be stacked against them. On the credit side, they possessed a couple of talented players in Ian Venn and Paul Merchant in addition to himself (and Damian was perfectly capable of making a realistic assessment of his own abilities at soccer as in other things). Davey Scott could be quite useful as a goalkeeper if only he could be persuaded to concentrate at all times and also exert himself when he had at least a thirty per cent chance of making a save.

Billy Sandford was useless as a captain but he could pass a ball and he packed a decent shot. If Mr Sandford really had decided to relinquish the managership of United then his son could easily be replaced as skipper. A majority vote among the rest of the players was all that was needed. So who should take over? Damian hadn't any doubt who'd get his vote. Ian Venn was a very positive player in everything he attempted and he would lead by example. The fact that he was so small shouldn't count against him: Ian was never afraid to speak up for himself and challenge anyone he thought might be in the wrong. So, if –

'Damian, what *are* you thinking about?' asked his mother, slicing through his theories like an axe. 'Honestly, you look as though you're contemplating the end of the world.'

'It's not quite as bad as that,' he conceded. 'But pretty serious, all the same.'

'Football, I suppose,' she said with a resigned air.

'Naturally. That's just about as serious as you can get – especially when you consider our position in the Sunday League. If we don't start to improve soon we've had it for good.' He paused briefly for dramatic effect. 'At the end of the season the bottom two teams are relegated from the League. And teams that do get kicked out hardly ever get back in again. New clubs are always queuing up for places and the Management Committee say it's their policy to give new blood a chance to circulate. You can read that in the League Handbook. So you can see why I'm worried.'

He handed her the folded *Echo*, indicating with a tip of a finger the plight of United.

'Yes, I do see,' said Mrs Tennant, looking and sounding suitably solemn. She always took his troubles seriously and gave whatever advice and assistance she could. On this occasion, however, she couldn't think of anything she might be able to do to help United. Their fate was surely in the hands – or perhaps the feet – of the players themselves.

'You wouldn't, I suppose, think of joining another team, Damian?' his mother asked hesitantly.

'No, certainly not! You know I've always said that loyalty is very, very important in any team. If we don't stick together we've no hope of fighting our way out of trouble – no hope at all.'

'Yes, I quite agree with that attitude, Damian. It's very commendable.' She smiled, glanced at the sports page again and then gently shook her head. 'Still – '

At that moment the telephone started to ring. Mrs Tennant got up from the table very quickly, looking relieved at the interruption. 'I'll get it. Finish your toast.'

A moment later she was back to announce that the call was for him.

'For me? But I never get telephone calls – well,

hardly ever. Who is it, Mum?'

'Your team-mate and equally devoted fan of United, Ian Venn. Says he has a most urgent matter to discuss with you. He was very polite, as usual.'

'Ian? But I was just thinking about him - you know, when you asked me about my thoughts. Hey, great minds think alike! But what does he want to talk about?'

His mother laughed. 'Don't ask me, ask Ian! I'm not surprised if there's been a bit of thought transference because I reckon you and Ian are two of a kind, a real pair.'

'Yes,' said Damian softly as he made his way to the telephone, 'I think we are.' That idea had never occurred to him before but now he recognised the truth in it.

'Listen, we've got to do something about United before it's too late,' Ian said in a brisk, businesslike manner. 'We can't hang around just hoping that someone will come along and save us. We've got to sort out our real problems and come up with a solution.'

'Hey, that's just what I was thinking while I was having breakfast,' exclaimed Damian, delighted by this further evidence of their shared outlook. 'In fact, I was just saying - '

'Yeah, but thinking's not enough, Damian,' interrupted Ian. 'We've got to *do* things. Take some action. That's why I've called you up because I'm organising a meeting this morning to plan our tactics – you know, a new approach to the way we play so that we start winning and get off the bottom of the table.'

'You mean a team meeting, with everyone there?'

'No, I don't! I mean just the best players – you and me and Paul Merchant and Alex Anson. When we've talked things out we can have a sort of training session to put our ideas into practice before telling the rest of the team what's got to be done. You know the Whitecliff camping site?'

'Is that the one near the old windmill, just off the Coastal Road?'

'That's it! Well, that's where we're going to meet. There won't be anybody up there now and there's a good sports area where we can do some ball work without being spied on. It's an ideal spot for us. Look, it's now 8.48. Can you get yourself up there by ten o'clock?'

'Er, yes, I expect so. Do you know if Paul and Alex will definitely be there?'

'Well, I rang you first, of course. But I know they're on our side so they'll get there somehow. O.K.?'

'O.K., Ian. See you.'

He returned to the kitchen looking well-pleased with himself and explained to his mother that he needed a lift if he was to get to the campsite by the appointed time. She was, he deduced, in a good mood that morning and so he was sure his plea would be answered.

'Well, as it happens, I am going to the shops, so I suppose I could drive round that way, even though it is a mighty detour,' she told him in a calculating way. 'But, in return, I want you to do something for me. You've been putting if off for ages but it needs doing before winter sets in: the front fence to be creosoted. By Monday morning, all right?'

Damian wrinkled his nose at the prospect but knew he was in no position to refuse. 'O.K., Mum, it's a deal. But if the smell of that stuff makes me violently sick all over – '

'That's enough! We've got an agreement, so stick to it. Now, if we're going to get to this secret meeting of yours in time, you'd better shoot upstairs and get yourself ready. Your car will be leaving in ten minutes.'

When Damian arrived at the camping site seagulls were swooping low over the sports area to catch chunks of bread being thrown upwards by Ian Venn and Alex Anson. He hadn't known that Alex was a keen ornithologist with a particular fondness for studying (and feeding, whenever possible) sea birds. A slimly-built boy of medium height with a rather dreamy manner, Alex normally played at full-back and his greatest asset, in Damian's opinion, was that he could kick equally well with either foot.

'I come up here quite a lot, mainly to watch

cormorants,' Alex explained when Damian said what a breezy spot it was. 'The air can be very invigorating. That's one of the reasons I suggested it to Ian as a suitable training ground. If you can control the ball up here in half a gale you can control it anywhere.'

'Have you two been planning this meeting for some time, then?' Damian asked.

'No, I only decided last night,' Ian replied. 'I just remembered what Alex had said when I realised we needed somewhere private. Oh good, here's Paul. Now we can get down to work.'

Paul, his round face beaming at the sight of them,

was the only one not in a tracksuit; and, he confessed, he wasn't even wearing his football shorts under his trousers.

'I didn't know we were going to have a kick-around,' he said guiltily. 'I thought we were just going to, you know, sort things out in a discussion.'

'I did explain on the phone that we were planning some ball work but I expect you weren't listening properly,' Ian pointed out. He smiled as he spoke, to take the sting out of the words, but it was still a reprimand.

'Sorry, Ian. Really I am. But I can still join in as I am, can't I? I mean, I often play at school like this. In fact, in break-time and lunch-time games I'm third top scorer! So ordinary trousers don't hold me back, you see.'

Ian nodded. Then, picking up his sports bag which contained a football as well as his boots, he led them across to a grassy mound overlooking the playing area. It was screened from the road by a row of bushes and so afforded them all the privacy they needed. From the way he began to talk, it was obvious to the other three that he had considered the background to United's plight very carefully before coming up with suggestions to improve matters. He stressed that they were only suggestions and that anyone was free to tell him that his ideas were crazy and couldn't possibly work; but if his listeners did agree with him then he hoped they could all act together to put them into operation. At the same time, he hoped that if anyone else had some good ideas they, too, could be discussed at this meeting.

'I've been thinking of some changes we ought to make,' Damian put in. 'But you go ahead. I expect we're working on the same lines.'

Ian exchanged glances with Alex and then said: 'Well, the first thing we've got to decide is who's going to be in charge of the team from now on. You see, after that shambles against Burnwood, I got Billy Sandford on his own and he confessed that his dad really has given up the manager's job. But he was too embarrassed to tell us himself, Billy says. Typical! I mean, he wasn't much good to us in any way, was he? Anyway, Billy wasn't going to say anything if he could avoid it because he wants to hang on to the captaincy. But he's useless, too: he couldn't lead a dog to a gate-post!'

They all laughed and no one disagreed with such a verdict.

'I've been analysing all the players and I think we're the only ones who can really run the team in the future,' continued Ian earnestly. 'So we should form ourselves into a committee and then find some adult to help us out with raising funds and taking us to matches when we have a long way to travel – that sort of thing. We need *somebody* who is really keen and organised and *believes* in us as a team that's going to get better. Won't be easy but we've got to start looking for a bloke like that.'

As he paused for breath, Damian quickly remarked: 'You've said we need a new captain and I'm sure we all agree. Well, I think you should have the job, Ian.'

'I second that,' Alex said before anyone else could speak. Paul nodded vigorously.

'Well, I was going to suggest, you, Damian,' Ian disclosed.

'Damian can be the vice-captain,' was the next prompt response from Alex. 'We need a deputy if ever Ian has to miss a match. We don't want to give Billy a chance to creep back in. I'm sure the rest of the lads will support us.'

'Thanks very much for your confidence in me,' said Ian in a manner that suggested he was pleased with what had happened but that he hadn't expected it. 'I'll do everything I can not to let United down. A cousin of mine - he's twelve years older than me - just might be able to help out on the management side. He's pretty keen on soccer and plays sometimes for a works' team. So I'll have a word with him next time he's at our place.

'But we've got to start putting some things right ourselves without wasting any more time. In my opinion, the first thing we've got to improve is our tackling.'

'Tackling?' queried Paul with obvious astonishment.

'Look, probably the chief reason why other teams walk all over us is that we don't tackle 'em properly when they've got the ball,' was Ian's emphatic reply. 'We just chicken out or something - or, as I think, our technique is wrong. We don't go in as hard and as direct as we should. We pussy-foot about and go in for half-hearted trips that just gets free kicks for the opposition. We've got to change all that, Paul.'

'But I'm really a winger, not a sweeper, as Mr Sandford made me last month. If I go back to being a forward then I don't have to bother about being a good tackler.'

Ian shook his head. 'Poor thinking, that, Paul. *Every* player has to learn how to tackle. Forwards should learn to tackle opposing forwards when necessary - and often forwards have to drop back to help out when their defence is under pressure. One of our weaknesses is that our forwards haven't helped out enough. They've stood around and done absolutely nothing at times.'

Paul really had no answer to that. In the past he himself had complained about team-mates not dropping back to become extra defenders when needed.

'If we can start winning the ball in one-to-one situations, especially in midfield, then we can start going forward in strength - midfielders alongside the forwards,' declared Alex, a light of endeavour in his grey eyes. 'I might even get into an attacking position myself!'

'Exactly! I'm sure that as soon as we start going

forward in strength, we'll start winning matches,' Ian agreed. 'Anyway, that's enough talking. Let's get on with some work on the ball. *Hard* work. We've got to master the ball-winning tackle ourselves before we can teach the rest of the team.'

The three who were wearing them stripped off their tracksuits, put on their boots and went through a few loosening-up exercises. A wind had got up while they talked and now there was a distinct chill in the air. They divided into pairs, Ian and Alex on one side, Damian and Paul on the other, so that they could practise passing and dribbling together as well as tackling. Damian had long regarded tackling as one of his own weaknesses but had done little to improve it; trouble was, he tended to think of himself as an attacking midfielder rather than as an extra defender.

'O.K., let's get on with the important thing,' called Ian when he decided they'd done enough to warm themselves up. 'Just remember this about the tackle: you've got to watch the ball, not the man. You won't get fooled by a swerve or a dribble if you keep your eye on the ball, not the player's feet. Right, you've got the ball, Damian. So you and Paul come at us and one of us'll take it off you. That's a promise!'

On their first attempt to get past the opposition, Damian and Paul succeeded easily because Alex was caught off balance by Damian's body swerve ('I told you to watch the *ball*,' Ian hissed at his partner); but the next time, Ian went in with a crunching tackle to take the ball off Paul's instep. Paul was so surprised that he stumbled and sat down.

'See what I mean?' Ian grinned. 'Total determination, that's the secret! You've got to believe you can't fail to win the ball. Now it's your turn. So, watch out, here we come!'

They moved forward at a brisk pace, switching the ball between them as rapidly as possible. Damian, who was directly facing him, was sure that Ian would retain possession at the critical moment. He eased back a step or so, trying to pick the perfect moment to go for the ball. Paul, equally keen to do well, was on Damian's left and now he moved closer to his fellow defender as if he knew for certain that Ian would hold on to the ball.

Suddenly, Ian swerved to his left and then appeared to hesitate, perhaps fearing that he hadn't got the ball under complete control. In that split-second Paul leapt forward. As he crashed bodily into his opponent his right foot came down heavily on Ian's left leg, just above the ankle.

The sound that they all heard was like the crack of a rifle.

Three

For all his clumsiness in the collision, Paul Merchant was quick to get to his feet. He had fallen across Ian Venn and his first thought was to help his victim to get up.

'No! Leave him where he is,' Damian ordered fiercely as he saw Paul reach out for Ian's hand.

One look at Ian's face, contorted with pain, was enough to tell him how bad the injury might be. He glanced down at Ian's legs and saw that there appeared to be a bulge above the ankle on the left one: and Ian wasn't wearing shinpads under his long socks. Although he'd never seen one before, he felt certain that Ian's leg was broken. The noise they'd heard was of the bone snapping.

Ian's face was as white as his shorts when Damian bent over him to ask how he felt. Even though his eyes seemed to be drowning in tears, Ian still managed to sound as calm as ever when he spoke.

'The pain's pretty bad. In my left leg. I think – I think I must have broken it, Damian. I daren't try to – to move it.'

Paul was kneeling beside them, desperate to be believed as he repeated over and over again that it had been an accident, that he'd do anything, if only he knew what to do, to make up for his stupidity. Alex, meanwhile, was fetching his anorak to put over Ian to keep him warm.

'I could do with a drink, more than anything,' Ian gasped. 'I'm feeling a bit odd, my head's a bit swimmy.'

'No drink,' said Damian crisply. 'The, er, hospital wouldn't want you to have one before they, er, look at you. Look, Ian, we've got to get help. I'm going to ring for an ambulance – dial 999. They'll be getting here in no time, I expect. You won't have long to wait, I promise.'

He sensed that Ian was listening though now his eyes were closed and he seemed to be sweating; even his hand felt clammy. Damian, who'd once read a book about sports injuries, guessed that United's new captain was in a state of shock because of the severity of his injury.

'I came up on my bike – you can borrow that, Damian,' Alex told him. 'There's a phone kiosk just down the coastal road in a lay-by. Oh yes – have you got some money? I think – '

'You don't have to pay for an emergency call. While I'm away you two keep Ian warm. That's vital. And don't move him, whatever you do. Oh, and thanks for the bike, Alex. Makes a lot of difference. O.K., I'll be back as soon as I can.'

As he built up speed across the camping area Damian prayed that the telephone would be in good working order, that it was one the vandals had missed. He knew that Ian needed to be treated in hospital without delay; probably he would have an anaesthetic so that the bone could be set and that was why he wouldn't be allowed anything to drink before the operation. Fervently he hoped that the break was a clean one; then, with a bit of luck, Ian would be playing soccer again before the season ended.

On such a normally deserted stretch of road, unbelievably, the phone box was occupied when he reached it. He propped the bike against the side of the kiosk and stalked round and round in sight of the man within; should he risk opening the door and pointing out that he wanted to dial 999? The steely look in the eye of the man when he caught sight of him was a deterrent. Undoubtedly he would a) tell Damian he was being impertinent; b) order him to be patient; or c) simply employ strong language. In fact when, half a minute later, he vacated the box it was with a friendly grin and the comment: 'All yours now, son.'

For the first time in his life Damian called the emergency number.

'Which service, please?' asked a cool, clear voice.

'Er, we need an ambulance. Soon as you can.'

There was a momentary hesitation and then the

voice inquired: 'Is this a genuine emergency? You sound very young. You can be in a lot of trouble if you make a hoax call, young man.'

'It IS an emergency! My friend's broken his leg. His name is Ian Venn and mine is Damian Tennant. We play for the same soccer team. Oh, please, hurry up. He's in a bad way and needs to get to hospital.'

This time there was no delay. A split-second after answering the operator's request for the location of the telephone box, he was put through to the ambulance station. They didn't doubt his word for a moment: as soon as they knew what had happened they promised instant action. An ambulance would be with them within minutes.

It was, too. Damian barely had time to check on Ian's progress during his absence before the ambulance, headlights blazing, blue light flashing, was sweeping into the camping ground, followed almost immediately by an equally frenzied police car. That was nothing to worry about, the police driver assured the boys, it was standard procedure for the nearest police vehicle to check out any emergency call for an ambulance.

With as much tenderness as speed, the ambulance attendants lifted Ian on to a stretcher after examining his leg. Before he disappeared from sight into the vehicle Ian somehow summoned up a wan smile. He murmured something but the boys couldn't catch his words.

'He was probably saying something about

United,' Alex explained to Damian. 'While you were phoning for the ambulance he kept saying that we must stick together. We must keep on playing whatever happens. He said when he's fit again he'll want his place back in the team.'

'You know,' said Damian softly, 'he'd have been a terrific captain. He's got real guts as well as talent.'

'Well, you've got to forget Ian for the time being,' Alex pointed out with unexpected candour. 'It'll be weeks before he's back playing for United. From next Sunday's match, *you* will be captaining the team.'

Four

Damian tried to quell his nervousness by imagining what the England manager would say in similar circumstances. Doubtless he would tell his players to go out there and do their best for their country; but, above all, they should enjoy themselves. If they were enjoying themselves then, automatically, it followed that they'd be playing well. Top managers were always saying things like that and, usually, their teams got good results. The only big difference, as far as he could tell, was that most managers remained on the bench throughout the match whereas he, Damian, would actually be out on the pitch, playing in the match.

He glanced round the rickety dressing-room, with its scarred walls and broken clothes-hooks, licked his lips and launched into his first ever pep talk as captain of Darton United.

'Look, I'm really grateful to you all for agreeing that I should be captain and I'll do my very best for you – for United – at all times,' he began. He knew that he was speaking much too fast but that didn't matter as long as they got the message: and it was gratifying to see that most of them were listening intently. 'But personalities aren't as important as the team itself. We've got to go out there and play as a team, with everyone helping everyone else. It doesn't matter who scores the goals, or makes fantastic saves at the other end. The only important thing is doing well as a team.'

Damian paused to see if anyone wanted to make a comment but they all appeared to have been struck dumb.

He resumed: 'O.K., we've had some horrific results in the last few weeks, I know. But we've got to forget them and think only about the future. We've got a new spirit in the side from today and we must make it work for us.' At that point he couldn't resist glancing directly at Billy Sandford, the deposed captain. Billy, however, was apparently worried only about a hole in his left sock. 'Well, we have a great chance to get off to a good start. Turnbridge Rovers aren't a good team. That's why they're in the middle of the table because they aren't anything special. No hopes of promotion, no worries about relegation. We should be able to beat them because they're not ambitious and we are. So, lads, let's get out there and show 'em. Let's give 'em a few big surprises.'

As they reached the playing area Alex Anson moved alongside Damian for a quiet word. 'You did that well, skipper. I think they've got the message. Remember, I'm always ready to help you in any way.'

Damian was greatly impressed by the support he'd already received from the full-back. He hadn't realised what an ambitious boy Alex was but as soon as Damian had suggested he should be the new vice-captain Alex accepted with alacrity. What's more he'd taken the leading role in persuading the rest of the players to vote for Damian as the new skipper. Billy hadn't objected too strongly because he knew he was in a weak position in the absence of his father; and, anyway, he wanted to keep his place in the side. Alex said little but he didn't hesitate to act. One of his first self-imposed tasks had been to find a new player for United. He had chosen one of his school friends, Jonathan McGuigan, who hadn't played regularly for a team at any level. Jonathan, tall and strongly built, was a natural left-footer and that alone was a bonus to United.

No sooner had Damian joined in the shooting-into-goal kick-about than he was being summoned to the centre circle by the referee to toss up with his rival for choice of ends. Damian correctly called heads - that alone seemed a good omen - and decided that United would play with the slope in their favour. It wasn't a severe gradient but the tilt was towards one corner flag, which made things difficult sometimes for wingers.

'There's one thing I want to stress to you both,' the referee told the captains. 'I won't stand for any bad behaviour, not by anyone. Bad sportsmanship will be dealt with in the strictest fashion. Understood?'

They nodded – and then, when the referee turned away to whistle up the rest of the players, they exchanged conspiratorial winks. Both knew their teams would play as they normally did whatever anyone said before the match began.

In their smart black-and-white striped shirts, black shorts, and scarlet socks Turnbridge Rovers didn't look like a team without ambition – and they didn't start like one, either. From the kick-off they kept possession very skilfully with their strikers exchanging one-twos at bewildering speed. Then, in a sudden change of direction, the ball was driven out to the right flank. Alex Anson rushed across to make a tackle but slipped on the greasy surface and simply slid humiliatingly into touch, on his back.

Without hesitation, the winger crossed the ball into the front area of the box. Davey Scott jumped up and down on his line but didn't come out; it wasn't really a goalkeeper's ball. But Paul Merchant didn't agree with that viewpoint. Fiercely he yelled at Davey to 'come out and grab it!'

Paul should have gone for the ball himself and the delay was fatal. Rovers' centre-forward, who had started the entire movement, nipped past the stationary defender, took the ball under control, moved on a couple of paces and then fired it home to the goalkeeper's right.

Turnbridge had scored the first goal in thirteen seconds without a United player so much as getting a touch of the ball. Darton's defence had instantaneously proved to be just as feeble as its goals-against record suggested. Rovers, having tasted sweet success so swiftly, were now determined to make the most of it.

'What were you *doing*, standing there like a dummy?' Paul demanded of the goalkeeper. 'You just handed that goal to 'em on a plate, Scottie. You're as useless as ever.'

Davey was furious. He'd only agreed to remain in goal for the next couple of matches because Damian and Alex had been so flattering and persuasive. Rovers' goal, he knew very well, was not his fault but Paul's. He'd never liked Paul and always regarded him as a trouble-maker.

'Don't you talk to me like that,' he yelled as he rushed from his net towards Paul, on whose face he detected a sneer. Well, he'd wipe that off for a start. Without another moment's thought, Davey swung his right fist.

As so often was the case when he tried to punch the ball clear, he missed his target. But he struck Paul on the collar-bone: and Paul, as much through surprise as the force of the blow, fell flat on his back.

The referee, who'd been about to re-start the

game, had a clear view of the incident. At top speed he tore up the field to administer justice and, simultaneously, set an example to the other ruffians in the United team (as he assumed them to be on this evidence).

'We're not having that!' he thundered at Davey Scott, now utterly astonished at his own conduct and the outcome of it. 'If you can attack one of your own players like that what on earth would you do to the opposition? I dread to think. But you're not going to have the chance - oh no. Leave the field immediately! But take off your jersey first. Another player is going to need it, unless your team intends to continue without a goalkeeper.'

Damian sprinted up to see what salvage work he could carry out. By now, Paul had picked himself up, totally unscathed, and avoided Damian's eye. He had wanted to return to being a winger instead of acting as sweeper but had agreed to play on at the back to please his new captain. After what he'd done to Ian he could hardly dictate his own terms.

'Can't you give him another chance, please?' Damian politely asked the referee. 'I'm sure it was all a mistake. It'll be very difficult for us without a proper goalkeeper.'

'That should have been thought of before this hooligan was selected for your team,' was the official's unbending attitude. 'Now hurry up and decide who is to wear the green jersey. We've been held up long enough by bad conduct. Oh yes, and

you should understand that I won't hesitate to remove other offenders from the field if anything like that occurs again. You must learn to control your players.'

It had never occurred to United's new skipper that he should have a replacement goalkeeper in mind in case of emergency. However, as he glanced round at his players to make a choice, a volunteer stepped forward.

'I don't mind having a go if you like,' said Jonathan McGuigan. 'I used to play in goal often at my previous school.'

'Oh, great – thanks,' replied a relieved Damian. 'I'll have to keep my fingers crossed and hope we don't get any injuries. Honestly, I think there's a jinx on this team. But good luck with the saves, Jonathan.'

As if to prove that he had skills the equal of any Turnbridge players, Neil Dallimore made a supreme effort to keep the ball from the kick-off. The gangling striker went weaving across the centre-circle and into the heart of Rovers' midfield. After half-stumbling over his own feet, Neil dribbled past one player and then was brought to the ground by a sliding tackle. At the very least, that should have brought a warning to the Turnbridge offender but the referee just flapped his arms to indicate they should play on.

Damian's heart sank a little lower. It didn't need a genius to work out that this wasn't going to be

United's day.

With United down to ten boys the skipper himself had to drop back deep into defence. Additionally he needed to give support to Paul, still shaken by being the unwitting cause of Davey's dismissal. Even so, they weren't, between them, able to prevent Rovers scoring again. Elated by that instant success, their strikers combined fluently when the ball reached them and this time the progress was down the left flank. Then, with a neat change of direction, the ball was hooked into the middle. The centre-forward chested it down, beat off a challenge and aimed for the top of the net. And he found it – despite a quite heroic effort from Jonathan to tip the ball over the bar.

Damian wondered what he could do to stave off another crushing defeat for his side. They were so used to being overwhelmed that they'd almost lost the will to fight back. It could have been so different if they'd got off to a good start and proved they had the skill and enterprise to rattle the opposition. As it was they'd blundered into disaster in practically record time. His own stature as the new skipper would be meaningless unless United adopted a positive approach and at the very least created scoring chances for themselves.

Their first need was to keep possession: if they held on to the ball, instead of simply whacking it anywhere, then they had hopes of making progress. The captain himself ought to set the example and so, as soon as possible, Damian took command of the ball. The strength in his legs and his balance were great assets as he rode a couple of tackles and ploughed a diagonal course towards goal. Twice he faltered because of lunging challenges from Turnbridge midfielders but he parted with the ball only on his own terms. He flicked it accurately to Billy Sandford with the instruction: 'Push it back, Billy, push it back!'

Billy did as he was told. The deposed skipper still feared that he might be left out of the team altogether and he was determined to avoid that fate. He wasn't sure what Damian had in mind but he respected his footballing ability as well as his intelligence. Mr Sandford had more than once remarked at home that young Tennant was 'the thinker' of the side.

Ignoring Neil Dallimore's frenzied screeches for a pass, Damian went off on a solo run in another direction. This time, Turnbridge defenders tended to stand off and wait for him to make a mistake. After all, he wasn't exactly heading for goal.

What Damian hadn't realised was that Rovers had instinctively relaxed. Their instant two-goal lead, coupled with Darton's abysmal playing record, had convinced them the match would be a walk-over. They could probably score at will. Certainly they didn't have to exert themselves. It was that sort of lazy attitude that kept them in the middle of the table. With the talents they possessed they ought really to have been pressing for promotion. Now their defenders expected Damian to run out of steam very quickly; in any case, he was going into no-man's-land near the corner flag – he was no threat at all because he was on his own. No other United player had thought to give him close support.

Damian suddenly had the impression that he was playing a game of his own. With no one to pass to, he had to turn and try a new path parallel with the dead-ball line. A full-back lumbered at him like an earth-mover but Damian simply jinked one way, then the other, and the full-back fell over his own studs. Then Damian spotted Stevie Pailthorp running through the middle towards the edge of the box. Officially, Stevie was United's right-winger but for some reason he'd hidden himself in midfield. He felt he was lucky to be in the team at all. Even he, however, recognised that he could run – and run fast.

'Yours, Stevie!' yelled Damian, sending him a long, and splendidly judged pass.

Stevie swooped on to the ball, pushed it forward for a couple of long paces, and then let fly with his right foot. He hit it beautifully, and he hit it with surprising power.

The ball appeared to be passing just over the crossbar when, without warning, it dipped and then buried itself in the top of the net – before gently falling to the ground behind the astounded goalkeeper.

For a few moments Damian was equally stupefied. He hadn't even expected Stevie to try a shot let alone score a goal. On the basis of the way he'd played in recent matches, who would have guessed he was capable of such enterprise? However, that didn't prevent his intoxicated team-mates from rushing up to pour congratulations all over him. It was only United's sixth goal of the season - and undeniably it was the best.

'I just thought I ought to test out their goalie - give 'em something to think about,' was Stevie's modest reaction to his success. 'I mean, Damian said we must attack whenever we had the chance.'

It was just the inspiration Darton needed. From then on there was real bite in their tackles, real purpose in their passing: the aimless kick in a scramble for the ball became a rarity. That 'thunderbolt out of the blue', as their manager described it, didn't have a chastening effect on Rovers, after all. The players seemed to treat it as the sort of fluke that couldn't be repeated: and so they continued with their casual approach to the game. They felt they could work their way into the United penalty area at will and so, when attacks broke down, they patiently waited for the opportunity to build another one.

All the time, Damian was shouting encouragement to his players, neglecting no one who made a firm tackle or an accurate pass. He even wondered if he was overdoing it but the important thing was to keep up their morale. In Mr Sandford's time as manager they scarcely ever heard a word of praise: sarcasm was the whip he kept cracking. The players hadn't responded very effectively to that so perhaps a different style of leadership was necessary.

The most heartening development was the display by their stand-in goalkeeper. Twice when Rovers broke through into the box, Jonathan McGuigan came off his line to foil them, diving bravely for the ball at the forwards' feet. On another occasion he palmed away a fierce shot with almost nonchalant ease. His height was an advantage but it was his competent handling that counted. If he were happy to continue in goal after this match then that would be a real bonus for United, Damian reflected.

Stevie, now that he was a hero, was doing all he could to become the first United player ever to score two goals in one match. Eagerly seeking the ball, at one point he even vied with a team-mate for possession so that he could launch, and participate in, another attack. His speed carried him past midfielders who had to turn but the Turnbridge left-back was a useful sprinter, too, and he was tending to shadow Stevie. During one raid Stevie insisted on trying to do everything himself when Neil Dallimore was screaming for a pass – and was in just the right position to make the most of it.

At half-time the score was still 2–1 to Rovers and

Damian could feel satisfied with that after such a dreadful start for United. The players didn't leave the field for the break but huddled in groups on opposite sides of the pitch. Alex Anson had thoughtfully provided a plastic bag containing oranges already cut in halves. That was more than Mr Sandford had done for them and the players gratefully sucked them dry as they listened to Damian's remarks. Much of the time he simply praised their performance. He couldn't think of any tactical changes they could, or ought to, make, apart from mentioning, as casually as possible, to Stevie that the attack might function better sometimes if he released the ball sooner when another forward was up with him.

'We can get a really good result from this match if we keep on playing in the same way,' he concluded as they were about to troop back on to the pitch. 'I told you Rovers weren't so great. Now I think we can prove we're the *better* team. So let's get at them right away.'

Not surprisingly, Turnbridge had been given a roasting by their manager at half-time and so they, too, were determined to resume at a scorching pace. Neil Dallimore blinked at the ferocious manner in which his opposite number hacked the ball away from him to set up the first attack. In what was almost a duplicate of the first move of the entire match, the ball was switched to the wing before being hooked cleverly into the penalty area. This time, though, Jonathan McGuigan reacted instantaneously. With bounding steps he came out, gathered the ball above his head as if removing an apple from a tree, dodged round an opponent and then hoofed the ball to his own right wing. He gave neutral observers the impression that he'd spent his life keeping goal.

Stevie combined neatly with Billy Sandford and, in the course of the next few minutes, United began to look at least the equal of their opponents. For the first time that he could remember Damian found that he had the time to play exactly as he wanted to: he was able to control the ball, look for an opening or a team-mate to pass to and generally run the game for his side. It became an exhilarating experience: and it was crowned by the equaliser.

Billy Sandford started the move just inside Rovers' half after picking up a sliced clearance. His long pass to Damian on the right was hit hard and true – and Damian outwitted his marker by side-footing the ball immediately to Stevie, who accelerated towards the box.

In his enthusiasm the speedy winger allowed the ball to run too far ahead of him. It was directly in the path of a defender and he should have dealt with it easily: instead he tried to boot it clear and missed his kick completely – and spectacularly. Somehow the ball caught the heel of his non-kicking foot, spun sideways and fell appetisingly in front of Neil, who'd sensibly made up a lot of ground in support. Even Dally-a-lot at his worst couldn't miss an open goal like that for the keeper was well out of position. Even so, Neil contrived to hit the ball against the inside of the far upright before it entered the net.

For the first time that season, Darton United had scored two goals in a game; even better, they were now on level terms with Rovers. Every single member of the team had a vision of United collecting their first League point.

'Hold on now, lads,' Damian urged his players. 'Don't let 'em get back into the game.'

While Rovers' defenders argued among themselves about who was really responsible for giving (as they saw it) United the equaliser, their forwards battled furiously to regain a winning position. The manager's fevered orders to 'knock the ball about and stretch their defence' were obeyed whenever possible. Turnbridge tried to attack down the wings but first Paul Merchant and then Alex Anson defied them with critical tackles. After his tragic start to the game Paul was beginning to play with keenness and composure. He still preferred being up-front but for the present he was doing his best as a back-four player. One well-timed tackle that saved a dangerous situation brought warm congratulations from Alex, who'd decided he should do a bit of shouting, too, now he was vice-captain.

With their manager anxiously looking at his watch to see whether enough time remained for them to snatch the winner Turnbridge launched their last attack. From a mêlée just on the edge of the United box their centre-forward emerged with the ball. After jinking one way and then another to find an angle for a shot he lost patience with Alex's close marking and simply blasted the ball towards the net. It was going straight for Alex's face, and, instinctively, he flung up an arm to protect himself. The ball struck his wrist and bounced harmlessly away.

When the referee's whistle shrilled and the official pointed theatrically at the penalty-spot Damian couldn't believe what was happening.

'It can't be a penalty!' he protested. 'He didn't handle the ball. He just acted in self-defence, ref.'

The official frowned at him. 'Don't argue with me, son, unless you want your name in my little book. Now, remove yourself from the area before the kick is taken.'

Inevitably, it was the centre-forward himself who took the kick and, equally inevitably, he scored, in spite of Jonathan's dive along his line to reach the ball. A split-second after signalling the goal, the referee blew to end the match. Rovers 3, United 2.

The Darton players seemed stunned, and none more so than Alex. In an effort to console him as they trudged from the pitch, Damian put an arm round his shoulders.

'I'll tell you something,' he said, saying the first thing that came into his mind. 'The way things happen to us I reckon there must be a *diabolical* jinx on our team.'

Five

They sat in the Canary Café, the three of them, and wondered whether they should go. It had been Alex's idea but even he was beginning to have doubts about the venture. Damian supported him, because he felt anything that might help was worth trying. And Paul Merchant was willing to do whatever might be asked of him because he believed he was the cause of all the trouble in the first place. Paul's concentration on the discussion wasn't total, however, for he kept eyeing the rest of the chocolate fudge cake on the serving table by the counter.

'Probably he won't be in and then it'll be a wasted journey,' Alex said gloomily. 'Or if he is in he'll be too busy to see us without an appointment. The Secretary of the Football League is the sort of guy who'd only see *anybody* by appointment.'

'Mr Rayner is secretary of Redbourne Sunday League, not the *entire* Football League, and he works from home not in a colossal luxurious office in Lancashire,' Damian pointed out. 'And as it's eight o'clock at night he's not likely to have many people queuing up to see him. Honestly, it's worth a chance. He can only say no, forget it, if he doesn't like the idea – or if the rules won't allow it. He certainly won't bite our heads off just for asking. Right, Paul?'

Paul, at the mention of the word bite, had cast another longing glance at the rich cake and wasn't prepared for the question. Damian sighed with exasperation and nudged him back to reality.

'Quit thinking about feeding your face and concentrate on more important matters – if there is anything more important to you than stuffing yourself with cake,' Damian added with a touch of asperity. Somehow, Paul never seemed to do the right thing at the right time. 'I'm asking your opinion.'

'Oh yes,' said Paul, looking thoroughly guilty again. He really hadn't been listening properly. 'Look, I've told you what I think: I'm the one who's brought United all this bad luck. I broke Ian's leg and got Davey Scott sent off. So if you drop me for good the luck'll change. I'm ready to be sacrificed, you know.'

'Oh, stop wallowing in self-pity!' Damian responded. 'We can all do that very easily. We've already told you that things were bad before Ian got crocked. They've just got worse, that's all. We've got to do something *positive* to change our luck. We won't get anywhere if all we do is leave people out of the team. I'm ready this minute to go and see Mr

Rayner and tell him we want to change our name. It was Alex's idea but now he seems to be having second thoughts for some peculiar reason. So your vote is vital. Do we go or don't we?'

'We go,' replied Paul very promptly. He'd just made up his mind that he shouldn't have a third piece of cake after all: since buying a present for Ian, his money had almost run out.

'Right, that's two-to-one in favour, so let's not waste any more time.'

'No, it's three-nil,' declared Alex, draining the remainder of his pineapple juice and then getting to his feet. 'I was only being a bit cautious because I didn't want to talk you into something you were against. If this is a success I've got lots of other ideas we can work on, too.'

The proprietor of the Canary grinned at Paul as the boys edged past the counter on the way to the door. 'I'll keep the biggest piece of choc cake I can find for next time you're in,' he promised the young customer who returned with unfailing regularity. Paul was undeniably good for his business.

'Oh thanks – I'll try to look in tomorrow night,' replied Paul, distinctly cheering up again.

With Damian setting a pace that inhibited second thoughts, they walked briskly to the end terrace house that was the home of Richard Rayner. Carefully Damian mentally rehearsed his opening line for when Mr Rayner answered the door. He knew it was vital to give the right impression from the start. As it turned out, however, it was some moments before he was given a chance to say anything at all.

'Well, what a pleasure! A deputation of young gentlemen to see me,' was the instantaneous greeting from the tall, exceedingly thin and silver-haired secretary of the Sunday League. 'Please come right in and tell me what I can do to help you, gentlemen. I must say, you've chosen your moment well. I was just resting between labours, you see, so you've interrupted nothing of any consequence. Not at all, not at all.'

As they followed him down the passageway to a room at the back of the house the boys exchanged amused glances. Already they had the firm impression that Mr Rayner would never stop talking for anything. It also occurred to Alex that he hadn't even inquired whether it was him they wanted to see: but then, if he hadn't a wife or family any callers were bound to be seeking him. So perhaps he was lonely and glad of a chat with anyone and would be sympathetic to reasonable requests. Alex's hopes rose.

'Well, now, what can I offer you in the way of refreshments?' Mr Rayner inquired once they were all seated.

'Oh, I don't think we need anything to eat or drink, Mr Rayner,' Damian was starting to say when their host cut him off with a raised hand and ascending eyebrows.

'Nonsense, my dear young chap! Can't have people calling at my residence without offering them something, er, cheerful. Wouldn't do at all. How about a fizzy drink and a slice of plum cake?'

Paul's face immediately lit up at the prospect of something sweet to eat and it was really his response that sent Mr Rayner off to the kitchen with the promise that it wouldn't take a minute.

'Hey, he's very friendly, isn't he?' Paul said enthusiastically. 'He must really like us. Bet he'll agree to whatever we ask. I reckon this is the start of a whole new chapter for Darton United.'

Damian didn't say anything. He was still feeling somewhat overwhelmed by Mr Rayner's hospitable manner. There might, he feared, be a catch in it. On the other hand, perhaps the League secretary made a habit of welcoming every visitor with wide-open arms.

'Well now, you have my undivided attention,' said Mr Rayner quite formally after providing them with the refreshments and then settling in a high-backed leather armchair. 'But first, please tell me your names and the team you represent. If, as I have been assuming, you *do* represent a particular team in our League.'

Enthusiastically, Damian reeled off the introductions and explained what he had in mind. 'You see, Mr Rayner, we believe that if we change our name we'll definitely change our luck. Anyway, United is a bit old fashioned, isn't it? I mean, if we called ourselves Sporting Darton - like Sporting Lisbon, you know, the team that does well in European matches - well, that'd be modern, really up-to-date. Or the other name is Dynamos - like Moscow and some other Russian outfit that I can't quite remember. Personally, I favour Darton Dynamos as the best choice but Alex and Paul here think it should be Sporting Darton. So do you think we could do it, then?'

Mr Rayner regarded him solemnly and silently for a few moments as if making up his mind exactly how to phrase his reply. Then, quite mildly, he inquired: 'Do you mean you wish to make a formal change so that in forthcoming fixtures your opponents will officially be playing Sporting Darton instead of Darton United?'

'That's right!' said Damian and Alex simultaneously.

'Out of the question, I'm afraid,' the secretary replied, to their considerable surprise. 'There is no provision in the rules of the Sunday League for any team to change its name in the middle of the season. Such a move would be bound to sow confusion and doubt all over the place. Your opponents wouldn't be at all sure whom they were playing if you turned up under a new guise. I'm sorry gentlemen, but your request cannot possibly be granted.'

Paul had suffered so many setbacks recently that he'd become almost used to them. He was beginning to learn how to face up to disappointments.

On this occasion, too, his enjoyment of the fruit cake helped to make him bolder than usual.

'Well, if we can't change our name, do you think we could change our shirts – I mean the colour of them?' he asked. 'You see, we think green is an unlucky colour – my dad says he never backs any horse with a jockey wearing green in *his* shirt colours. Dad says most racing people think that green brings back luck to the person wearing it.'

'Does your team have an official alternative strip?' Mr Rayner wanted to know.

'No chance!' said Damian with a half laugh. 'We can hardly afford one set of shirts between us. Any spare money we can get hold of is usually spent on travelling expenses. We're already saving like mad to buy another match ball for emergencies. We've only got one.'

'Oh dear.' Mr Rayner was now looking quite sad. 'I'm dreadfully sorry to have to turn you down again but the rules don't allow for colour changes in mid-season, either, except of course in dire emergency. And I hardly feel that your alleged bad luck qualifies as a dire emergency.'

'It does to us,' Damian muttered, half-hoping that Richard Rayner would choke on the orangeade he was now swallowing and so have to be replaced by a more sympathetic Sunday League secretary. 'If our luck gets any worse we'll have to pack up playing. I reckon that'll be an emergency.'

'A tragedy, Damian, a tragedy,' Mr Rayner corrected him with a wan smile. 'It is a tragedy when *any* team has to drop out of our League, whatever the reason. We must all strive to prevent that happening. But, I must tell you this: I invariably believe that when people talk about being dogged by bad luck they are simply failing to recognise their own shortcomings. They know a problem exists but they're not tackling it. They're trying to cover it up. And that won't do.'

'But what can we do?' Paul wanted to know. 'We've tried everything we can think of and nothing seems to work.'

'You've told me you've lost your manager. Well, have you thought of finding another one, somebody who has perhaps more expertise and would undertake to coach you in a more professional manner? Failing that, you could employ new tactics, a new approach to your playing skills. I'm quite sure that if you set about repairing the recent damage in a determined way then things will be bound to improve. But you have to *work* for success. When you meet an obstacle you have to find a way round it or over it. If you stick at something and do your best you'll come up with a solution eventually.'

He paused and then added: 'The fact that you've taken the trouble to come and see me tonight shows you have the right attitude. You've already proved to me that you're not the sort to surrender just because you're going through a bad patch. Gentlemen, I admire your spirit. But now....'

Richard Rayner stood up and the boys followed suit. The meeting was over.

'Well, thanks very much for giving us so much of your time, Mr Rayner - oh, and for the cake and drinks,' said Damian.

'My pleasure. As I told you, I was just having a break when you arrived. But now I must get back to my twitching.'

They all stared at him, sure they must have misheard. But Alex couldn't resist asking for an explanation.

'Ah, you've not heard of the twitchers before?' said Mr Rayner, his eyebrows leaping high again above smiling eyes. 'Well, I suppose we are very rare birds, if I can put it that way. I always find that young people enjoy a good pun. Twitchers are bird watchers and twitching is our name for passing on vital information to one another about the location and the observation of unusual visitors to our shores. If we see something special we ring our pals so they can leap into their cars without delay and have a chance of a look for themselves. Before you came I was ringing round - and after you've gone I'll be contacting a few more friends. Monday is my favourite night of the week for this little task. Monday night is when most people seem to be at home, I find, so a bit of gossip is always welcome.'

Only Alex knew what to say in answer to that unexpected revelation. 'Actually, Mr Rayner, I'm a bird watcher myself. I'm often up on the cliffs studying seabirds. Have you, er, ever seen any really fantastic bird? You know, that hardly ever is seen in Britain?'

He nodded with remembered satisfaction. 'Indeed, yes. I was once exceedingly fortunate to get a call from a friend in Yorkshire who had just identified a desert wheatear. I was able to dash there and get a glimpse for myself. Really, it shouldn't have been anywhere near our country. It should then have been in North Africa. But we decided it must have become disorientated – lost its sense of direction, I mean, and flown north instead of south. That sort of thing can happen with birds. And with humans too, I shouldn't wonder. Still, I musn't delay you all with my ramblings. You'll be wanting to get back to your homes. So – '

Alex, however, had decided that a final appeal might still stand a chance of being successful.

'Mr Rayner, as we both have the same hobby,' he began tentatively, 'do you think you could do us a great favour and change your mind? I mean, let us change our name so that we can change our luck? Please.'

His fellow players turned back and looked expectantly at the tall figure of the League secretary. But now, with an air of some sadness, he was shaking his head.

'I'm afraid that would be quite improper. I really

couldn't make an exception, not even for a fellow ornithologist.'

'No, of course not,' Alex agreed. 'We do understand. Goodnight, Mr Rayner.'

Six

Ian Venn was demonstrating how adept he was at getting around even without the usual support of a crutch or walking stick. His main difficulty at first, he said, had been in keeping his balance because of the extra weight on one side of his body. But, he added in typical fashion, he'd quickly taught himself how to cope with that situation.

When, at last, he sat down and put his leg up on a footstool his visitors admitted they were impressed by his progress. None of them had ever broken a leg and so they hadn't been sure what to expect when calling on the boy who so briefly had been captain of their team. Paul had even suggested that Ian might be too drowsy to talk to them because he'd been under the influence of pain-killing drugs.

'So you don't get any trouble with it, then?' asked Damian.

'Well, not much. Some sharp twinges of pain now and again – bones knitting together again, I imagine. But everybody says the plaster makes you itch like mad after a time. And, of course, you can't have a jolly good scratch when you want to under there! Hey, I think it's time you guys put your autographs on my plaster – if you can find a space!'

Ian himself offered a pen and they lined up to sign.

'Got anybody famous among this lot?' Paul inquired.

'Not since I started the whole thing off with my own signature,' Ian laughed.

'It'd be great if you could get some famous First Division players to drop in and sign up for you,' said Alex. 'You often see pictures in the papers of top stars signing the plaster casts of other players in hospitals or clinics or wherever they finish up. Then, when they're removed, the casts are auctioned for charity, aren't they? If we did that, we could raise some cash for United.'

'Hey, that's not a bad idea, not bad at all,' Ian enthused, and the others nodded their agreement. 'But first, tell me about the visit to Mr Rayner's. I realise it didn't work out. If it had, you'd've been bursting to give me all the details as soon as you got here.'

That couldn't be denied. Damian explained how hospitable the League secretary had been but that he couldn't amend the rules for the sake of United.

'We all liked him but, frankly, he wasn't much help,' he concluded. 'The only thing he could sug-

gest was that we found ourselves another manager or a coach. Somebody with expertise – a professional, really.'

'A professional *footballer*, did he mean?' Ian asked immediately. 'Hey, that's good thinking, too. Maybe that's what we should do right away. It'd give the rest of the players a great boost, wouldn't it?'

'What, you mean to come and sign your plaster cast so that it'll be worth a lot more money when – '

'No, you idiot, Paul!' Ian rolled his eyes heavenwards. 'Forget the plaster. We're talking about getting a *coach* – a top player who would turn us into a better team. Come to think of it, that shouldn't be hard for anybody!'

'No *professional* would give up his spare time to looking after us,' Alex declared. 'I mean, they only want to be involved with successful teams.'

'Not necessarily,' replied Damian with the air of one who was thinking things through. 'Lots of League teams have boys of our age as mascots. Well, this would be the situation in reverse. A good player would be bound to think that he could do something for us because we *are* at the bottom. He'd get a kick out of lifting us up – and he'd be sure to do that, all right. If we were right at the top then he might reckon he'd only be jumping on the bandwagon – or that a top team didn't need him. No, I believe it's got a good chance of working.'

'Exactly!' said Ian, warming to the idea which had come to him almost by accident. 'If we go the right way about asking for help – you know, not ask too much – then I'm sure we'll succeed. But we've got to be enthusiastic in our approach. I was reading yesterday – I get a lot of time for reading at present – that enthusiasm is catching, like measles! It always rubs off on people.'

'You can't rub measles spots off, though, can you?' Alex remarked drily. He knew he had to say something funny to recover lost ground.

They discussed whom they should choose. Because of the travelling that would be involved, they had to go for someone who lived in the area. Redbourne City were the local Second Division club, and, by common consent, Bryn Marsden was the star player. Earlier in his career he'd played for Liverpool and then West Ham United but, according to newspaper critics, it was only in the last couple of seasons that his skills had really blossomed. He was the inspiration behind City's recent surge up the table and, what's more, he'd scored in six successive games.

Bryn Marsden was the unanimous choice of the newly- (and self-) elected Management Committee of Darton United F.C. to be their coach and honorary President. He was to be informed immediately by letter.

'But how do we start it off?' Ian wanted to know. 'I mean if we call him "Dear Bryn" he might think we were being a bit cheeky because we don't know him personally. Well not yet, anyway. But "Dear Mr Marsden" sounds too – what's the word? – oh, formal. He might think it's just a begging letter for extra money. My dad always chucks those sort of letters into the bin without even reading them all through. We don't want Bryn Marsden doing that.'

They debated that point and the rest of the contents during the next half-hour. Six drafts were made before they settled on the final version of the letter. Paul, who had his own typewriter, offered to type the original and four copies but that was turned down because the consensus of opinion was that a handwritten letter had more personal appeal. They used Ian's address and enclosed a list of United's fixtures. The letter read:

Dear Bryn Marsden,

We, the undersigned members of Darton United F.C., would like you to be our official coach and honorary President. We play in the Sunday League every Sunday afternoon. We have to confess that we're not a very good team. Actually, we're pretty dreadful because we're bottom of our section. But we are very determined and are keen to do our best at all times. We think that if you came to coach us we would improve terrifically.

We are all keen fans of Redbourne City F.C. and go to matches whenever we can. You, of course, are our favourite player and always have been. So we are really looking forward to seeing you at our next match - or when you can make it. We know we'll start improving after that.

We send you all our best wishes and hope you score a hat-trick on Saturday.

Yours sincerely,

(*Signed*) Damian Tennant, Alexander Anson, Paul Merchant and Ian Venn

PS The address above is Ian Venn's. He's broken a leg and so can't play for a few weeks. Damian is the team captain.

They all read it through several times to see whether it contained any faults and whether it could be improved upon. Alex, who claimed that English was his best subject at school, pointed out that the word 'keen' had been used twice; but Ian said that 'keen' really summed up their attitude as committee and so there was nothing wrong in repeating that word. Damian and Paul agreed with that view and so Alex withdrew his objection. Because, by common consent, his handwriting was the neatest and clearest Alex wrote the final copy that was to be posted. Ian, meanwhile, hobbled off to persuade his mother to part with a first-class postage stamp.

'Well, all we can do now is keep our fingers crossed that he'll turn up at our next match,' remarked Alex as the letter and fixture list were sealed into the envelope which was then addressed to Bryn Marsden at City's football ground. As an afterthought Alex added 'Urgent' in the top left-hand corner.

'If he looks at the Sunday League tables in the *Echo* and sees how rotten our playing record really is, he probably won't come within ten miles of us,' Damian said in a moment of pessimism.

'We'll just have to risk that,' was Ian's philosophical reply. 'But even if he doesn't come to help us we'll at least have done *something* to try and change our bad luck. We're not lying down and letting disaster roll right over us. We'll be proving to everybody that we're not giving in, whatever happens. Right?'

'Right!' was the firm and unanimous reply.

Seven

With a flick of his wrists Damian tipped another shovelful of snow over the touchline and then took a long look at the sky. It was the colour, he decided, of a lump of old plasticine, and just about as cheerful. If there wasn't a lot more snow up there he'd be amazed. Even if only a little of it fell during the next hour or so, United's away match with Eppleby Village Colts would surely have to be abandoned. On reflection, though, that might not be the worst thing that had ever happened to United.

On arrival at the ground, which was actually part of the attractive village green beside a railed duck pond, Damian had been informed by the home team's skipper that Billy Sandford wouldn't be turning up. Mr Sandford had telephoned to say that his son couldn't play because he was suffering from tonsillitis. Damian wondered how true that was. It could be that Billy was sulking because he was no longer captain; or that his father simply preferred to sever all family connections with the team he formerly managed. Still, at least Mr Sandford had let them know what was happening. Nowadays the Darton players made their own way to matches and so until they all assembled the captain had no way of knowing, in advance of the kick-off, who'd be present. As it was, they'd now have only the minimum number. Davey Scott, who'd served his period of suspension for attacking Paul Merchant, would have to be promoted from substitute to makeshift striker. So it was to be hoped that they all avoided injury during the game.

In spite of the Arctic weather of that weekend, the pitch, under its covering of snow, was not nearly so hard as the players supposed. The groundsman, who was intensely proud of his handiwork, wasn't too pleased when the referee insisted that some at least of the snow should be removed before the game began so that the touchlines and other markings could be seen clearly by the officials. Reluctantly, he'd handed out shovels and brushes to every boy within reach and then stalked from one group of workers to another to make sure none of them damaged his precious turf. More than once he could be heard trying to persuade the referee to postpone the fixture because 'there's a cartload of snow up there still and half of it's sure to come down before this game's over. Best to take sensible precautions now.' The ref, however, had been abroad for a couple of weeks on a business trip and was keen to get back into action again.

Eppleby were equally anxious to play. They were having a run of success and could see a chance of snatching promotion after an indifferent start to the season. Their star player was their skipper and top goal-scorer, Gareth Green, who had played several games for Redbourne City Boys' team and was soon to have a trial for the county. The Colts – or the VC's as their supporters preferred to call them – had every reason to believe that they'd easily demolish Darton United, still without so much as a single League point. True, United had also shown some recent improvement but not enough to achieve a draw let alone a victory. There'd been no

response at all to the letter to Bryn Marsden and even Damian was beginning to feel a little depressed by the lack of success. He couldn't see what more he could do to lift the team. Only victory would do that now, he supposed.

Light flakes of snow were swirling across the pitch when, at last, the match began. As Damian had anticipated, Eppleby had a strong tendency to play every ball they could to Gareth Green. That didn't particularly help their cause because even Gareth at his best couldn't outwit a posse of hard-tackling defenders. Usually he tried to as if he had perpetually to prove to himself how many skills he possessed. In training sessions, United had concentrated on tackling quickly and forcefully. For the first time, it began to look as if all that hard work was paying off. Damian had nominated himself and Paul Merchant as the first line of defence against Gareth's wiles and, by good fortune, both had got their timing right in the early stages of the match. Gareth began to collect a few bruises for he scorned the use of shinpads. Several times the ref blew up for fouls on the star striker but none of them was severe enough to merit a caution. Then, when he did escape the attentions of Damian and Paul, Gareth found that Alex Anson was just as tough a proposition. Inevitably, Gareth had to start laying the ball off if his team was going to succeed.

When Eppleby at last broke through and had a clear sight of goal they discovered that Jonathan

McGuigan was in superlative form. He'd been improving rapidly ever since taking over from Davey Scott and now he excelled himself. Within a minute he'd fingertipped round the post a searing shot from Gareth's co-striker; and then, with a startling reflex save, blocked a piledriver from Gareth himself at point-blank range.

'Terrific, Jonathan, terrific!' Damian sang out as he hurried to take up a defensive position for the resultant corner kick. He couldn't remember seeing a better save than that one.

Even the Colts' supporters vigorously applauded the goalkeeper's performance. 'Well, of course, he must have had plenty of practice considering the state of their defence – it's always been like a sieve,' remarked one man, unaware of the fact that Jonathan was a relative newcomer to the side.

There wasn't much doubt, in Damian's view, that Jonathan was proving to be an inspiration to the rest of United's defence. Their growing confidence in his ability to keep the opposition at bay was now extending to their own play. Determination to succeed was replacing desperation: their first instinct was no longer to clear the ball from their penalty area at all costs. They had started to pass the ball to a team-mate decisively and accurately. Panic was in the past.

Unhappily, there wasn't any sign of improvement up front. Neil Dallimore was as clumsy as ever and though Stevie Pailthorp was still prepared to run hard and fast he wasn't getting anywhere. Discouragingly, it was already beginning to look as if Davey Scott was a better goalkeeper than a forward! So far he hadn't even managed to trap or kick the ball properly when it reached him. At present, United's attack was no better than a joke. Damian wondered whether he dare switch roles in the second half with Neil. If Neil could be persuaded to mark Gareth Green, sticking to him like superglue, then his height and unpredictable awkwardness just might put the Eppleby skipper out of his stride. The whole ploy was a risk - but perhaps one worth taking if it enabled United to set up some attacking moves.

Damian decided to postpone any decision until the interval. He might even ask Neil what he thought of the idea, though he could guess the striker's reaction. Dallimore believed that only sheer bad luck prevented him from being one of the League's most prolific goal-scorers but that one day his real talent would be recognised.

Every gesture of the referee's was flamboyant and he brought the first half to an end with vigorous scissors movements of his arms following a piercing blast on his whistle. United had the greater cause for satisfaction: after all, they had not conceded a goal in spite of all the pressure they'd been under right from the kick-off. For their part, Eppleby felt they had the measure of their opponents. It was surely only a question of time before they got the ball in the net. Gareth Green would break out of his personal stranglehold in the second half. That was what his manager told him, anyway.

'Look, we've done terrifically so far – especially the defence,' Damian said as his players gathered around him. A few had brought their own refreshments but by now the spirit of the side was such that they offered to share them with those who had nothing. 'But we mustn't relax in the second half. We've all got to concentrate, really *concentrate*, just as much as ever. If things go our way then we can hit Eppleby on the break and win our first match. I really mean that.'

It was a matter of great satisfaction to Damian that not one member of the team looked as though he doubted that statement. Then he explained the tactical change he had in mind if United didn't manage to score within ten minutes of the start of the second half. This time Neil himself had some reservations about the plan, just as Damian had anticipated.

'Yes, I realise you feel you're wasting your talents just marking somebody out of the game,' Damian told the gangling striker calmly. 'But a good player should be able to play *anywhere* in the team. The main thing is, though, this move is for the benefit of the whole side. That's what counts most. O.K.?'

Even Neil found it impossible to argue against that view and so, albeit sulkily, he agreed to do his best. Predictably, Eppleby resumed like the weather: driving forward relentlessly in fierce gusts. Once again, however, Darton's defence held firm. Of course, by now they were becoming specialists in rearguard actions. Then, just when it seemed that they might be getting the upper hand, things went dreadfully wrong.

Damian had made his switch with Neil and twice had sent Stevie Pailthorp on challenging runs to the edge of the Eppleby box. Davey Scott was trying to make his own impression on the opposition when, quite savagely, he was cut down by a wild tackle. Anticipating the award of a free kick Damian darted forward to grab the ball – and was knocked to the ground by a blow from the referee's hand that caught him across the throat. The official, who hadn't seen Damian's approach from behind, had simply been demonstrating in his customary dramatic style, his disapproval of the Eppleby player's tackle before awarding a free kick.

The pain was terrible. Damian was sure he was going to be sick – and yet he was also gasping for breath as he writhed on the ground. The whole thing had happened so suddenly he didn't even know what had struck him.

'Son, I'm sorry, truly sorry!' the referee was saying over and over again as he knelt on the turf and tried to cradle Damian's head in his arms. Already Eppleby's manager was rushing on to the pitch with the medical bag. He had seen the entire incident and was aware of how serious the injury could be.

'How does it feel now?' the two men asked but, for the present, Damian was quite unable to answer. The pain was receding a little but he still felt as if he were dying. His throat was on fire.

Someone was offering him a drink. Although he heard a voice inquiring 'Is it wise to allow him to drink?' he swallowed some of the orange juice. He needed it. For a moment he thought he was going to bring it straight back but, luckily, it stayed down. Marginally, his throat felt easier; but he still didn't dare try to speak.

'Look, let's get him to the touch-line - and for goodness' sake put a coat or a rug over him,' the Eppleby manager was saying.

A woman spectator also came forward to help. She claimed to have nursing experience and carried out a gentle but thorough inspection of Damian's mouth and jaw and neck. Gradually he began to feel better although his throat felt very sore.

'I don't think anything's damaged,' the young woman told him comfortingly. 'Just take things easy and you should soon be perfectly all right again. You've been very lucky it wasn't worse. It looked awful when it happened. But it was a pure accident. The referee just didn't see you coming up behind him. He's a bit of an extrovert, isn't he? Should be on the stage!'

'Lucky' wasn't a word Damian would have used. His team was down to ten men - and, as he began to focus on the game again, they also went a goal down. Gareth evaded another of Neil Dallimore's unco-ordinated tackles, sprinted into the penalty area, cleverly slipped the ball past Paul Merchant, rounded the defender on the other side and then crashed an unstoppable shot past Jonathan's right shoulder. His team-mates greeted him like the hero he was. With time running out they'd feared Eppleby were going to be held to a humiliating draw.

Damian started to get to his feet to rejoin his team; now they needed him more than ever if United were to salvage anything from the match. His temporary nurse, however, restrained him.

'I think you'd be better off resting because you still look very pale,' she told him. 'It's getting near the end, anyway. And, after all, it's only a game! Your health comes first, young man!'

He would have gritted his teeth at that remark if only his mouth wasn't so sore. It was true that he was still feeling a bit groggy. On the other hand, a captain should be prepared to overcome the pain barrier for the sake of his team.

'You know, it's really bad luck on Darton to lose a goal just when their best player's been carried off after a karate chop from the referee!' remarked one of the men on the touchline within Damian's hearing. His friend laughed and said that 'karate chop' just about described the blow. Damian was marginally comforted by knowing that someone, at least, considered him to be United's star player. But that would count for nothing if they didn't score a goal in the remaining few minutes. He felt he should be urging his side on but he didn't want to risk further damage to his throat.

Alex had automatically assumed the leadership but he was being kept busy trying to subdue the revitalised Eppleby forwards. What they'd done once they felt they could do again: and it was plain that another goal would clinch the match for them. Gareth was seeing plenty of the ball again and, inevitably, making good use of his opportunities. Dallimore was totally bemused by his opponent's skills and against them could offer only brute force.

After bringing Gareth crashing to the ground on the edge of the penalty area, Neil received a severe warning as well as a booking and Eppleby had a free kick from a dangerous range. Damian desperately wanted to be on the pitch to organise the defence. He sensed that this time Gareth, ruefully rubbing a bruised knee, would act as a decoy. Pulling away from his medical adviser, Damian darted down the touchline to attract Alex's attention.

At that moment Alex, looking towards Damian, caught sight of someone else approaching the playing area from the path by the duck-pond.

'Hey!' he cried excitedly. 'Bryn Marsden's here! He's come to see us at last.'

Simultaneously the referee signalled for the kick to be taken. The ball was floated perfectly for the tallest Eppleby midfielder to head it back across the box to where Gareth, oblivious of the ache in his knee, could collect it and, in the same fluid movement, drive the ball through the gap between the stationary Jonathan and the far upright. It was one of the simplest goals Gareth Green had scored for several matches.

Of course, the whole thing had been made a good deal easier for him by the attitude of the Darton defenders. Most of them had been completely distracted by Alex's dramatic announcement. Beside the arrival of the man they believed was going to be their official coach and honorary President, everything else was fairly insignificant. Even Damian, as elated as anyone by the appearance of the Redbourne City star, missed seeing Gareth Green's goal. When it dawned on him what had happened he covered his dismay by going forward to introduce himself to the familiar tall, slightly stooping figure of his favourite player.

'Good to meet you, Damian.' The words were as warm as the handshake. 'Sorry it took me so long to get round to it. But we've just moved house and every spare minute away from playing and training seems to have been taken up with sticking tiles on walls or painting anything that stands still for five minutes on the trot! Anyway, I seem to have chosen a bad moment to turn up. Sorry about that. Better fill me in on what's been happening overall.'

Within two minutes it seemed to Damian that he and Bryn Marsden had been friends for years. He was amazed how easy it was to talk to him. Bryn, however, appeared to be genuinely interested in the progress (or lack of it) of Darton United and concerned about Damian's own mishap with the referee. Then, when the final whistle blew, he made a point of applauding the United players from the field and sympathising with them in their defeat. Players from both sides crowded round for autographs as soon as they could lay their hands on anything that could be signed; patiently he signed for every one of them. Eventually, however, the Eppleby Village Colts and their supporters departed. By now, the snow had stopped falling and, as far as Damian and his fellow committee members were concerned, the day had begun to improve enormously.

'Are you going to accept our invitation to be our coach and President?' asked Damian anxiously, voicing the question that was in all their minds.

'Sure I am!' was the enthusiastic response. 'Do you know, I get all sorts of invitations from all sorts of people but nobody's ever asked me to be President of their football team. I think it's terrific and I'm really flattered, boys. When I played in a schoolboy side we had a marvellous chap helping us. So if I can give you something of what he gave us I'll feel I'm really putting something back into the game.'

'But you know we're not a very good team, don't you?' said Alex. 'I mean we've just lost again this afternoon and we must be hot favourites to be

relegated at the end of the season. Sympathy alone is not going to be enough, is it?'

'You've hit the nail right on the head, son! We've got to be practical and find positive ways of improving in all departments of the team. O.K., you're on the deck now but you've got spirit and you're keen – you told me that in your letter and I believe you. Well, we'll build on that for a start. We'll get down to some really organised training with he aim of developing individual skills *and* teamwork. How about that?'

They nodded, eagerly.

'I can get the use of a sports hall for a couple of

hours on Monday nights,' Bryn continued. 'I think that's the ideal time because we can analyse what happened on Sunday and then plan the improvements for the week ahead. If you can make it then, I think we should start as soon as possible. Which means tomorrow night. O.K.?'

'O.K.!' they chorused.

Eight

'Are you absolutely *sure* you're feeling all right?' Damian's mother asked him anxiously as he swallowed a piece of apple with, apparently, some difficulty. 'If your throat's still bothering you I'd rather you went to see the doctor instead of traipsing off to *another* football meeting. Now tell me the truth.'

'No, it's fine now, honestly,' Damian tried to assure her. 'I mean, I just bit off a bit more than I could chew - if you see what I mean. Shouldn't have swallowed it all in one go. Anyway, it's not just a *meeting*. We're going to be coached at the Sports Centre by Bryn Marsden himself. I can't miss that - nobody can. Even Ian's going to be there and he's still got a broken leg. Look, I told you, Mum: the throat's only a bit sore if I swallow a lot at once. Otherwise it's improving all the time.'

Mrs Tennant gave him a dubious look but let the subject drop. Normally she allowed him to judge his own fitness for football but the knock on the neck worried her. Damian himself would never have mentioned it but Alex had rashly referred to the incident in Mrs Tennant's hearing during a visit to the house the previous evening. Since then Damian had been obliged to give his mother regular reports on the state of his health. He just wished she would believe him when he said that he was feeling perfectly fit again.

Deliberately he took a long swig of milk, making sure that she noticed; normally he liked milk no better than yogurt but it was supposed to be a body food. Moreover, he'd improved it first by adding soda water from a siphon.

'Right then, I'm off,' he announced with great cheerfulness. 'Shan't be late because Ian's dad has promised to bring me back in their car. Oh yes – and I finished my homework before tea. Bye then.'

At the Sports Centre on the edge of town they didn't have to wait for Bryn Marsden to turn up; he'd arrived ahead of any of them. What impressed them still more was that he was wearing his official Redbourne City strip of scarlet shirt and shorts with white-banded black socks and training shoes.

'Proves you've got guts if you turn up for training when you've got a broken leg,' he remarked with grin as he shook hands with Ian Venn. 'No trainer can ask for more than that. Right then, boys, gather round and I'll tell you what the master plan is for tonight.'

He explained that they were going to begin from

the beginning with the most fundamental part of the game of soccer: passing. Everything was built on that and therefore if a player couldn't pass the ball properly he was no good at all to any team. Even the goalie had to learn that skill because, if injured, he might have to become an outfield player. In the few minutes he'd been present at Sunday's game, Bryn went on, he'd seen some examples of poor passing, particularly with the toe-end. That had to be banished, for a start. The ball should be passed with the inside or outside of the foot. Accurate passing had to be achieved as soon as possible but there was no point in moving on to other skills until it had been mastered.

'So,' he concluded, 'the first part of this session may become a bit boring for you. But we've got to work at it until we get it right. And when we do get it right you'll already have become much better players. *Much* better.'

Twelve players had turned up, including Billy Sandford, who sheepishly explained to Ian and Damian that it hadn't been his wish to miss the match against Eppleby; and yes, his tonsillitis seemed to have cleared up by itself with remarkable speed. Bryn Marsden split them up into pairs and then had them form parallel lines a dozen or so metres apart. The object was to keep each ball in motion with the partners passing to each other, first using the favoured foot, then switching to the weaker foot.

On the unyielding artificial surface of the sports hall it wasn't easy to judge the bounce of what appeared to be a fairly light ball and so initially the passing was pretty ragged. One or two of the players soon started to joke about their incompetence when a pass was badly misdirected or someone stumbled over the ball. Bryn, however, instantly clamped down on what he described as 'a totally unprofessional attitude'. He added: 'the only time to laugh is when you've beaten the opposition hollow in a Cup Final or a top-of-the-League clash. And you haven't done that yet.'

He moved easily from pair to pair, from time to time demonstrating how to apply the right technique, and gradually a rhythm built up. Then, just as they had got used to their partnerships, the pairings were switched. Damian, who'd been linked with Alex Anson, now found himself having to combine with Davey Scott. Passing had long been one of Damian's specialities and he'd even begun to feel a bit superior about his accomplishment in this company. Working with Davey quickly helped to change that outlook.

'Oh, come on, Scottie, you can do better than that!' Damian called in exasperation after retrieving the ball from the back of the hall following another wild kick from his companion.

'Look, you're not the teacher,' Davey snapped back. 'Just because you're captain – *temporary* captain – doesn't give you the right to – '

'Hey, simmer down, simmer down!' Bryn Marsden interrupted. 'We're not going to get anywhere as a team if you're at each other's throats *in training*. Discipline in a team is very important and Damian *is* the captain, Davey. He's simply wanting to get the best out of everybody for the team's sake. Well, now I think it's time we had a break. You've all been working pretty hard so you deserve a rest. Now, who'll volunteer to fetch us all some drinks from the cafeteria? Oh, and before anyone starts to argue, I'm paying for the first round because I'm your President!'

While they all sipped coffee and Cokes and fruit

juices he talked to them about team morale and tactical matters. It was easy to forget, he pointed out, that soccer was a team game because spectators and commentators were always referring to the skills and performances of individuals. 'But a team will only be successful if they play as a team. That's true at whatever level you play, from your Sunday League to international matches. However brilliant, one player can't win games on his own. I saw last Sunday that too many times you played, many of you, without much thought for your team-mates. Not passing when *they* wanted the ball, not looking up to see who was being marked before giving the ball to a team-mate. Once we all start thinking alike, thinking about *our* team, then we'll be making great progress, I promise you. As I've seen tonight, most of you have skills as well as an aptitude for learning how to improve. We're going to build on all that, week by week.'

They found him very easy to get on with and, gradually, they stopped thinking of him as simply a star player they were lucky to have met in person. They began to accept him as their coach or manager: the man who would guide them to success. When they made a mistake or said something foolish, he told them so. Praise was something he gave only when it was earned.

In the second half of the evening he stepped up the tempo. The players formed groups and had to pass the ball while on the move and then when challenged by opponents. In the final minutes Bryn himself joined in and interest soared as individuals made supreme efforts to deliver the perfect pass to him. But he turned down a plea that there should be a six-a-side game, involving everyone, as a finale.

'I've had a long day,' he said with a grin, 'and I'm sure you have, too. Look, I want you to enjoy these sessions and you won't enjoy them if you finish them feeling totally exhausted. At City we always like to keep a bit in reserve and I think you should do the same. O.K.?'

'Will you be coming to all our Sunday League matches, Bryn?' Paul Merchant wanted to know.

'I can't promise that, son. I've got a family of my own, you know, as well as a new house to work on. I'll turn up when I can because, naturally, I want to see how the coaching sessions are going to help you when the chips are down. But there are going to be times when I just can't make it for one reason or another. But I promise you this: only an absolute emergency will keep me away from these Monday night training spots. And if I am unable to get here, well, I'll do all in my power to get a team-mate from Redbourne City to stand in for me. And he'll be given a copy of the programme I've worked out for you.'

'What will we be doing next week, then?' Billy inquired a split-second before Damian could ask the identical question.

'Ah, that's what I like – keenness! If you're already looking forward to the next session things must be good. Well, first of all we'll see how much you've remembered about passing the ball. So after we've revised that I hope to move on to controlling the ball – trapping it, checking it, not just with the foot but with the body, on the chest, in the tummy and on the thigh. Very useful skills at all times.'

Bryn paused but they were all gazing at him so expectantly that he decided to summarize the rest of the training programme he had drawn up. Tactics, he explained, might come next, knowing when to run both with the ball and off the ball, when to tackle and when to stand off; and so on. Another session would be devoted to heading, a skill which few boys mastered at an early age. Then it would be time to specialise in tackling and dribbling.

'If you absorb all that lot then you'll be on the road to success,' he concluded. 'So, when the crunch comes, the entire *team* will be properly equipped to cope with it. O.K.?'

By now they were all used to his style.

'O.K.!' they agreed.

Then he added: 'But just remember this: you've still got to work on the things you've learned. They won't stay with you unless you keep polishing them. As one of my old bosses used to say, if you look after your talents properly they'll look after you when you need 'em most – when that crunch comes.'

Nine

The 'crunch' that Bryn Marsden mentioned turned out to be the game against Tinacre Rangers. It could not have been more vital. For the team that lost would be relegated.

In the weeks since the Redbourne City star had taken over as their coach and President, Darton United really had blended skills with endeavour. After picking up points with successive draws they'd achieved their first win of the season. True, the opposition had not been formidable. French Hill Eagles were the team directly above them in the League: but Darton triumphed 5–3 after being a goal down at the interval. That success was another inspiration for the following Sunday they won again, this time overcoming a team in the top half of the table with the help of a penalty awarded in the last minute of the game. Damian had taken that responsibility upon himself and, with a coolness he was still proud of, had slotted the ball into the net by the left-hand upright for the winning goal. Bryn had been present at that match and later rewarded Damian with the gift of a City shirt 'for playing a captain's part to the full'.

As the season reached its climax they clawed their way over French Hill and so lifted themselves from the bottom of the table for the first time in their history. Now, with just one match remaining, they were level on points with Tinacre Rangers. To some, it seemed as if fate had intervened to arrange the most dramatic fixture possible. For United's final match at home was against Tinacre – and Rangers' goal difference was superior to United's. So United *had* to win to survive.

While Tinacre had been having a very bad run of results – losing each of their previous six games – United had been in good form. The time they'd devoted to training and building up their skills under Bryn's direction had plainly been well spent. Practically every member of the squad had become a fitness fanatic and Paul, for instance, was able to announce proudly that he'd completely given up eating cake at any time. Ian Venn had made remarkable progress in recovering from his broken leg: he'd started light training again and declared that, in an emergency, he'd even be prepared to turn out in the Tinacre match.

Damian had pondered whether to choose Ian as substitute but in the end decided against it. The risks, for both player and team, were too great. But it would be good to have Ian on the touchline, giving the team all the encouragement he could, especially as Bryn couldn't be present until half-time at the earliest. Their inspirational coach had promised to attend a friend's birthday lunch party in a neighbouring village and had confessed to the boys that it might well be difficult for him to get back in time for the second half. In his absence, Damian and Ian would have to cope with the pre-match pep talk. The United players no longer needed to be motivated: they knew exactly what was required of them by now and how they should set about achieving it. On the other hand, there'd been ominous signs in the last two matches that several were being affected by nerves as tension built up. Some of the old elementary mistakes had occurred again; and more than once defenders had panicked under pressure. Both games had been won by a single goal after United had held a useful lead.

Against Tinacre Rangers, who would be just as desperate to win, any nervous error at all might prove fatal. And then United's gallant struggle against relegation would be lost.

It was Bryn Marsden's belief, which he had drilled into the United players, that a team should concern itself with building up its own strengths and ambitions and not waste time worrying about the quality and the plans of the opposition. All the same, Damian felt he couldn't ignore the menace of Rangers' best player, a tall, strongly-built mid-fielder called Lee Shoscombe, famous for his surging runs on goal from deep positions. Damian was reminded of the problem of trying to curb Eppleby's star player, Gareth Green: they'd kept him quiet for most of the time but, in the end, he'd won the match for his side. Since then, however, United's defence had improved greatly and so there'd be no need to use a striker, Neil Dallimore, to try and mark an opponent out of the game. Neil had actually learned quite a lot from Bryn Marsden and was now playing the best football of his life. What's more, he was also United's leading scorer.

No, Damian resolved at last, they wouldn't try to anticipate what Rangers might do: they'd simply play in their own style and hope to be at their best. And keep their fingers crossed that luck would be on their side, too.

'Right, then,' Damian told his team-mates as they were all about to leave the dressing-room, 'we know we're a better team than Tinacre. So let's just go out there and prove it.'

He licked his lips, hoped he'd concealed his own nervousness, and led his team out on to the pitch at a very fast pace. Deliberately he'd waited for Rangers to take the field first. Now they would see United coming at them, looking as determined and unstoppable as a fleet of green-and-yellow excavators. To add to the effect, United were greeted by prolonged applause from the biggest crowd ever to support them.

Damian, however, would thankfully have swopped at least half of those spectators for the presence of Bryn Marsden. On the other hand, if United could win without his guidance then it would surely prove that they really had matured as a team. Their success would truly be deserved.

Rangers, all in red, didn't give the impression they were riddled with anxieties. After winning the toss, they chose to defend with the sun in their eyes and calmly allowed United to launch the first attack of the game. When the ball ran clear to one of their deep-lying midfielders he didn't simply boot it up-field. Almost nonchalantly he took it round one United player, then another, before sending a splendidly-judged pass to one of his strikers. Such coolness drew appreciative applause even from United fans.

It occurred then to Damian that Tinacre, because of their recent bad results and the fact that they were playing away to desperate rivals, had resigned themselves to defeat. They would simply try their best and hope not to suffer too severely, which meant that they could play in a very relaxed manner. That could only make things harder still for Darton.

At the earliest opportunity Damian set up another attack and supplied Stevie Pailthorp with the chance to run at, and unsettle, Rangers' defence. Stevie's speed was still his chief asset, though now he'd learned to use it in bursts. Very sensibly, he kept to the touchline to draw the full-backs apart and then sent over a good-looking centre. Unfortunately, Neil's timing was not as good as his jump and the ball passed over his head as Neil was coming down to earth again. Still, the United fans had seen something to shout about for their own team and the cheers were further encouragement to Stevie.

For the next few minutes there was too much aimless play with neither side able to build up a movement worthy of the name. The first goal was probably going to be vital and each defence was absolutely determined not to be the one to concede it. Those in the middle of the field tended to push the ball around among themselves and almost inevitably it went to a player already heavily marked. So there was no progress in any direction. Of course, it would satisfy Tinacre to hold out for a draw and so they didn't need to exert themselves.

'Come on, let's get a grip on this game!' Damian yelled fiercely as Davey Scott gave away a free kick with a clumsy foul on a Tinacre striker. The offence occurred only just inside the United half but the ball was hammered right into the heart of the penalty area. Unnoticed by all the United players, Lee Shoscombe came through at panther-like speed to meet the ball and head for goal.

Jonathan McGuigan, who'd hesitated about whether to come out, just managed to get a fingertip to the ball – and that was enough to deflect it on to, and then over, the bar. United had given away a corner. But it had so very nearly been a goal.

Shoscombe himself, who plainly had his own fan club behind the goal, jostled with Jonathan for a prime position on the goal-line as the corner was about to be taken. Damian was deeply worried about the threat from the tall Rangers midfielder. He'd been furious that he hadn't spotted Lee's diagonal run into the box. Lee wasn't the sort of boy to miss twice from that range.

Fortunately, the kick was short and Alex Anson had no difficulty in heading the ball away from the danger zone. Then the ball was pushed across to Paul Merchant as the Tinacre players streamed back upfield in expectation of a counter-attack from United's forwards.

Afterwards, Paul wasn't able to give a convincing explanation of what he'd really been trying to do when he caused the disaster. As he faced his own goal on the edge of the box he appeared to onlookers to be attempting to side-foot the ball. Instead he got his foot under the ball so that it ballooned towards the net. Jonathan, aghast, hesitated a moment or two and then hastily dashed out to collect it. But then, just as he was about to take it in his arms, the ball swerved wickedly away from him because of the spin that was controlling it.

Despairingly, Jonathan dived full-length to try and catch it – and he very nearly succeeded. However, the ball struck his forearm and bounced away. Lee Shoscombe, alert as always, had missed

nothing of what was going on. His acceleration carried him into the box before anyone else could get there. For him it was the easiest task possible to collect the rebound, swerve past the prostrate Jonathan and slide the ball sweetly into the net.

Paul Merchant sank to his knees, praying for the earth to open up and bury him. Damian dare not look at Ian Venn on the touchline. The rest of United's players were simply stunned. None of them felt able to say a word, either in anger or despair. Like robots, they moved to their customary positions for the re-start. Because of their celebrations it was some moments before Rangers were ready for the resumption and the referee had to speak forcefully to them. Behind Jonathan's net a few supporters were actually dancing jigs.

It was in Damian's mind that the whole season had been blighted by defenders' errors but he didn't voice his thoughts. Instead, with both fists clenched he urged his players: 'Come on, come on, lads. That was just a fluky goal for them. We'll get a real one.'

When next the ball reached him he controlled it well, smartly jinked past a couple of opponents and then fed Stevie Pailthorp on the flank. With unexpected perception Stevie immediately transferred the ball to the unmarked Neil Dallimore. Neil galloped forward for several paces and then hit a humdinger of a shot. Although the goalie palmed the ball over the bar, the swiftness and the coordination of the move were heartening for United.

After the shock of Shoscombe's goal the home team's fans were coming alive again and the volume of noise began to lift the team. Even Paul Merchant could believe that Rangers were still a long way from claiming victory. He put his heart into his next tackle and emerged triumphantly with the ball. United's new team spirit, inspired by Bryn Marsden, was proving to be a true asset.

As the first half faded away Rangers appeared to be concentrating wholly on defence. They hadn't crossed the halfway line for several minutes and whenever the ball bobbed around their box they tended to boot it anywhere that looked safe. Twice United got in good shots, one that just whistled past an upright with the goalie clearly beaten, the other that struck the crossbar and ricocheted to a relieved defender who hooked it over the touchline for a harmless throw-in. Damian was constantly going forward with his attackers and providing a lot of vocal encouragement. His instinct was also to keep an eye on Lee Shoscombe, especially as Rangers' danger man had been subdued since his goal. Like a professional assassin, Shoscombe was prepared to be perfectly patient until the real moment to strike arrived. For the present, there was no point in wasting energy.

During the interval Damian asked his players if they had any bright ideas for getting the equaliser but no one could come up with anything really original. Several of them remarked on Bryn Marsden's absence and inquired if it was known when he'd turn up.

'Bryn thinks we're good enough to win this one on our own, so I reckon we should do just that,' Ian Venn pointed out. It seemed a fair comment. 'Rangers are just hanging on like rock climbers. One slip and they'll crash.'

Damian nodded. 'If we can get one goal we'll get two, I'm sure of it. So let's go at them all the time.'

Some spectators came up to offer advice but most just wished United luck as they returned to the pitch for the most vital thirty-five minutes of their season. If they failed to score at least twice before the final whistle sounded then there would be no future at all for a team called Darton United.

Rangers seemed ready to fall back on defence again. Their coach was a great believer in luck and it was his firm belief that on this day the luck was all with his team. As evidence he could point to Lee Shoscombe's goal: scored because of one of the luckiest breaks imaginable. Moreover, his horoscope in the Sunday paper had stated categorically that he 'would have a lot to be thankful for at the end of the day'. He didn't know then that his daughter was going to arrive after tea to tell him he was going to be a grandfather for the first time.

With a quarter of an hour to go, the visitors' defence was still looking quite composed when, rather carelessly, they conceded an indirect free-kick on the left-hand edge of their penalty area.

It was a moment Damian had been waiting for since the match began. As the Rangers defenders took their time about forming the conventional defensive wall, United's skipper conferred hastily with Alex and Billy Sandford. After appearing to give his instructions, Damian casually edged backwards across the front of the box. No one noticed that his fingers were tightly crossed.

As soon as the whistle blew Alex, who appeared to have been intently studying the one gap in the wall, flicked the ball to Billy on his left. Instinctively, goalkeeper and defenders began to move in that direction. But Billy hit the ball hard and low way over to the right. It arrived exactly as Damian had wanted it to: controlling it on the first bounce, he took one step forward and then cracked the ball into the vacant area of the net by the right-hand post. The manoeuvre, devised by Bryn and rehearsed so many times by the players involved in the training sessions, had worked brilliantly.

It was Damian's first goal of the season in open play and it was United's most vital equaliser.

As if on cue, Bryn himself arrived, dressed spectacularly in gold-coloured trousers and a dark green sweater. Within seconds he'd been updated on the state of the match and he looked as elated as Damian felt. He signalled his support and urged his players on to greater endeavour. Unless they scored again, they'd be relegated and face oblivion.

Inevitably, Darton surged forward again at the first opportunity until Lee Shoscombe made a timely interception in midfield. With a swift change of pace he headed into United's half. Lee still had plenty of energy in reserve and he was going to make the most of it.

Damian, who was on the other side of the pitch, could do nothing to stop the progress of Tinacre's star player. But, as if utterly determined to redeem his past errors, Paul Merchant charged in: and he had never produced a better tackle in his life. His timing was impeccable and, just as important, he kept his balance as Lee lost his: so Paul was able to collect the ball and launch his own attack.

'Keep going forward, Paul!' Bryn yelled at him and those words registered. When, at last, he parted with the ball it was in the form of a pass to Billy Sandford. Billy, who'd been playing as well as anyone in the team in recent matches, skilfully played a one-two with Neil Dallimore, took the ball into the penalty area – and was thwarted only by a courageous diving save from the agile goalkeeper. Still, Billy had gained a corner for his team.

'Take a short one and then push it across the box,' instructed Bryn, who'd dashed down the touchline after noting the height of so many Tinacre defenders. It was a ploy he'd advocated in training but none of the team had remembered it . . . until now.

When the ball reached Damian just inside the

penalty area he kept it tightly under control and weaved past a couple of challengers. Then, with the inside of his left foot, he pushed the ball strongly into the goalmouth. It was Neil who showed the fastest reaction. Jumping forward and stretching out his long legs he just managed to get his left heel to the ball before anyone else could make contact, and stab it over the goal-line.

It was one of the least elegant goals anyone would score - but it was enough to win the match for Darton United. Predictably, Rangers tried to switch from defence to attack but they had neither the ability nor the time to snatch a life-saving equaliser.

When, at last, the final whistle shrilled, Damian felt elated enough to turn a couple of somersaults. It was the most joyous moment of his football career.

Before he could attempt any more gymnastic feats, Bryn Marsden and Ian Venn had managed to reach him to express their own delight and congratulations.

'I feel as if we've won the Cup - and yet all we've done is avoid relegation!' Damian exclaimed.

'Maybe that is all you've done - for the moment,' Bryn Marsden responded with a grin. 'But now Darton United have a real future. We've got something we can build on.'

MASCOT

One

Damian Tennant replaced the telephone receiver with a sense of bewilderment.

'They're not going to believe this, they're definitely *not* going to believe it,' he said to himself, shaking his head. He was still standing in the hall, transfixed, when his mother came down the stairs, twirling her badminton racket and wearing an even shorter white dress than usual.

'Seen a ghost, darling?' she asked cheerfully, pausing to check her appearance in the full-length mirror on the wall beside the front door.

'Not exactly,' Damian told her. 'But just as unbelievable.'

'Must have something to do with football, then,' Mrs Tennant observed, with a lopsided grin. Damian knew she always put on that expression when she was mocking one of his obsessions.

'Of course it has!' he told her, a trifle irritatedly. 'What else is so important?'

'My badminton! And if I don't dash Jenny will be

looking for another partner. But you'd better tell me what's happened. Quickly, though.'

'Bryn Marsden's leaving City, that's what. Been transferred to Charlton. I don't know how we're going to manage without him. It's a total disaster.'

'But I thought City were having a good season, winning almost every match and –'

'I'm not talking about City,' Damian cut in. 'I mean *us*, Darton United. Bryn's still our coach, you know. Oh, and he's still our President.'

'Oh, but you'll manage to get somebody else, I expect,' Mrs Tennant said confidently. She was well aware that her son had a tendency to worry unnecessarily about his football life.

'I'm not sure about that,' Damian said doubtfully. 'It took us ages to find somebody like him in the first place. He made all the difference to our team. Without him we'd probably still be at the bottom of the Sunday League – or near the bottom, anyway.'

Sue Tennant scratched one slim, bare leg just above the knee and took another glance at her watch. 'Well, perhaps Bryn can suggest one of his team-mates as a replacement as a parting gesture to you.'

Damian gave her a calculating look. 'That's one of the unbelievable bits, Mum. He's already thought about a farewell present for me. He's fixed it for me to be the mascot for City's next home match. It's against Plymouth a week on Saturday.'

Mrs Tennant looked delighted. 'Well, that's marvellous, darling. Good for you. I know you'll really enjoy that. Surely that makes up for the disappointment over Bryn's leaving? So, look cheerful, stop being down in the dumps! Look, I just must fly. I – '

'There is something else,' Damian told her reflectively.

'Go on,' she said, trying not to let her exasperation get the upper hand.

'Well, the rest of the squad – the United squad, I mean – have been chosen as ball boys for the same match.'

'So what's wrong with that?' His mother was genuinely puzzled.

'They might be jealous because I've been singled out as mascot.'

'Oh, nonsense! You're the captain so you should get preferential treatment. That's only fair. They're bound to see that, Damian. I mean, you saved the whole team when things were really black for you last year – or last season, was it?'

'Last season. But Ian might not,' he told her flatly.

'Why on earth not?'

'Well, now he's fully fit again after his broken leg I think he wants to be captain again.'

'Has he said so?'

'Not exactly. But you see, Mum – '

'Darling, go I must! We can talk this over later – at supper time, if you like. It'll keep till then, won't it?'

'I suppose so. But can I ring the other players to give them the news? It's only fair to tell them as soon as possible.'

'All right,' agreed his mother, seizing her car keys from the wicker tray by the coat-stand. 'But keep the chat down, Damian. We can't afford another whopping phone bill like the last one. You and your vice-captain ought to share the information relay service between you, I reckon.'

Even when he'd seen his mother's silver saloon disappear from sight down the avenue, Damian hesitated over making the first call. He was thinking that he should speak to Alex Anson, United's vice-captain, first; and yet his instinct was to make contact with Ian Venn, his partner in midfield. The previous season, when United were in dire trouble at the bottom of the Redbourne Sunday League, Ian had become captain: but, as it turned out, only for a few minutes because in a training session his left leg had been smashed in a tackle by his team-mate, Paul Merchant. That was when Damian had taken over.

United had started the current season quite well and were in the top half of the table. They had a settled side, an inventive coach in Bryn Marsden, and most of the boys had a feeling they could even win a trophy before the season was over. For the first time in Damian's experience with the team, everything seemed to be in United's favour.

Ian had slotted back into the midfield as if he'd never been away and showed no ill-effects from his injury. So far he hadn't said a word (at least, not in Damian's hearing) about wanting to be captain again; he had simply followed Damian's leadership like everyone else. Ian didn't say much at any time but when he did open his mouth it was usually to say something sensible. In his conversation, as in his play on the field, he could be relied upon to make a worthwhile contribution. Nonetheless, Damian had a feeling that Ian would like to take over the team and run things his way.

Damian picked up the receiver, let his forefinger hover over the buttons, hesitated, bit his lower lip – and then plonked the phone down again. 'Go and see him,' he told himself. 'See how he takes things.' So, after checking that the cat was out of the house, he slammed the front door and set off up the avenue at a steady jog. It was only after he reached the junction with Sundial Hill that he remembered he ought to have brought an old tennis ball with him for dribbling and shooting practice. 'Whenever you're out, either on your own or in pairs, take a ball with you,' Bryn had advised. 'If you're on the move and you can train at the same time you're bound to improve your skills.'

Mrs Venn, who answered the ring on the side-door bell, seemed pleased to see him. 'Ian's in the sitting-room, watching some rubbish on television,' she announced, shaking her head sadly. 'I can't believe you've come to see the same programme, Damian. You're too intelligent for that.'

'Of course!' Damian grinned.

Ian managed to look apologetic as he lifted himself off the arm of a chair when Damian walked in with Mrs Venn peering over his shoulder. 'I sort of got hooked on this monster stuff when I was laid up with my broken leg,' he explained.

'Oh, you don't have to apologise to me, Ian,' Damian said in a tone of mock-superiority. Then, when he was sure that Mrs Venn was out of ear-shot, he added softly: 'I watch quite a lot of rubbish myself when nobody else is around to notice. Listen, I've just had some amazing news and I came round to tell you before anyone else.'

He studied Ian's face as he disclosed the details of Bryn Marsden's move to Charlton and the invitation to the United players to be the ball boys for the Plymouth match; but Ian's expression didn't alter much, although he kept tugging at a lock of his straw-coloured hair as if trying to make it still shorter. Damian recognised that as one of his regular habits. It was only when he mentioned being chosen as mascot that Ian displayed some emotion.

'You jammy devil!' he exclaimed. 'That's the one thing I've always wanted to be, ever since I went to see City play for the first time. It must be, well, fantastic to go out on to the pitch with the players and have the kick-around before the game begins. Oh, and you usually get the coin from the referee after they've tossed up – to keep, I mean. Sometimes it's a pound! Oh, the whole thing must be great.'

Damian was a little embarrassed by such fervour. 'I didn't know you felt so strongly about it,' he said quietly.

'I don't usually say how I feel about things, unless I really have to,' Ian replied in his more familiar cool manner.

Damian wandered across to a bookcase behind the television set and fiddled with the spine of a leather-bound volume. He didn't know whether he should say what was in his mind; but he wanted to be fair to a boy he thought of as a friend as well as a team-mate.

'In a way,' he said eventually. 'I suppose you ought to be the mascot. I mean, you would have been the captain if you hadn't broken your leg. I only got the job because of that, didn't I?'

'Yes,' was the blunt answer. 'So are you going to give the job up, then?'

Damian was taken aback by Ian's attitude but he responded immediately and instinctively. 'No, definitely not!'

'Well, that's it, then. You'll be the mascot and I won't. So I'll just be with the rest of the team, chucking the ball back when it goes out of play. Better than nothing, I suppose – and at least we'll get into the match free!'

'Er, Ian, what do you think we should do about finding a new coach?' asked Damian, anxious to change the subject.

'Have you asked Alex what he thinks?'

'You know I haven't! I just told you, I came round to give you all the news first.'

'Well, he's the vice-captain and I don't think he'll be very pleased with you if you don't consult him first. Alex likes to get involved in running things, you know. He often has good ideas. Alex is a bit of a thinker on the quiet.'

Damian had no doubt about that; he appreciated Alex's thoughtful contributions to team planning and the support he provided during matches if things were going against Darton United. Because Alex was the studious-looking type, and bird-watching was his chief hobby when not playing football, other boys tended to overlook the role he took in team affairs. In fact, Damian now recognised that he himself didn't always confer with Alex as often as perhaps he should. Ian's remark had made him feel more than a little guilty.

'Yeah, well I was going to see him after coming to you,' Damian said weakly.

'Got any other brilliant ideas?' Ian asked.

Damian was now distinctly disturbed by Ian's sarcastic tone. He hadn't imagined that Ian could feel so strongly about the captaincy. If this resentment continued, team morale would soon be affected.

'Well, I did ask you what you thought about getting a new coach – then I can tell Alex your views.'

Ian was now tapping his teeth with a pencil and seemed to be thinking very carefully what to reply. It was obvious to him that Damian was upset but Ian rarely allowed personal feelings to deflect him from getting what he wanted out of life. Now that he was fully fit again and, in his opinion, playing as well as ever, he believed strongly that he should be in charge of the team. On the other hand, he realised that Damian was popular with the majority of the United players and therefore they'd be unlikely to vote against him at any meeting. Ian guessed that the best way for him to regain the leadership would be to find some way of persuading Damian to resign the captaincy.

'It's my view that we don't need another coach,' he said positively. 'Bryn taught us a lot and I'm grateful for all he's done for the team. But I reckon we can get along fine without him or anyone else. I mean, the team's playing well. We don't want to risk somebody coming along and trying to change our tactics, our style. That would be – lunacy.'

'Yes, but – '

'Hang on! I hadn't finished. I was going to say that all we need now is a committee – say four of the players – to run the team and decide if we need to make any changes for any reason. Any reason at all.'

'A committee! Football teams aren't run by committees. That's crazy – '

'It isn't! My dad says all the best decisions are made by really good committees. And he should know. He sits on a few because he's got a top job in education.'

Damian was baffled. He was sure this wasn't a good idea at all and he couldn't think why Ian should be so enthusiastic about it; except that . . .

'I suppose you want to be on this committee, don't you?' he asked.

'Well, if you want me to be, yes, of course,' Ian replied without a second's hesitation. 'I'm also on a committee at my school so I know how they work. I think there should be four guys on our team committee – you, me, Alex and one other. If it were up to me I'd invite Jonathan McGuigan to join us. He's very keen on getting us up the League and improving our image. Jonathan's willing to help in any way. Look how he became our goalie when we needed one, even though he's really an outfield player.'

'I'd forgotten that,' Damian confessed. 'I just remember that Alex found him for us. They played in the same team at their school.'

'Jonathan really plays on the left side of midfield – like you,' Ian informed him. 'Anyway, what do you think about having him on our committee?'

Damian thought of saying that he hadn't exactly agreed that there should be a committee but he didn't want to risk upsetting Ian at this stage; in any case, if they didn't succeed in finding a new coach it might be a good move. At present all the responsibility for organising things was on the captain's shoulders; and, following Bryn Marsden's departure, his task would be harder still.

'I'll work on it,' Damian promised. 'Oh, and I'll see what Alex thinks. I'm going round to see him now with all the news. Then the three of us – oh, and Jonathan – can have a discussion after the match against Fyfield next Sunday. We'll have lots to talk about then, anyway.'

'Sure,' Ian agreed, accompanying Damian to the door.

Then, just as they were parting, Damian had a sudden thought. 'Hey, shouldn't we have somebody else on the committee to make it an odd number? You know, in case of a vote to decide anything that – '

'Oh no, I don't think that'll be necessary,' Ian cut in smoothly. 'I mean, we aren't likely to fall out over anything, are we?'

Two

The excitement in the Darton United dressing-room had nothing whatsoever to do with the match the team was about to play. Hardly anybody was even thinking about that: all the discussions were revolving around the news that the players were to act as ball boys at the Redbourne City v Plymouth Argyle match the following Saturday. Some, like Alex Anson and Jonathan McGuigan, had known about the invitation for several days, but this was the first time they'd been able to talk about it with the rest of the squad.

'Hey, I've just thought of something bad,' exclaimed Stevie Pailthorp, the speedy right-winger. He appeared quite crestfallen. 'We won't be able to wear our normal green shirts, will we, because Plymouth play in green? I mean, the referee will be worried about a colour clash, won't he?'

There was a momentary silence to greet the remark and then Billy Sandford said cuttingly: 'You nut, Stevie! Ball boys don't wear their own shirts. They're all in track suits. So – '

'But we haven't got track suits – not as a team, anyway,' Alex pointed out. 'The teams I've seen acting as ball boys at the City Ground have all been sponsored. You know, by a local garage or a supermarket or something. Maybe we should look for a sponsor quickly so that we can get track suits with our names on – oh, and theirs, too – for next Saturday.'

'That's good thinking, Alex,' Ian Venn told him. 'We should look into it right away.'

'I don't think there's going to be time to get that sort of thing fixed before next Saturday,' Damian pointed out as he pulled on his own No. 6 shirt and tucked it into his yellow shorts. 'Anyway, I expect City have some spare track suits, perhaps the ones the apprentices use. We can ask Bryn about that.'

'Bryn'll be too busy to think about us now,' Ian said. 'Anyway, he's already in London, isn't he? That's why he's not coming to our match today.'

'Er, yes,' Damian agreed. 'But his first match for Charlton is going to be next Sunday, so he's hoping to be at City's match with Plymouth – just as a spectator, of course. He's bound to want to see us at half-time and probably before the game begins as well.'

He could see that Ian wasn't convinced of Bryn Marsden's continuing interest in them, but he wasn't going to spend time arguing about that now. The vital thing was to concentrate on the preparations for their match against Fyfield Swifts; if they could defeat them then United would climb another rung of the Sunday League ladder to success. Bryn wasn't there to offer them any advice or to suggest changes of tactics if necessary during the course of the game. It was up to Damian himself to plan for everything as well as to lead the team both on and off the pitch. Although he had talked about this situation with the vice-captain, Alex hadn't offered to take on any of the responsibilities of running the team. He had given Damian the impression that his only real concern was his own form as one of the back-four players. Alex was two-footed but he tended to favour the right flank whereas Damian preferred him to stay in the middle of the defence.

'Listen, do you think we'll all get our pictures in the paper after Saturday?' Billy Sandford was asking everyone when Damian interrupted him by calling for silence.

'Look, I think we've got to forget about next Saturday and start to concentrate on today's game,' he said when he thought he had everyone's attention. 'If we don't get a good result today we won't be able to enjoy ourselves at the City Ground.'

'That's what you think!' Billy murmured, but loud enough for Damian to hear. He wanted to get his own back for being cut off. But this time nobody seemed to be listening to him.

'Fyfield are a pretty fair side and we won't be able to relax for a minute.' Damian carried on as if nobody had said a word. 'So I think we've got to attack right from the kick-off and put them under a lot of pressure. They've got a good home record so I expect they think visiting sides will be a bit nervous to start with. I mean, that usually happens.'

There he paused, not quite certain what to say next. Normally Bryn would have turned up by now and thrown in a few inspirational phrases to remember on the pitch. But Bryn wasn't here to inspire him or anyone else: and probably wouldn't be again. So Damian had to be coach as well as captain. He'd been looking at Stevie Pailthorp and now he remembered an idea he'd had.

'Stevie, you probably noticed as we came in how wide this pitch is. Well, that could help us if you make good use of your speed. I want you to stay out on the touch-line as much as possible. That'll drag their defence apart because somebody'll have to keep a watch on you. Then when you get the ball make for the corner flag – keep everything as wide as possible. OK?'

'And what do you want me to do when I get to the corner flag, then?' Stevie asked in a tone that just might have contained a hint of sarcasm.

Damian frowned. 'Well, what you usually do, of course: either send in a good cross or cut inside for a one-two with one of the other strikers. The point I'm making is that we want to keep their defence stretched. Right, anybody else got any questions?'

Deliberately he looked at each of his players. The only one not to meet his gaze was Ian, bouncing a spare ball near the entrance to the showers and seemingly counting each bounce.

'Any ideas, Ian?' he inquired.

Ian looked surprised and shook his head. 'No,

nothing.'

'Right,' Damian said positively. 'Let's go and get at 'em.'

That didn't sound right, coming from him, and he knew it. The phrase was what Bryn Marsden called their battle cry: he'd coined it and uttered it before the start of every match and the players reacted to it eagerly. Damian recognised that all he himself had done was remind them of Bryn's absence. That wasn't helpful at all. In future, he'd have to come up with a battle cry of his own.

As soon as he saw the assembled Fyfield team Damian wished, for the umpteenth time, that he was at least a couple of inches taller. Although he had strong thigh and calf muscles and could jump to a good height, there were times when he felt much too short: and this was one of them. By comparison with United, the Fyfield players, in their blue-and-white hooped shirts, seemed enormous. All Damian could hope was that their play wasn't as powerful as their appearance. Because Fyfield had been relegated at the end of the previous season, Darton hadn't encountered them before (Darton never having played in a higher division of the Redbourne Sunday League).

The Swifts were determined to get promotion at the earliest opportunity and they had plenty of vocal support from enthusiastic parents and other supporters; in contrast, United hadn't a single person off the pitch to shout for them. Damian's mother had promised many times to turn up to an away match but she hadn't made it yet and on this Sunday morning she was playing in what she told her only son was another 'absolutely vital' badminton game. Perhaps, Damian reflected, if he went to watch her in action her conscience would compel her to return the compliment.

Light rain was falling as the match began and the Swifts immediately lived up to their name by darting all over the place, unpredictably and at rare speed; with the ball skidding off the wet long grass, control wasn't easy and United's defence committed several uncharacteristic errors in the opening minutes. It was only by good luck and the length of Jonathan's fingers that Fyfield didn't score three times in that period. Damian, dropping back to help his beleaguered back-four, praised Jonathan and patted him on the back as they waited for a corner kick to be taken. Fyfield's tallest player, their centre-back, got in a header which skimmed only just over the bar with, this time, Jonathan ill-positioned to cope with it had the ball been on target.

'You ought to have been marking their centre-back, you're almost his height,' Damian murmured to Neil Dallimore, United's main striker, when they met moments later in midfield. 'We can't afford to let them get in free headers from set-pieces.'

'Somebody has to stay up front in case of a breakaway,' Neil muttered. 'I mean, I am here to score goals, you know.'

There was no time to say anything further. Damian had to move quickly to pick up a loose ball and fire it at

Ian Venn.

For once Ian wasn't paying attention. When he failed to trap the ball properly he turned slowly to try to retrieve it and was far too late. Fyfield's left-winger had already snapped it up and, urged on by the baying home crowd, was making rapid progress down the flank.

'Wake up, Ian!' Damian yelled in exasperation as he chased back towards his own penalty area to provide additional cover.

Ian shot him a fierce and surprised look but didn't retaliate. He knew he'd been at fault and he hated to make mistakes. All the same, he didn't care to have those mistakes pointed out in public. Rapidly he set off in pursuit of the opponent who'd taken the ball off him. By now, however, the winger had cut inside and then, after selling a dummy to Alex Anson, he drove the ball all along the ground towards the far side of the penalty area. There to meet it was the Swifts' smallest and nippiest attacker. Cleverly he stopped the ball, dragged it back under his foot as Paul Merchant tried to dispossess him, jinked sideways and then, with splendid accuracy, drove his shot beyond Jonathan's despairing reach into the far corner of the net.

'Oh, great goal, great goal!' yelled the boy's father, one of the most vociferous of the spectators. He firmly believed that his son would play for Arsenal (and probably England) one day and his only regret was that no scout from Highbury was present to see such clinical finishing.

Damian didn't know what to say as Jonathan

retrieved the ball. The goalkeeper hadn't really been at fault and although he thought that Paul should have tackled his opponent sooner he wasn't to blame, either. The goal chance had actually stemmed from Ian's failure to take a pass, but no good would come from harping on that: he'd already made his view plain on that point.

Fyfield hadn't been lacking in confidence before that goal, but now they set about Darton United as if they believed they could slaughter them. For the next ten minutes or so the green-shirted visitors were penned in their own half of the field – and mostly in and around the penalty area. Every booted clearance from there was almost always promptly returned by Fyfield's sweeper, now operating just inside United's half. To his ill-concealed disapproval, Neil Dallimore had been ordered to help the defenders and it was his clumsiness which very nearly cost Darton a second goal: a goal that, Damian believed, would have killed off their hopes of getting any points out of the game.

The gangling striker had improved his play greatly since the end of the previous season, but he was still liable to make the most ridiculous mistakes in any quite ordinary situation. Alex had once remarked that Neil was simply 'disaster-prone' and that was a fair description. If anyone was going to fall over because of standing on the ball instead of trapping it, that player was Neil Dalli-a-lot, to use the nickname several of his team-mates favoured. Now, on the edge of the United box, he intercepted a pass from a Fyfield forward, failed to control the ball, lost it to another player and, in his desperation to regain it, lunged at his opponent and knocked him to the ground.

It was clearly a foul and, in spite of Neil's protests that it was a fair tackle, the referee pointed to a mark barely inches outside the penalty area. Hastily Damian organised a defensive wall. Neil was ordered to station himself right in the middle of it so that whoever took the free kick would have difficulty in chipping the ball over him. Jonathan, dancing up and down on his line, was pleading for a clear view of the kicker.

Fyfield summoned up one of their midfielders, who could strike the ball with the force of a cannon. Clearly the team didn't believe in subtlety where the taking of free kicks was concerned. The ball was blasted at the wall, causing Paul Merchant to double up with the agony of taking the impact in the midriff, and then bounced invitingly for an attacker to try a lob into the top corner of the net. Although he saw the shot coming only at the last second, Jonathan's reach was enough for him to palm the ball round the post.

The corner kick had to be delayed, however, for Paul to receive prolonged treatment from Fyfield's coach. It was one of Damian's perpetual worries that United lacked a regular supporter who possessed medical knowledge or healing powers or both. If one of their players was injured then they invariably had to rely on the opposition or casual spectators for help. Paul was really only severely winded but he was giving the impression that he felt he should have been rushed to hospital for emergency treatment.

'Come on, Paul, you'll live,' Damian told him, a trifle unsympathetically. 'You should learn to protect yourself better at free kicks.'

Fyfield, having grown impatient at the delay, wasted the kick when it was taken and Alex was thankful to hoof the ball to the half-way line. It was soon back in United territory again, however, and the siege was only relieved when Damian himself collected the ball and began a mazy dribble that took him out to the right wing; there he dummied to pass to Stevie and made further progress before hitting a beautifully-judged long pass to Neil Dallimore. For once Neil kept his feet and control of the ball; his only mistake was to hit his shot far too soon because he could have taken the ball another few yards before shooting. But at least United had the satisfaction of launching an attack on the Swifts' goal.

A couple of minutes later Damian was wondering how soon the referee would blow for half-time. He, for one, would be glad of a rest. Fyfield, too, seemed conscious of the time factor and were pressing hard for a second goal that would surely demoralise the opposition. The ball was switched to Tim, their goal-scorer, and this time he was intent on a solo run. Paul Merchant was his nearest opponent but he made no attempt to go in for a tackle. He was backing off, backing off, all the way into the penalty area. Jonathan, too, took no purposeful action – until it was too late.

Tim, with the goal now in his sights, suddenly and

dramatically accelerated. Because he'd been retreating at a slowish pace Paul couldn't react quickly enough and he simply fell over when he tried to change direction. Jonathan belatedly decided to come off his line to narrow the angle for the shot; but by then the astute Tim had picked his spot and was slotting the ball past the goalkeeper and into the vacant net.

'What do you think you were doing?' Damian stormed at Paul. 'Why didn't you get in there and tackle him?'

For a moment or two Paul made no reply at all. His round face was pink with embarrassment. 'Well, I didn't want to go in hard and risk getting hurt again,' he admitted.

Damian was staggered. 'What d'you mean?' he demanded.

Paul looked unhappier still, if that were possible. 'Well, you see, Damian, I was thinking about – about next Saturday. I don't want to miss being one of the ball boys. That'd be – well, a disaster.'

This time Damian was speechless. He would never have believed that a player would calculate his chances of being injured before going in to tackle an opponent when his team was in danger of conceding a goal. He turned and trudged back to the centre for the resumption.

At half-time, however, he had to find something to say: something to encourage the team to keep trying for victory and something about tactics for the second half. A pep talk was expected of him as it would be of any coach or manager in similar circumstances. If he, as the captain, appeared downhearted then the team couldn't be expected to fight for survival.

'They're not as good as they think they are, you know,' he said, thinking aloud between mouthfuls of banana, his favourite food on match day. 'We're just letting 'em over-run us, we're not hitting back. We've got to believe in ourselves.'

He knew that Bryn was a great believer in believing in yourself and that he'd probably expressed the same thought dozens of times; but that didn't matter. The only important thing was to make his team-mates think about the match and their own game.

Ian, now bouncing a spare ball from one forearm to the other in a new style of juggling, waited for the pause and then said: 'Well, you know what's wrong, don't you, skipper?'

Damian, ignoring the deliberate emphasis on the word skipper, asked what Ian had in mind.

'More pace down the middle, that's what's lacking,' Ian told them. 'If we don't get some real attacks in then we can't hope to score, can we?'

'And where are we going to get that from?' Damian wanted to know.

'Well, for a start I think Stevie should move inside, up alongside Neil,' suggested Ian. 'We're too spread out to make any worthwhile attacks.'

'Yeah, I agree,' Stevie contributed. 'This pitch is a bit too wide. When I put a cross in there's nobody there for it if it drops a bit short.'

Damian could have pointed out that this was because Stevie wasn't putting enough beef into his centres but he decided that remark mightn't be helpful. Stevie was the sort of player who responded to praise, not adverse criticism. Still, Ian's idea had some merit and Damian was perfectly willing to try it. He asked if anyone else had suggestions and, as he did so, he looked at Alex. But neither the vice-captain nor anyone else offered a single thought.

'OK,' he announced, 'we'll do that. Stevie you can move inside and combine with Neil. But don't get in each other's way!'

Ian, who had begun bouncing the ball on his right instep, grinned his approval and exchanged glances with Alex, which was something Damian didn't notice.

The rain was much heavier when play resumed so that the surface was becoming very slippery. Yet, to his team-mates' surprise, Neil displayed exceptional control after picking up a loose ball on the perimeter of the centre circle. Rounding Fyfield's centre-back with ease, he set off on a direct run to the penalty area with Stevie in close support and Ian just behind them. Another defender slipped out of contention after missing an attempt at a sliding tackle and Neil, following an exchange of passes with Stevie, had a clear sight of goal. His fierce drive was only parried by the goalkeeper whose reflexes were slow after being out of action for so long. Neil was unable to reach the rebound but Ian, following up, very coolly slammed the ball into the back of the net and then spun away, both arms aloft to signal his delight at scoring his first goal of the season.

'Hey, terrific goal!' yelled Damian, running across to congratulate the scorer. 'And well done, Neil. That was a great run of yours.'

Ian exchanged a cool shake of the hand with his captain and didn't say anything although he naturally looked well pleased with himself. Neil, inevitably, was telling team-mates, really, the goal ought to be credited to him because he'd done everything except put the ball in the net after hitting 'the hottest shot that goalie's ever had to handle'. Damian didn't mind who scored just so long as United were back in the game.

Surprisingly, Fyfield seemed to wilt instead of redoubling their efforts to restore their two-goal lead. Most of the players had written off Darton as no-hopers and now they couldn't immediately cope with the reality of United's skilful and successful counter-attack. They tended to rely on their band of adult supporters to encourage them instead of taking their lead from their captain; and now those adults were shouting conflicting advice. Some wanted the Swifts to 'close the game down and shut Darton out'; others urged 'attack, attack, attack and get another goal. A one-goal lead is never enough!'

In spite of their own renewed zeal and an abundance of attacking opportunities, United were finding it impossible to get the equalizer. More than once Neil and Stevie actually got in each other's way and good chances in front of goal were squandered. Ian, now that he had the taste for scoring, was pressing further and further forward. Nonetheless, the Swifts somehow managed to contain United's attack. Damian sensed that it would be a good idea to tell Stevie to exploit the width of the pitch again to pull Fyfield's defence apart. But if he did that Ian would probably regard the manoeuvre as treachery. What they lacked most of all was a left-winger with pace and penetration; but then that had always been so since Darton United was formed.

'Billy, keep out on the left touch-line as much as you can when we're going forward,' Damian instructed Sandford, who'd been having a fairly aimless time in the middle of the pitch. 'We've just got to change the point of attack.'

That was the sort of ploy that Bryn Marsden would use, Damian was convinced. But for him it back-fired almost at once. For, when Ian swept the ball out to the left flank Billy failed to control it with his left foot and, in the most obvious and painful fashion, he used his right foot to gain possession and then try and take on an opponent. With contemptuous ease the Fyfield player dispossessed him, leaving a dejected Billy sprawled on the grass. Billy, whose father had once been Darton's manager, didn't have much fight in him and he was inclined to sulk if things went badly wrong for him.

Gradually Fyfield had recovered their composure. They had repelled all the Darton raids, such as they were, and their own attack was beginning to function again. Best of all, there was no more helpful advice being offered from the touchlines. Their supporters restricted themselves to handing out praise when it was deserved. The Swifts were confident again of improving their promotion prospects. Then, with only three minutes of the match remaining, they had no doubt at all of a comfortable victory that would even improve their goal difference.

Because the Swifts' attacks had been so rare in the second half, Jonathan McGuigan had taken to straying further and further from his line as he tried to urge his team-mates to keep going forward. So he was ill-positioned when Tim received a speculative long pass out on the right wing where no one was marking him. Tim, noting the goalkeeper's wanderlust, took only a couple of steps before, with excellent aim, hitting the ball as hard and high as he could in the direction of the yawning net.

Jonathan was slow in seeing the danger. But even if he'd moved immediately, and at top speed, there was no hope of his getting back to the goal-line before the ball crossed it. Tim had completed his hat-trick with the most satisfying of his goals and, at the same time, sealed the Swifts' success. He thoroughly deserved the heaped congratulations of his team-mates and their enchanted supporters.

'What were you thinking about?' Damian asked his goalkeeper, more in dismay than in anger, as the teams left the field after the final whistle. 'You just about gave 'em that last goal.'

'I never expected him to shoot from there,' was

Jonathan's only reply.

'You know, we definitely ought to have won that match – or at least grabbed a draw,' Damian said to Ian Venn as they arrived at the entrance to the dressing-room together. 'We ought to have *built* on your goal. Instead . . .'

'We would have done if we'd had some strength and pace to help the attack down the left,' Ian replied. 'That's the sort of player we're missing.'

'Well, we've no hope of getting one,' Damian responded gloomily.

'Oh, I think we have,' Ian said quite chirpily. 'In fact,

I'm sure of it.'

Damian stood with his hands on his hips and stared at him. 'What have you got in mind?'

Ian grinned. 'Tell you at our first committee meeting. That's where we ought to have a proper discussion of tactics, isn't it?'

Three

It had always been Damian's dream to stroll through the players' entrance at Redbourne City's ground. He had imagined driving his luxurious sports car into the reserved space with his name on it in the private car park under the North Stand, and then receiving a salute and a friendly welcome from the official on duty just inside that desirable entrance. Probably he'd be asked to sign a few autographs for patiently-waiting youngsters and, of course, he would do so with a flourish and a word of encouragement for the autograph-seekers' own sporting careers. He'd smile his appreciation when they gushed 'Thanks a *lot*, Damian'. Somehow it wouldn't sound at all right if they addressed him as Mr Tennant.

Now, as he approached the huge grandstand after dropping off the bus in City Road, he wondered what sort of reception he'd receive. Already scatterings of spectators had arrived for the Second Division match and some were standing around in groups, waiting to see something worth seeing and Damian had to ask some older teenagers to move aside so that he could reach the players' entrance. He was relieved that none of them made any rude comments.

'Oh, you'll be one of the ball boys, I take it,' was the greeting he received from the dark-suited figure standing just inside the doorway.

'Well, actually, I'm the mascot,' Damian explained. He didn't know who this man was but he'd half-expected to be met by City's manager, Alistair McAndrew (or MacAndy as Bryn Marsden always called him when he talked to the boys at coaching sessions).

'Oh, that's even better, isn't it?' said the club official. 'That makes you a VIP for the day.'

'Pardon?'

'A Very Important Person – which of course you are anyway, I expect. Now, if you come through here and then go down that corridor to the second door on the right, you should find Ricky Bennett in his office. He's our Promotions Manager, as I expect you know and he'll look after you.'

'Thanks very much,' said Damian, setting off.

'Oh, by the way, I hope you bring us some luck, son,' the man called after him. 'Mascots are supposed to be lucky, you know.'

Damian had never met Ricky Bennett but he knew a good deal about him for the Promotions Manager had once been City's most prolific goal-scorer until his career was ended by a serious ankle injury which caused him to hobble even now. The door was wide open and

Ricky was speaking on the telephone; but he was alert to Damian's arrival and beckoned him in.

'Well, son, nice to see you,' he said when at last he put the phone down. He held out his hand for a firm and welcoming shake: 'You must be Damian. Heard a lot about you from Bryn. Says that your team is going places. Well, today they've come to the *right* place! I'm sure you're going to see a great match and you're going to help us win it. I mean, that's what you're here for, son, isn't it?'

Damian, finding it easy to respond to Ricky's warmth and enthusiasm, agreed that it was. Then he listened carefully as he was told exactly what was going to happen to him during the course of the afternoon, though more than once Ricky had to break off to take another telephone call or have a brief word with a visitor.

He was disappointed that he wasn't going to be allowed to change in City's dressing-room with the players for that is what he'd wanted more than anything; he would have felt part of the team. But he didn't let that disappointment show as Ricky reached into a cupboard and then handed him the strip normally worn by the mascot; it was, of course, identical to that worn by the City players: scarlet shirt and shorts and white-banded black socks. In fact, Damian had once been presented with a City shirt by Bryn Marsden and he wished now that he'd brought it with him to wear on this momentous occasion. But perhaps his club would think that was showing-off.

'Right, I'll take you along to the kit room where the ball boys always change and then when you're ready you can return to my office and I'll introduce you to the players just before they go out on to the pitch,' Ricky said, leading him down the endless-seeming corridor that ran almost the length of the grandstand. 'You'll be able to wave to your mum and dad from the pitch as well as join in the kick-about. Oh yes, and you'll get your photo taken. We'll give you a big blown-up print for your bedroom wall as a souvenir. It'll help you to remember the day.'

'I don't think I'll ever forget it as long as I live,' Damian said feelingly.

Several of his United team-mates had already arrived and were changing into club track suits when Ricky and Damian reached the narrow, triangular-shaped room hidden under the main concrete stairway at the far end of the stand. Because he was putting on a team shirt and shorts instead of the same outfit as everyone else, he soon felt on his own. Alex and Ian were deep in conversation and it was clear to Damian that they wouldn't welcome an interruption. Some of the others were chattering excitedly about the prospect of getting autographs or being spotted by League scouts as prospects for the future.

'Anyone seen Bryn?' Damian inquired generally, more in the hope of joining in a conversation than in getting information.

'I should have thought you'd see him before any of us,' replied Billy, 'seeing as you're mixing with the top people. We're just the slaves, you know, kept out of sight at the bottom of the ship.'

That provoked a laugh, much to Billy's delight because he wasn't renowned for possessing a sense of humour. So he immediately tried to crack a few more jokes and that made Damian feel completely excluded.

'See you,' he called out as he left the kit room but he didn't hear anyone respond.

He cheered up when Ricky, in a change of plan, took him along to the home team dressing-room a minute or so before the players were due on the pitch. Alistair McAndrew, who'd just delivered his pep talk, came across to present him with a City pennant and most of the players made a point of shaking his hand. Damian didn't have time to catch more than a glimpse of the famous deep bath which could take all the team and more. Moments later the referee looked in, exchanged quips with Mr McAndrew and said it was time they were all out in the sunshine to entertain the millions who'd come to see them.

'You go first, Damian – let the crowd see our latest record signing,' City's skipper told him cheerfully. Damian, grateful that his name had been remembered, was surprised to note that the player didn't appear to be feeling any tension at all. Yet Damian himself always felt nervous when he was about to lead United into a match.

The sun really was shining very brightly now and the roar that greeted the home side as they emerged from the narrow tunnel was much louder than Damian had expected. He very nearly dropped the spare ball he was carrying – that would have looked terrible.

As soon as he was on the hallowed pitch he drop-kicked the ball and then chased after it into the penalty area where City's goalkeeper and one of the full-backs fielded the shots that rained in on them during the shoot-in. Damian was presented with one or two good shooting chances and with the second of them he succeeded in putting the ball into the net, hitting it hard and low with his left foot. That provoked a small outburst of cheering and whistles from spectators behind the goal and Damian acknowledged it with a nonchalant wave.

He was so absorbed in the kick-about that he almost missed hearing his own name over the loud-speaker system but, after listing the Redbourne and Plymouth teams and the match officials, the announcer added: 'And today's mascot is Damian Tennant, who captains Darton United in the Junior Sunday League. Damian's team-mates, the other United players, are today's ball boys, so our sincere thanks to Darton United for their support.'

Damian wondered what his parents were thinking about all this. They, too, had been invited to the match and provided with seats in the main stand, close to the directors' box, where Damian would join them once the game started. He would have preferred to be a ball boy, too, but Ricky Bennett said that it was traditional for the mascot to be with his folks in the stand; and Damian felt it wouldn't be polite to try and argue against that.

ON FE

The match had attracted a good crowd and it was quite impossible for him to pick out his parents from the pitch but he knew they'd be watching and so he gave another wave in that direction. He'd always imagined it would be marvellous to step on to City's pitch before a big match and so it was; now he decided it was the greatest thrill of his life. There could hardly be a greater one until the day he signed for City as a full-time professional player.

'Right, son, let's go and do the toss-up,' City's skipper called to him and they made their way to the centre circle where everybody shook hands with everyone else. An awful lot of time was taken up with hand-shaking, which seemed quite pointless to Damian.

'You can call if you like, Damian,' the skipper told him as the referee prepared to spin the coin.

That was totally unexpected and, suddenly, it seemed to Damian to be an awesome responsibility. Suppose he called wrong and . . . 'Heads,' he said firmly, shutting unwelcome thoughts out of his mind.

They all had to move as the ten-penny piece bounced down and then rolled so far it almost went out of the centre circle; but when they all stooped they discovered that City's mascot had made the right choice.

'Fine, we'll play towards the city end,' the skipper declared and then turned to grin at Damian. 'You seem to have got us off to a good start, Damian. Hope you enjoy the match. Nice meeting you.'

'Here you are, son, that's for you to keep,' said the

referee, handing Damian the coin and accompanying it with the inevitable handshake.

'Thanks a lot,' Damian replied and then turned to make his way off the pitch.

As he neared the touch-line he saw that Ian Venn had stationed himself as close to the managers' dug-out as possible as if hoping to pick up some useful advice.

'Hey, I told you you'd get the money,' he called to Damian. 'Going to buy us all a Coke after the match?'

'I don't think ten-pence will exactly run to that,' Damian told him before he entered the tunnel that would take him back under the main stand.

By now, of course, the place was practically deserted and Damian experienced a sense of isolation as he changed back to his ordinary clothes in the odd-shaped kit-room. More fiercely than ever, he wished they'd allowed him to be one of the ball boys; he thought he'd have sacrificed the glory of being the mascot for the chance to stay close to the pitch. Instead, he made his way up the stairs to the seats where his parents were watching the match with every sign of interest.

'You looked really good out there, just as if you belonged on the pitch,' his mother greeted him. 'You seemed to be part of the team.'

'I think I'm a bit on the short side for that,' Damian remarked wryly.

'You won't always be!' his mother assured him, squeezing his arm. 'Honestly, we feel very proud of you.'

Damian, after glancing quickly at the pitch to see

how City were getting on, switched his attention to the directors' box. There he hoped to see Bryn Marsden, perhaps sitting beside the Club's chairman as a farewell gesture. But there was no sign at all of Darton United's President and honorary coach. Perhaps, after all, he'd been detained in London; at that moment he might even be training with Charlton and getting to know his new team-mates before playing his first match the following day.

'I think your lot have got a fight on their hands this afternoon,' said his father, cutting into Damian's thoughts.

'Oh, they're a bit like us, they don't always make a brilliant start,' Damian replied. To Damian's abiding horror, his father actually preferred rugby, both to watch and to play. He was always inclined to make disparaging remarks about soccer when he was sure Damian was listening.

However, it was true. City were pinned in their own half by the fast-moving, inventive Plymouth side which kept up the pressure with considerable skill. The only surprise to date was that the green-shirted Devon side hadn't scored a goal to underline their superiority. Even when City managed a breakaway movement Argyle's sweeper, a Danish international, was always on hand to make a telling interception. Yet, at half-time, there was still no score.

'I suppose you're off to join your mates for a free feast,' said Damian's father, offering his wife a toffee.

'Well, nothing was said about that,' Damian

admitted rather sorrowfully. 'Ricky Bennett told me to take the kit back to his office and that's what I did. I mean, I've no idea where our team's gone. Probably they're just in the kit-room, waiting for the second half.'

'Oh, well, you'd better have a toffee, too!'

Damian chewed away and thought that being the mascot wasn't such a wonderful thing after all. It was all over so quickly and he didn't have much to show for it, apart from the Redbourne City pennant. No one had even taken his photograph with the two captains and the referee, something he'd seen happen at a televised match. Worst of all, he hadn't seen Bryn and he was separated from his team-mates. To avoid having to make any further conversation he studied the match programme with unusual intensity. Then he discovered his own name in it, along with a reference to the fact that he captained Darton United, and immediately he felt quite cheerful again. He casually pointed it out to his mother.

'Oh, I know,' she said, 'because I've read your dad's programme. But we didn't tell you because we wanted you to find out for yourself.'

The good news came abruptly to an end just two minutes after the second half began when Plymouth scored the goal their dominant play deserved: a diving, almost horizontal, header from an unexpectedly early cross by their right winger. Damian groaned aloud but made a mental note to tell Stevie Pailthorp to hit some low crosses from time to time.

Although he kept an eye on the directors' box in case Bryn turned up, Damian began to watch the ball boys in action. In fact, they rarely had anything to do because when the ball went out of play it was usually a player who retrieved it (or a spectator in the crowd if it went as far as that). So perhaps he wasn't missing much after all by sitting in the stand, he consoled himself.

'Come on, City!' he urged under his breath. 'Everybody'll think I let you down if you lose. I'll be the *unlucky* mascot.'

Five minutes of the match remained when, in trying to hook the ball clear of an opponent, a Plymouth defender sliced it out of play and then fell as he tried to recover his balance. As the ball flashed over the touch-line Ian caught it at full stretch and, without a moment's hesitation, lobbed it straight to a City player who was well-positioned to take a throw-in. He accepted it gratefully, threw it to a team-mate who, taking advantage of the absence of cover around the Plymouth penalty area, hit a high cross to the far side of the box.

The timing of that centre, as it turned out, was superb. As if in anticipation of receiving the ball, City's leading striker had begun to race towards the penalty area as the throw-in was taken. Now, right on cue, he arrived on the ideal spot to rise above his solitary opponent and direct a powerful header into the top right-hand corner of the net for City's equalizer.

Damian was on his feet an instant before the spectacular goal was scored, eager to applaud the movement, and Ian's quick thinking, which had led to it. He had sensed that the ball was going to finish up in the net. His only regret was that it wasn't Bryn Marsden who'd applied the finishing touch.

'Well, that was worth waiting for, I must say,' Mr Tennant commented, much to his son's surprise. 'I suppose you'll be happy for the rest of the week after that, will you?'

'Happier,' was all Damian would concede. 'I mean, we haven't won, have we? Just like Darton United, City need to win every match they can if they're going to get anywhere in the League.'

But City couldn't manage the winner although in the final moments of the match Plymouth were defending desperately. His parents assured Damian they'd thoroughly enjoyed the match in addition to seeing him on the pitch as the mascot.

'You going to catch up with your pals now, then?' his father inquired. 'You'll all have a lot to talk about.'

'Well, I don't know,' Damian said doubtfully. 'I mean, nothing was fixed about after the match and – '

'Oh, go on! You might have a chance of another word with the players. No point in missing out on things if you can join in.'

So, grateful for the insistence, Damian pushed his way through the crowd leaving their seats and then dashed down the wide stairway to the kit-room. And the first person he saw there, just inside the doorway and holding a gift-wrapped package in his hands, was Bryn Marsden. The rest of the United players, some of them already changed out of their track suits, were all looking at the coach expectantly.

'Ah hello, Damian,' Bryn greeted him with a wide smile. 'I was wondering what had happened to you. I mean, I can't open my present without the captain being here, can I? Or a parting gift I'd better call it, hadn't I?'

'Er, um, yes, I suppose so,' Damian stammered, baffled by what was going on. He tried to catch Alex's or Ian's eye but both were staring intently at Bryn.

'Well, how about that! A wallet – and in red leather, too,' he exclaimed, plainly delighted, when he'd torn away the wrapping. 'Just what I need. Honestly, boys, it's really very kind of you to give me this but you shouldn't have spent your hard-earned pocket money on me.'

'We thought you'd need another wallet now you've joined a London club and you'll get lots and lots of money,' Jonathan joked.

'I don't know so much about that! Anyway, it costs about five times as much to live in London as it does in Redbourne so I'll probably be even worse off there. One thing's for sure, though: I'll miss Darton United. So you've got to promise to keep me up-to-date with results. OK?'

'Oh, we'll do that, Bryn,' Ian promised before anyone else could say a word. 'We can send you a report on every match and the League table from the local paper if you like.'

'Fine, fine. Oh, and Ian, that was a really smart bit of

work of yours when you caught that ball and gave it to Charlie Miller for the quick throw-in. I reckon that was why we scored! Really good work, son.'

'Yes, I thought so, too, Ian. I had a very good view from the stand and *everybody* thought it was terrific,' Damian added, thinking it was about time he said something.

'Well, boys, I'm afraid I've got to say cheerio for now. Got to have a word with some of my mates – oh, and Ally MacAndy as well, of course. Got to keep in with your old boss, you know. Never know when you might need him again!'

But, before he actually hurried away, Bryn made a point of shaking each boy by the hand and wishing him well in the future. Damian was the one he reached last and for him he had a slap on the back, too.

'Well, son, I hope you enjoyed being mascot – you looked good out there, I must say. I was a bit late getting here so I sat at the back of the stand, otherwise I'd have come down to meet you. Anyway, if you keep leading United the way you have been doing, things can't go far wrong. So all the best, Damian.'

'All the best to you, Bryn – and thanks again for everything you've done for us,' Damian told him fervently. 'And you'll still be our President, you know.'

As soon as Bryn was out of earshot, Damian turned to Ian and demanded to know why he hadn't been told about the plan to make a presentation to their departing coach. After all, he was the captain and it was his job to hand over a gift like that. It was obvious to everyone that he was angry at not being involved.

'Well, it was just a spur-of-the-moment idea yesterday and you weren't around when Jonathan and I discussed it,' Ian replied calmly. 'We paid for it out of our own money but the rest of the team have all said they'll chip in their share. It's 60p each if you want to join in, Damian. But you can give us the money later if you haven't got it on you.'

Damian swallowed his wrath. There was no point in losing his temper, especially over something he approved of. He dug into his pocket for his contribution.

'But you could have told me in advance,' he pointed out, handing over the money. 'I mean, I saw you all in here before the game began.'

'Well, I just forgot,' admitted Ian, pulling on his favourite red-and-blue sweater. 'Anyway, we didn't know if you were coming back here, did we? You were off up in the stand doing your own thing. You weren't with the rest of us and *involved* in the match, were you?'

'I *wanted* to be! But the club fixed it that way, saying I should sit in the stand with my parents.'

'Yeah, well, it doesn't matter now, does it?' said Ian, heading for the exit. 'See you at the committee meeting on Tuesday. There'll be plenty to talk about then. Come on, Jonathan, let's get back to my place and play some pool.'

As Damian set off on his own journey home, a few minutes later, he began to worry about the Tuesday meeting. He sensed that his leadership of Darton United was now under threat.

Four

Damian was demolishing a doughnut when Ian Venn walked in to the Canary Café with Jonathan McGuigan. He had known they would arrive together because it was obvious that their friendship was growing all the time. Yet, originally, Jonathan had been Alex's friend and he'd been introduced to the United team when Ian was out of it. Lately Damian had been wishing that he had a close friend in the side, but none of his team-mates went to his school; so he had very little contact with them except on match days.

'I'm going to have a slice of fly cemetery,' Jonathan announced loudly. 'It's the best food there is.'

None of the other customers appeared to take any notice of this peculiar taste, rather to Jonathan's disappointment. Like many goalkeepers, he was always happy to show off when he was assured of an audience.

Ian, shrugging his shoulders resignedly at Damian, accompanied Jonathan to the counter and there took some time in choosing what he wanted; eventually he settled for a large slice of chocolate cake displayed in a bell-shaped glass case beside the tea urn. The Canary Café had built its reputation with the town's afternoon tea-takers on its distinctly old-fashioned style. Its proprietor even addressed his adolescent customers (who were in the majority at this time of day) as 'Young sir' or 'Young lady.' His courtesy was so plainly sincere that no one was ever rude to him.

'Paul Merchant used to eat a lot of that stuff until he realised it was making him fat –and unfit,' commented Damian, pointing to the chocolate cake, as the others joined him at the table beside the leaded windows.

'No danger of that with me,' Ian replied confidently. 'I never put any weight on whatever I eat. I'm twice as fit as you – at least!'

Jonathan wasn't wasting eating-time on words: he was devouring his slice of treacle-and-currant tart with evident satisfaction. So far he'd hardly even glanced at Damian; it was almost as if he was embarrassed at being in his company. Damian, for his part, was wondering what had happened to Alex.

'Well, what are these ideas you've got about improving the team – in attack, anyway?' Damian inquired. He took only a small sip of his Coke because he was determined to make it last. He was desperately short of pocket money this week and he'd already had an advance on the following week's in order to buy some new football socks.

'I – well, we – think Jonathan here should move up front. He's got plenty of speed and he's the right height. I mean, that's just what we need most, isn't it?

Dalli-a-lot's got to have somebody to help him out and who else is there?'

Damian took a deep breath before replying. He'd watched a programme on mental and physical health and learned that it was very damaging to your system to explode with anger over anything. Take a deep breath and think carefully before speaking if you're upset: that was the advice he'd absorbed.

'I know this is saying the obvious,' he said in a deliberately slow tone, 'but Jonathan *is* our goalkeeper and, as far as I can remember, we don't have another goalkeeper. Am I right – '

'I wasn't *always* a goalie,' Jonathan put in quickly. 'I only took over last season because it was an emergency – you know, when your regular goalie was sent off. I used to be an outfield player and I was pretty good. Alex would back that up because we used to play in the same team when I scored quite a few goals. Well, I want to play up front again. I reckon I deserve the chance after all I've done for United.'

'But, Jonathan, we *need* you in goal. You've been brilliant there. You know – '

'You didn't say that last week!' Jonathan interrupted heatedly. 'You told me I *gave* Fyfield their last goal. You said I wasn't thinking about the game.'

'I don't think I put it quite like that, Jon,' Damian muttered, wishing now that he hadn't made that criticism.

'Well, maybe I *wasn't* thinking about goalkeeping,' Jonathan retaliated. 'I was probably thinking about getting really involved in the game in the middle of the park, not stuck out of the way between the posts. I think I've had goalkeeping up to here,' he added, putting the side of his hand against his throat.

'There is one other thing,' Ian said. 'Jonathan's a natural left-footer and you know we need somebody on the left flank. Well, with his height and speed *and* a good left foot he's exactly what we need. You know that's true, Damian. You've said the same thing yourself.'

Damian nodded. That couldn't be denied: United had to have a balanced team if they were to be successful. It had been in his mind to ask Alex Anson if he'd like to have a spell up front on the left flank because he was a two-footed player. But Alex was slightly built and didn't have much acceleration. He wouldn't be such a good prospect as Jonathan in that role.

'OK, I suppose we could give it a try,' the captain agreed reluctantly. 'But what do we do about getting somebody else to play in goal? We haven't any spare players and nobody else has any experience between the sticks.'

There was a significant pause before Ian, after a quick glance at Jonathan, made his next suggestion.

'I think you should have a go in goal,' he said to Damian.

'What! I'm not even tall enough to be a goalie! And – and I'm needed in midfield. That's my best position.'

'You don't *have* to be tall to be a goalkeeper – you've

got to be alert and, and athletic. Ready to jump and throw yourself about,' Ian argued. 'Well, you're pretty fit, I'll admit that, and you can jump a good height. I've seen you.'

Damian was still flabbergasted by the idea. To give himself time to work out the implications he took a longer sip of his drink. Of one thing he was beginning to be sure: that Ian, aided by Jonathan, was scheming to take his place as captain of United. It wasn't easy to lead a team from the goalmouth and if that's where he found himself then it would be much easier for Ian to take charge in midfield and influence the rest of their team-mates.

'Look,' said Ian, impatient to know what Damian would decide to do, 'a good captain ought to be willing to play *anywhere*. Yes, anywhere, for the good of the team. I know I am – would be, I mean.'

'If it's an emergency then *of course* I'd be willing to play in goal,' Damian told them. 'But I think we ought to try to find an experienced goalkeeper if we can. We can sign up another player as long as he's not registered with any other team in the League.'

'There won't be time for that before next Sunday, even if you could find anybody good enough,' Ian countered.

'No, I don't suppose there is but we can start looking,' Damian agreed. He turned his attention to Jonathan. 'If you've been wanting to give up goalkeeping why didn't you say something before now? You could've mentioned it when we were together on

Sunday.'

Jonathan interlaced his fingers and then cracked his knuckles audibly. 'Well, everyone was a bit down after our match was cancelled. So I didn't want to make things worse. I was also, well, er, a bit keen to get away.'

'To play pool with Ian, I suppose,' said Damian. He watched the other two exchange glances but neither of them spoke. But it wasn't worth pursuing so he changed the subject. 'Do either of you know why Alex hasn't turned up?'

Ian shook his head. 'Not a clue. He didn't say anything to me about not coming to our committee meeting.'

'I've no idea, either, but I saw him at school today so he must be OK. Perhaps he's charged off to the beach to see if he can spot a Gigantic Red-necked Sand Dune Hopper,' joked Jonathan in a reference to Alex's hobby of ornithology.

'You weren't thinking of putting him in as goalie, were you?' Ian asked sharply.

'No, not – '

'He'd be absolutely *useless* there!' Jonathan razored in. 'He couldn't catch anything – not even a cold! I know, I've seen him try.'

'No, that wasn't what I was thinking at all,' Damian replied mildly. 'But I did want to ask his opinion about things, including whether we should try and find another coach. After all, Alex is vice-captain, you know.'

'No, I don't think we need anybody now – we can sort things out for ourselves,' Ian remarked. 'OK, I know we lost out last match, but Fyfield are a pretty fair side and now we've decided on some changes up front things'll improve. What do you think, Jon?'

'Oh sure, I agree. I mean, I'll be livening things up in the forward line and we could get a stack of goals against Brattleby.'

Damian wasn't at all sure about their coaching; Bryn had taught them a great deal and they were a much, much better side as a result. What's more, they had to make their own way in the League and the Cup. All the same, even European Champions had at least one coach on their staff, which proved that top professionals realised they still had things to learn.

'Well, I'm not too sure we oughtn't to have somebody to help out, even if it's only giving some advice occasionally,' he told them. 'It'd be useful just to have some grown-up around to support us and look after any player who's injured during a game. I believe that just having Bryn on the touch-line gave us confidence – even if he'd never said a word.'

'I suppose we could look around and see if anyone is available,' Ian said without much enthusiasm. 'It'd be different if any of the City players wanted the job, but they don't. So – '

'How do you know that?' Damian wanted to know.

'Bryn told me. He said he'd asked 'em but they're either fixed up with other teams or don't want to be bothered with junior football. We asked Bryn about it when we gave him the wallet.'

'Oh, I see,' was all Damian could say. He felt quite deflated.

'Well, look, I've got to go now,' said Ian, who had been eyeing some rich fruit cake; but he decided it might spoil his tea after all. 'But are you going to play in goal for us, Damian?'

'Well, yes, I suppose I'll have to. As you said, a captain's got to give a lead. But in this case I'll be leading from the back, won't I, not the front. And you can't get any further back than being in goal!'

'Great!' Ian declared, getting to his feet. 'But you'd better get some practice in before we play Brattleby. They may have a leaky defence but they've got some fairly big guys in their attack and they'll be trying to swarm all over you.'

'Yeah,' said Jonathan with a grin and holding out his hand to Damian. 'Best of luck.'

'Thanks a lot,' replied Damian rather dolefully as he accepted another handshake.

Five

As he pulled on the scarlet goalkeeper's jersey in the makeshift dressing-room at Coolington Sports Ground, Damian pondered on the problems he was going out to face. He'd been thinking about them for most of the week, ever since he'd agreed to go in goal, but thinking hadn't made them any easier. He was still fearful of making some utterly stupid error that would not only cost Darton United a goal but provoke gales of laughter at his expense. Like everyone else, apart from professional clowns, he didn't want to look idiotic.

During a couple of lunch-breaks at school he'd managed to persuaded Carl, a form-mate, to go with him to the remotest corner of the school grounds so that he could practise some saves. Carl, who played for a top team in another division of the Sunday League, was renowned for the power of his shooting; and Damian saw no point in trying to cope with anything but the best that could be fired at him. They had put coats down for the goal posts and Damian had flung himself around with enormous energy and determination. His luck was in because a couple of boys, who were passing by, wanted to join in and so the new goalkeeper was forced to deal with close-range headers and fling himself at players' feet in order to stifle tap-in shots almost on the line.

At the end of the first session he felt utterly exhausted and his shoulder ached from an accidental knock he'd taken from someone's shoe while he was trying to grab the ball. But Carl was very complimentary: 'Your handling's not bad and you showed a lot of guts. But things'll be different in a match, you know.'

Damian did know that. He realised that the real test would come when he was under pressure from a crowd of players during a corner kick or when a free kick was taken from the edge of the box. It wasn't so much his height, or lack of it, that was worrying him because he thought that his ability to jump well might compensate for that. One thing he couldn't train for was coming off his line at precisely the right moment to make an interception. A goalkeeper's sense of timing was instinctive: either that or it was developed and refined over a long period.

'Feeling nervous?' Ian asked with a crooked sort of grin as the players drifted out on to the pitch.

'Not much point in that, is there? If I feel nervous I'm bound to make mistakes. So I've got to feel confident. Then the rest of the defence will feel confident, too.'

Ian didn't make any reply but moved off with Jonathan to get some shooting-in practice that was clearly going to test Damian's reactions. Alex came to stand on the line beside his skipper. Damian had already asked him about his absence from the Canary Café meeting and Alex, giving nothing away, had merely said: 'Look, there's lots to tell you so let's have a talk after the match. We can go to my house if you like and you can eat with us.' That was such a surprise that Damian hadn't tried to question him any further.

When, a couple of minutes later, Damian went to the centre to toss-up, he saw that Ian hadn't been exaggerating when he described Brattleby's strikers as 'fairly big'. They looked like giants, towering over everyone else in their own side, so it was no wonder they'd scored a sackful of goals between them.

With the sun slanting across the pitch, Damian decided that he might as well let the other goalkeeper suffer its worst effects in the first half and so it was Brattleby who kicked off after losing the toss. There were several other matches taking place at the Coolington Ground, but Brattleby were unique in their choice of colours: chocolate-and-orange halved shirts and lighter brown shorts and socks. It was already, as one of the handful of spectators remarked in Damian's hearing, a colourful match. He hoped for an early touch of the ball to give him confidence in his handling: and he hadn't long to wait.

On their first real raid deep into United's half, Brattleby were awarded a free kick only a metre or so outside the box when Paul Merchant floored Matt Carter, the bigger of the two strikers. Damian had remonstrated with Paul after his feeble display in the

Fyfield match when the full-back was trying to avoid an injury before making his debut as a ball boy at the City Ground, and it seemed that Paul had learned his lesson. Now he was tackling with determination but, unhappily, without complete legality. Matt was accustomed to getting his own way against smaller opponents, but if ever they outwitted him or put in a clumsy tackle that caused him to lose the ball then he didn't hesitate to bellow that he'd been fouled. This time the referee had no option but to agree with him.

'Move over, move to the right!' Damian yelled to his defensive wall. He couldn't see anything of what was going on just outside the penalty area. If he didn't have some indication of where the shot was going his chances of saving it wouldn't be high. But, obstinately, the wall wouldn't co-operate; two opponents had joined in and the United defenders were rightly suspicious of their intentions.

At the last moment the Brattleby players duly broke away from the wall in a well-rehearsed movement and the ball, struck fiercely and accurately, came whistling through the gap they'd left. However, the kicker hadn't been able to keep it as low as he'd hoped and Damian was able to take the ball in his arms without having to move a centimetre. Even so, the force of the shot rocked him back on his heels and he was thankful he hadn't fumbled it as Matt Carter came bursting through the scattering defenders to challenge him.

'Well held, son,' said a voice behind the net as if he'd taken a catch on the boundary at cricket. Damian was genuinely pleased by the praise: it confirmed that he'd reacted well to his first test as a goalkeeper. Alex, too, nodded his approval and Damian nonchalantly bounced the ball a couple of times in his area before punting it well down the field. He'd been practising his drop-kicking and now he was able to achieve a good distance, though not as far as Jonathan could manage with his best efforts.

At the first opportunity, Ian Venn clipped the ball into Jonathan's path and yelled at him to run, run, run. So Jonathan ran, ran, ran – and no one seemed able to stop him as he swerved round one defender, cheekily nutmegged another and then cut into the penalty area. Damian, with his distant view of events, couldn't tell how close to the goalie Jonathan was before he fired in a shot; but, sadly for United, it was easily saved, the keeper plucking the ball out of the air as though reaching for an apple on a low branch. Nonetheless, Jonathan had every right to look pleased with his performance. Ian and one or two others applauded him heartily. It was obvious that he could control a ball, could run and was willing to take on defenders.

Most of all, it was the United forwards who were encouraged – and Neil Dallimore was inspired. Within moments of that McGuigan raid the ball was at Stevie Pailthorp's feet and he, too, decided to take on the Brattleby defence. Instead of passing to Ian, as Ian was demanding loudly and almost threateningly, Stevie sped down the touch-line, drew the full-back, put the ball past him on one side and scooted round him the other and then cut inside. The figure he'd picked out on the other flank to pass to was, naturally, Jonathan. The only trouble was that Stevie made his intention so clear to the Brattleby defenders that they had no trouble in intercepting that pass long before it might have reached Jonathan.

'I told you to give me the ball,' Ian complained bitterly. 'Do as you're told next time, Stevie.'

Stevie gave him a sharp look and made the predictable reply. 'You're not the captain. I don't have to obey your orders.'

'I'm thinking about *the team*,' Ian replied between clenched teeth. 'I was the nearest to you. Between us we could have ripped their defence wide open. And I had a better view than you.'

Those two raids had certainly given the chocolate-and-orange-shirted team the impression that United possessed some talented players; and, for the moment, their own attacking ambitions faded. Ian and Billy Sandford were beginning to dominate midfield and, whenever there was a fifty-fifty ball, it was one of them who emerged with it. To his astonishment, Damian was nothing more than a spectator; and he began to wish that he was playing up-front to capitalise on some of the mistakes their opponents were making.

Neutral observers – if such existed – wouldn't have been one whit surprised that, in the tenth minute of the match, Darton forced a succession of corners on the right. The first two were fruitless because the ball didn't even reach the goalmouth from Stevie's kicks but, for the third, the kick was taken by Ian who could unleash a lot of power when it was needed. Stevie hadn't argued when Ian asked, rather than demanded, to take the kick and he himself was the one who rose to head the ball when it came over at the perfect height. He was directing it towards the top right-hand corner of the net but, as the ball began to loop down, Jonathan, with faultless timing and initiative, jumped to divert it with his forehead into the opposite side of the net past the stranded goalkeeper.

The scorer was so ecstatic he actually turned a cartwheel – and then was mobbed by every Darton player who could reach him. It must, to the Brattleby team, have seemed like the winning goal in a Cup Final instead of simply being the first goal in a fairly ordinary Sunday League match.

'I told you this could happen!' Ian yelled to Damian when at last he returned to the centre circle for the re-start.

'Great!' Damian yelled back. He had advanced to the edge of his penalty area but knew it wasn't wise to go any further. Yet he wanted to caution his team to stay cool; one goal at this stage wasn't enough to guarantee victory. They needed another goal but, before that, they'd have to defend against Brattleby's inevitable determination to score the equalizer.

Billy, who was having an excellent game, stemmed the first onslaught with a timely tackle but only moments later the referee blew for an infringement when, unluckily, the ball struck Billy on the hand. Billy

naturally protested that it was an accident but the ref waved him away.

Unhappily, Billy couldn't accept that warning and, continuing to demand justice from the referee, was booked for dissent. 'Oh, you idiot!' Damian murmured under his breath. Now, if Billy committed another bookable offence, he'd be sent off and the team as a whole would suffer. In training sessions with Bryn their coach had emphasised umpteen times how stupid it was to try to argue with referees. 'It's the ref who *always* wins,' Bryn pointed out; but Billy seemed to have forgotten that.

A Brattleby full-back swung the ball into the goalmouth. It was really a 'keeper's ball, to move out and jump for, but Damian had hesitated because he thought Paul Merchant was going to get there first and head it away. With the instinct of the striker for a half-chance Matt Carter flung himself headlong at the ball as it fell to waist height. What he couldn't control was his aim and all he succeeded in doing was turning the ball sideways towards Graeme Roustoby, his co-striker. Roustoby lunged at the ball just as Damian, deciding he must seize his chance, dived forward.

The Brattleby striker tumbled headlong over the goalkeeper as Damian tried to gather the ball which, in the mêlée, bounced out of his hands. Paul, recovering his composure after his own error of judgment, tried to clear the danger: but he missed the ball and instead his boot went into Damian's ribs. At the moment of impact Damian didn't realise how hard he'd been struck: his one concern was to grab the ball and, still on his knees, he reached out and succeeded in smothering it. Then, as he tried to get to his feet, he felt the fearful pain. Hugging the ball into his midriff, he sank to his knees again. The referee, spotting the contorted expression on Damian's face as he went down, promptly blew his whistle to stop the game.

'How do you feel, son?' he inquired with genuine concern as he tried to raise the injured player to his feet.

'Like death!' Damian gasped, which caused a couple of players to laugh and the ref to frown warningly. He knew from wide experience the kind of player who told the truth and the one who was a malingerer.

'Let's have a look at the damage,' said the ref, rolling up Damian's jersey and exploring his ribs with surprisingly tender fingers.

Damian, wincing with the pain of the blow and certain that something was smashed, found it hard even to stand upright. He didn't even realise he was still tightly clutching the ball until the ref, smilingly, persuaded him to surrender it to someone else.

'I don't *think* there's anything broken but if it stays very painful perhaps you ought to see your doctor,' the referee told him. 'Probably you'll just have a bad bruise there – a battle scar, if you like!'

Damian couldn't share in the smile but he was thankful the injury wasn't as bad as he'd feared. Perhaps, too, the pain was receding a little. At least he was able to stand up straight and walk about.

'D'you think you can carry on, son?' the referee

wanted to know. 'But don't try to be too brave just for the sake of it. If you feel in trouble we can certainly find somebody else to wear that smashing red jersey of yours.'

Damian could see that several of his players were looking alarmed at the possibility of being asked to take over in goal, though he noticed that Jonathan McGuigan was keeping well away from the penalty area. Doubtless he wanted to avoid the risk of having to resume his old role; and doubtless, too, he would claim that, now he was a goal-scorer, he was too valuable in the forward line to be replaced.

'You'll be all right, won't you, Damian?' Ian asked with a trace of anxiety in his voice.

Damian did momentarily think of saying that he'd be glad if Ian himself would take over but he sensed that Jonathan, for one, would simply believe that was a trick to put pressure on him (Jonathan) to volunteer. In any case, he suspected that Ian would be a hopeless goalkeeper because he lacked concentration – and he probably couldn't jump very high, either.

'I'll just about manage, I reckon,' Damian said to Ian's obvious relief. 'Oh, and who was it who whacked me?'

'Paul Merchant!' three players exclaimed simultaneously.

'Huh – the Merchant of Death,' joked Alex, remembering Damian's first words when the referee asked how he felt. Paul himself looked aghast but the rest of the group around Damian laughed.

'Well, next time, don't kick me, kick one of the opposition,' Damian told the moon-faced full-back.

By now the game was about to be re-started with what the referee had decided should be a free kick, although that was hardly a strict interpretation of the rules as no Brattleby player had committed any offence; but he wasn't going to drop the ball on the goal-line and risk another injury to the goalkeeper.

Fortunately for Damian, who was trying to ease the pain by massaging his rib cage, the ball was detained in midfield for two or three minutes as both sides struggled to dominate the game. Brattleby had the feeling that the fates were against them and none of their players had the confidence to retain possession and outwit opponents with sheer ball skills.

Then the deadlock was broken by the unexpected enterprise of Stevie Pailthorp who, up to that moment, had contributed hardly anything to the game, not least because Ian was tending to feed Jonathan on the left flank rather than Stevie on the right. It was this sense of isolation that made the speedy winger keep possession when he picked up a sliced clearance; he had plenty of energy in reserve and he was going to use some of it up. The mazy run he began was a revelation to his team-mates as well as to Brattleby. He edged in to the penalty area and then out again; seemed to make for the corner flag but then back-tracked to the eighteen-yard line; and then, after defeating two attempted tackles with quite audacious sleight-of-foot, he suddenly accelerated into top gear, swerved round the last defender and, noting the goalkeeper's uncertainty, fired a fierce shot that kept low and stayed on target all the way. A second before the goalie decided to dive, the ball was zipping past him on its way into the far bottom corner of the net.

Even Stevie himself seemed to find it hard to believe that he'd scored such a goal. Open-mouthed at his own accomplishment he stood, transfixed, as, first, spectators erupted into loud applause and, second, his team-mates rushed towards him to submerge him in praise.

'Fantastic goal!' Ian exclaimed. 'Out of this world!'

That seemed the right description. The Brattleby players were actually walking around, blinking or shaking their heads, as if they'd just arrived from another planet. Even the referee, after making a note in his book, made a point of going up to Stevie to say: 'Well done, son. That was a fine achievement. Pity the television cameras weren't here to record it!'

When, three minutes later, the whistle shrilled for half-time, Steve Pailthorp's goal was still all anybody could talk about. Because he was modest by nature he didn't care for all the fuss and he insisted: 'Look I didn't *know* I was going to score like that when I picked the ball up. I mean, it just, well, sort of *happened*. I could've missed just as easily, couldn't I?'

'Well, that's sewn the game up, no danger,' Ian chortled. 'We ought to get plenty more goals in the second half because they're shell-shocked. Don't know what's hit 'em!'

'I think they'll be pretty dangerous in the second half,' Damian declared. 'They'll have to attack, won't they, because they've got nothing to lose now they're two down.'

'Aw, come on, *skipper*, you can do better than that!' Ian said with plain sarcasm. 'Don't start talking as though we're going to *lose*. When we're winning like we are you should look on the bright side.'

Damian, who was munching his potassium-rich banana to ward off any risk of fatigue, shook his head violently. He was beginning to get tired of Ian's assumption that he was the only one with all the answers.

'You didn't listen to what I said,' he told him. 'I'm just being realistic. But at soccer, anything can happen. You should know that.'

'Complacent, that's what teams can get when they're in front,' Alex Anson put in much to Damian's surprise. 'We musn't be complacent. If we do we're in trouble. I agree with what Damian said.'

Damian gave him a grateful look and waited to see what Ian would come up with next. But the midfielder simply shrugged his shoulders and then went into a huddled chat with Jonathan for the remainder of the interval.

In fact, Damian's prediction was totally accurate. Brattleby began the second half as if they'd been threatened with execution if they didn't score a quick goal. Graeme Roustoby appeared determined to emulate Stevie's feat and he almost succeeded. His run, however, was more direct but he shrugged off the attentions of Ian and Billy and then sent Paul the wrong way with a delightful dummy before hammering in a ferocious shot. Afterwards Damian wondered how he'd reached the ball but somehow he managed to palm it against the angle of the upright and the crossbar: and when it rebounded he gratefully caught it.

'You lucky devil!' Roustoby yelled at him and Damian could hardly deny it. For once luck did seem to be on his side.

That was only the first in a wave of attacks and Damian guessed that his luck couldn't hold out for ever, especially after he'd diverted one shot to safety with his heel while lying on the ground after a mêlée. The United defence had been doing their best to protect him in every way and Alex had never played better or more intelligently; he seemed to know what an opponent was going to do before the opponent himself knew. In contrast, Matt Carter was having absolutely no luck at all and then, when presented with an open goal, he mis-kicked completely and skyed the ball over the bar. Damian was just starting to feel that being a stand-in goalkeeper wasn't so terrible after all when Brattleby got their long-awaited goal and he took another painful knock. This time the referee could do nothing to help him: and, in any case, in his opinion the goalkeeper had acquitted himself exceptionally well in his new role.

For once the full-backs were caught unawares as Roustoby pounced on a poor pass from a team-mate and sprinted clear of everyone into the penalty area. Damian, on his line, now experienced the goalie's classic dilemma.

His instinct was to stay on his line and hope that the striker would hit his shot within reach; but then he decided he must rush out to unsettle him and try to grab the ball. He very nearly succeeded in his aim but Graeme was cool enough to pull the ball back as Damian dived and then take it round the prone goalkeeper before sliding it into the net. Yet, as he did so, Damian's despairing hand caught his ankle and Graeme, knocked off balance, fell backwards on top of his opponent. For the second time in the match Damian had the breath squashed out of him and pain came flooding back. Graeme, of course, was on his feet in an instant and charging back to the centre, waving his arms in glee at putting Brattleby back into the game.

'You nearly got there and stopped the goal,' Alex told his captain. 'Honestly, you were a bit unlucky.'

Damian, receiving further ministrations from the concerned referee, shook his head. 'I don't agree,' he said when at last he could speak again. 'My timing was wrong. Goalkeeping isn't my game, I've decided.'

But, after Darton had hung on, if at times precariously, for a 2–1 victory, the rest of the team tried to convince the skipper that he'd not only done a fine job in goal but brought them some welcome luck. The overwhelming view was that he should stay between the posts for the remainder of the season.

'No way!' Damian replied decisively. 'I think *I* was lucky, apart from getting bashed about. We need a goalkeeper who *really* knows what he's doing all the time and isn't just hoping for the best. So if Jonathan is going to stay up front we'll have to find somebody else.'

Six

Damian took a long sniff. 'Hey, that smells good, *really* good!' he exclaimed. 'What is it?'

'Nut roast, I expect,' answered Alex, slinging his sports bag neatly on to a couple of coat hooks in the hall. 'It's what we usually have on a Sunday.'

'Nuts! What sort of nuts?' was the disbelieving question.

'Oh, I don't know: hazel, brazil, walnuts, all sorts. You can mix 'em up and get lots of different flavours. If we're lucky we might get some chips as well. I know they're not supposed to be good for you but Mum often makes some just for me.'

Mrs Anson appeared in the kitchen doorway at that moment to greet them, brushing strands of her long, black hair away from her eyes with the back of the hand that was holding a wooden spoon.

'Hi, nice to see you, Damian. I'm glad you're here because I've kept telling Alex it was time he brought his boss home for lunch!'

'Boss?' Damian was genuinely baffled.

'Well, you're the captain, aren't you? And Alex is vice-captain, right? So you're in charge. Alex is a great one for chains of command in my experience. He thinks highly of you, Damian.'

'Oh,' was all Damian could say. He glanced at his friend but Alex didn't look to be embarrassed in the slightest. He went up to his mother to give her a kiss and then ask if Damian could phone home to say that he was lunching out. Of course, he was told, and Mrs Anson pointed to the study before returning to the kitchen to put the chips on.

Mrs Tennant seemed relieved to hear her son's news because, she said, she was leaving early for an important badminton tournament and Damian's father was away playing golf all day.

'So they didn't want me around anyway,' Damian said to Alex with wry amusement. 'Listen, I didn't know you thought much about being vice-captain. I got the idea you felt it was meaningless.'

'Oh no!' Alex, reclining in his father's black leather office chair, replied indignantly. 'It's my job to back you up at all times.'

'Well, I didn't notice you backing me up at the Canary Café meeting. You didn't even turn up!'

'That was on purpose,' Alex explained solemnly. 'You see, Ian hoped I would help him and Jonathan get rid of you as captain. No, hang on! Let me finish. It's been obvious to everybody that Ian wants to be captain again. He got Jonathan on his side and he thought that would influence me to support him as well because Jon

and I used to be mates. But Jonathan's got big-headed and is going around with a different crowd now. So – '

'But if you'd turned up at the meeting you could just have stood by me and said what you've said now,' Damian cut in.

Alex shook his head. 'No, that wouldn't have worked. Ian wanted to have a vote. If you and I had voted together against those two it would have been 2–2. But that would have caused a bad split and more trouble in the future. It was best to make sure there wasn't going to be a vote at all. Don't you see that, Damian?'

'Well yes, now you've explained it. But I expect it'll happen again in the future so it might have been best to have sorted it out then at the Canary.'

Again Alex disagreed. 'I don't think it will crop up again. The rest of the team really admire you for taking over in goal. They think that shows real leadership. I know because I've been round everybody, asking them what they think. If there was a vote you'd win at least 9–2. They wouldn't want Ian as captain because they know he wouldn't have become the goalie.'

'He said he would!'

'Maybe he did. But he didn't mean it. Ian's always willing to say anything to get what he wants. I'll tell you something else, Damian: Ian claimed he'd got you to go between the sticks because you couldn't shout at him from there! He hated it when you told him off but you were right to do it. You see, Ian only thinks of himself but you, well, you think of the *team*. That's why you're a good leader and Ian never would be.'

Before Damian could reply Mrs Anson called them to lunch and he was introduced to Alex's younger brother, Scott, who looked even more studious than Alex usually did. The nut roast and *mange tout* and chips were as delicious as anything Damian had ever eaten and, because he was ravenous after the game, he was thankful there was enough of everything for second helpings.

'Look, if you two want to natter away about soccer, that's fine by us,' Mrs Anson remarked. 'Alex normally doesn't get much chance of that because the rest of us aren't exactly mad keen supporters. Alex apart, we aren't a sporty family, except for the odd game of ping-pong.'

'Table tennis, Mum!' Alex corrected her fiercely, but his mother merely laughed.

'Look, do you reckon Jonathan is determined not to play in goal any more?' asked Damian, taking up Mrs Anson's invitation.

'Oh sure. Now he's scored a goal he'll want to become a striker. He always did fancy himself as a great goal-scorer.'

'Well, in that case, we'll just have to find another goalie. But where do we begin . . .?'

He paused as Mrs Anson gave him a generous portion of lemon meringue pie which proved to be too good to linger over.

'I think I can help,' Alex disclosed. 'There's a lad from our school who plays in Saturday games for Farnfield. They play at Sundial Hill near you and I think Hajinder is pretty good. If you went to watch him next Saturday you could see what you think and then talk to him.'

'Great! We could go together and – '

'No, sorry, I can't,' Alex interrupted. 'You see Scott is playing his fiddle in a concert in Peterborough and the whole family's promised to go and support him. As I say, I've seen Hajinder but it's what you think that matters. You're the skipper. Anyway, now you've played in goal yourself you'll know exactly what to look for.'

'You can say that again!' Damian responded feelingly, tenderly exploring his ribs.

Seven

Standing under the shower in the bathroom at home, Damian was alternating the hot water with the cold and gasping with exaggerated pleasure at each temperature change. The hot-and-then-cold water treatment was, he'd read, excellent for toning up the whole body and especially beneficial to sportsmen. Although he wasn't playing in any game that day he'd decided he might as well test the idea and see how he felt as a result.

He was just about to switch off when his mother walked in.

'Hey,' he exclaimed, 'I thought bathrooms were supposed to be private places!'

'Oh, that's just an old-fashioned idea,' she replied airily. 'Anyway, you can't have any secrets from me. I've known you since you were born! Oh, and you were making such a row I feared you were drowning or something.'

Damian grinned and, stepping out of the stall, took the towel his mother had removed from the heated rail. 'I was just proving how terrifically fit I am,' he said, starting to rub his hair dry.

'Damian! What on earth have you been up to? How did you get that colossal bruise on your side – and that other one on your leg? You haven't been fighting have you?'

He was taken aback by her concern; so far as he was concerned the yellow and purple patches were fading nicely and the pain had just about gone. But then he realised she hadn't seen them before.

'Oh, I just took a couple of minor knocks when I was goalkeeper last week,' he said dismissively. 'Honestly, they're fine now, Mum. It was just a bit of bad luck at the time.'

'Honestly, I'd no idea football was such a dangerous game. If that's what – '

'Mum, I told you: it was just bad luck and I wasn't used to being in goal. And I won't be again if everything goes well today. That's why you're dropping me off at Sundial Hill, so that I can find a replacement goalkeeper.'

His mother gave him a doubting glance. 'Well, it had better go well. I don't want to see you covered in bruises again, darling. Sport should be for pleasure, not physical endurance and pain. Now listen, I want to be away from here in five minutes. So you'd better get some clothes on pretty smartly.'

Of course, she was in a hurry because she was going to play yet another badminton game, but Damian didn't mind leaving earlier than he'd planned because it would give him time to see more football at Sundial

Hill, where, on a Saturday, as many as a dozen matches would be taking place.

'You're very quiet,' his mother remarked in the car. 'You're not worrying about anything, are you? I mean, if it's your football with all these problems about injuries and other people wanting to be captain, maybe you *ought* to give it up. The captaincy, I mean. Then you'd probably start enjoying the game again.'

'No way!' Damian replied emphatically. 'I'm going to go on being captain and everybody knows that – or they soon will. I'm going to lift United, even if I have to do *everything* myself.'

'But your friend Alex is going to help, isn't he? I think it was very thoughtful the way he took you off to lunch at his home last Sunday.'

'Oh, sure, Alex is going to help. But it's up to me to make all the important decisions. Well, this'll do fine, Mum – and thanks a lot for the lift. Hope you win *your* game.'

He thought about Alex as he wandered between the games, looking for the one in which Hajinder was taking part. Until the previous weekend he'd never appreciated how much United meant to Alex and the degree of loyalty that he possessed. But for Alex's clever move in absenting himself from the Canary Café meeting, a deep division might have appeared within the ranks of the United players with Ian and Jonathan trying to win votes for Ian as captain. Instead, he had played creditably in goal (Damian saw no point in being falsely modest), Jonathan had demonstrated that he *could* play up front and team spirit was excellent. Now, if they kept on winning, no talk about changing captains could possibly be justified.

As it turned out, he timed his arrival beautifully. His first view of Hajinder was as the scarlet-sweatered goalkeeper flung himself bodily across the goalmouth to turn a shot round the post. Then, from the resulting corner, he jumped bravely through a crowd of attackers to punch the ball effectively out of the area. Because he himself had twice failed to connect when trying to punch the ball clear the previous Sunday Damian was impressed by Hajinder's effort. A few moments later the ball was at the other end of the pitch and so, when Hajinder glanced round, Damian gave him an encouraging smile and called: 'Terrific save you made there.'

Hajinder nodded his thanks but didn't allow his concentration to lapse in spite of the fact that play was going entirely in favour of his team. Damian had already spotted some skilful ball control by one of their forwards who seemed to have plenty of time to do whatever he wanted to do, whether it was to pass or take on an opponent or to shoot. That, he knew, was always the mark of a talented player. Damian started to wonder whether he, too, was free to join United.

Damian waited until half-time before he made any approach to Hajinder and even then he inquired whether the goalkeeper was needed to take part in any team talk. But, it turned out, he wasn't; and, it also turned out, he wasn't too keen on playing for United when Damian, after introducing himself and mentioning his friendship with Alex, broached the subject.

'You're not doing very well, are you?' he pointed out. 'I look at the League tables regularly so I know where you are. Only just in the top half. Yes?'

Damian had anticipated that answer. 'That's because we need a top-class goalie like you, Hajinder. We've been letting in too many goals. You'd've stopped nearly all the ones that Jonathan let in. Oh, and the one that got past me last Sunday, too.'

Hajinder didn't respond immediately to such flattery. He appeared to be pondering some point. Damian decided he must press his case as enthusiastically as possible. If Hajinder turned them down Damian hadn't a clue who else he might approach.

'All the rest of the team are dead keen to have you in the side,' he added. 'You'd give us all bags of confidence.'

Hajinder began pulling at the lobe of his left ear, something his father always did when he was being persuasive. 'If I agreed, then you'd have to keep me in goal for every match. Whatever happens.'

Damian stared. 'What, even if you, er, had a run of bad games – made a lot of mistakes?'

'That's right. You're not allowed to drop me, not for any reason.'

'But not even the captain of England is guaranteed his place in the team for *every* match,' Damian pointed out. 'Managers are always telling top players that they still have to play for their places. The manager of Arsenal said last week that a player's only as good as his last match. I know, I heard him on the radio myself.'

'But you're not a manager,' Hajinder said softly.

'I know, but I'm the captain. I pick the team, more or less.'

'Then,' Hajinder said triumphantly, 'there's no problem, is there? You just keep choosing me and no one can argue.'

'Well, I don't know about that, Haji. There's a bit of a risk in it and – '

'But you just said yourself that I'm a top class goalie. So how can you speak of risks?'

Damian paused, reflecting. 'Well, I mean, you could suffer a loss of form. That could happen to anybody. Even the captain of England. Look, I'll have to think about this, Haji.'

The dark-skinned boy shrugged. 'Well, please yourself, my friend.' He hesitated and then added: 'Anyway, Scale Hill Colts, are *really* interested in me.'

'Have they actually asked you to play for them?' Damian wanted to know.

'Almost. They said they'd be round to sign me up as soon as their regular goalkeeper left. His family's moving to London, you see.'

Damian scratched his head, trying to remember something. 'Isn't that Tony Hooberry?' he asked.

'Perhaps,' said Haji indifferently.

'Well, he won't be leaving for a long time!' Damian

announced with some satisfaction. 'His Dad's decided not to move after all. Mrs Hooberry says she can't bear the thought of leaving Darton. I know that because she meets my Mum at the Leisure Centre. They play badminton together. Sometimes she comes to our house.'

'Oh' said Hajinder, defeated for the moment.

But at that point negotiations had to be suspended anyway because the referee was signalling the start of the second half.

Hajinder was soon in action and dealt very competently with a couple of long-range shots as well as an almost suicidal back pass from one of his side's central defenders. Certainly he wasn't afraid to throw himself about when necessary and the risk of getting kicked in a mêlée didn't deter him. There were moments when he appeared to have a nonchalant, almost arrogant, attitude towards his role; but Damian knew that a confident player was a skilful player. In any case, he had an idea that Hajinder was simply showing off in order to try and impress him.

Eventually, however, Damian decided he ought to see what else was going on. After all, if he was here as a scout then he should be sizing up other possible signings for United. Hajinder's remark that Damian wasn't a manager had had the effect of making him realise that he was virtually in complete charge of the team. Nobody argued about his selections: or, at least, not until recently when Ian suggested changes and Jonathan elected to play as a striker. So if he could now provide them with a reliable goalkeeper and perhaps one other new player his position as captain would be beyond any challenge.

Of all the players he saw while strolling round the various pitches at Sundial none could really begin to compare with the striker he'd noticed in Hajinder's team. Long-legged rather than just tall, he made whatever he did look remarkably simple. There was economy of effort and precision in all his moves and when he scored his side's winning goal a couple of minutes from the end of the game with a deft lob over the goalkeeper's outstretched arms Damian instinctively applauded. Yet the scorer himself seemed quite unconcerned about his achievement.

He was behind Hajinder's goal again when the match came to an end and by then Damian had decided that United had found the goalkeeper they needed. His one problem now was to convince Hajinder that he would be doing the best for himself by joining Darton.

But, to his surprise, Hajinder had already reached his own decision.

'I've noticed you studying other goalkeepers today,' he said, coming to stand close to Damian and look him straight in the eyes. 'Am I the best you've seen?'

'Yes, definitely,' Damian replied truthfully.

'In that case, I will play for your Darton United. I think you are an honest person and you will play fair with me. So I will always play my best for the team.'

'Great!' Damian was delighted. Then, quickly, he added: 'Look, I'll fill you in on all the details about

Darton after you've got changed. But what's the name of the boy who scored the winning goal for you?'

'Warren Snowball.'

'What! I don't – '

'It's true! But you mustn't make jokes about his name. He hates that, though some of the boys call him Icy and he doesn't mind that, I think. We all think he is a very cool player, you see.'

'Yeah, you can say that again,' Damian agreed. 'D'you know if he plays for anybody in the Sunday League?'

Hajinder shook his head. 'I doubt that. He has, you see, only just come to live in this town. So I think he will not have made many friends yet. Also, he is a bit of a loner, doesn't mix with many people.'

'Well, could you tell him I'd like a word? I'll wait for you both to get changed.'

'OK, Damian, we won't be long,' Hajinder promised before dashing off to the distant changing-rooms.

When they met, a few minutes later, Damian wasn't at all surprised by the nickname Warren had been given. His eyes were a startling light grey and his look distinctly cool and rather calculating. Yet his voice and his manner were friendly enough when he responded to Damian's invitation to join Darton United.

'Sure, I'm interested. I wanted to play regularly when I came to Redbourne. But I was off sick for three weeks and I didn't get the chance. Are United any good? I mean, I don't want to go to a useless team. I want to be with a team that's going to win things.'

'Oh, yes, I'm the same!' Damian told him emphatically. 'Darton are definitely getting better all the time. We had a bad time last season but then we got Bryn Marsden as coach and he made a terrific difference to us. He also arranged for the rest of the team to be ball boys at the Plymouth match and I was mascot. So we're really ambitious, Warren. With you and Hajinder in the side I reckon we can be the best in the Division.'

Warren nodded, his eyes now beginning to glow a little with enthusiasm. 'Can you – we – get promotion this season?'

'I don't see why not, if we keep winning. There are enough matches left to get the points we need. Tell you what: come to the Canary Café after school next Tuesday. Both of you, I mean. Then you can meet Alex Anson – well, I think you already know him, Haji. He's our vice-captain. And there'll be a couple of other players there, too, Ian Venn, who plays in midfield alongside me and Jonathan McGuigan, who is also, er, a striker. We can really get down to talking about tactics and future matches and things like that.'

'Sounds a good idea,' Warren commented. 'Let's do that, then. Do you think there's a chance I might get invited to be City's mascot?'

'Er, I've no idea,' Damian confessed. 'Now that Bryn's gone we don't have the same contact with City. But, well, I suppose it's possible if we can keep in touch with the club.'

Warren had noticed, though Damian hadn't, that a

car was making its way along the boundary of the sports area towards them. It pulled up alongside them and the front passenger door was opened.

'This is my dad, come to pick me up,' Warren said off-handedly. 'And Hajinder, too. See you then, Damian.'

Damian waved them off. It didn't occur to him that he hadn't been offered a lift home; but then he didn't really want one. He was going to enjoy a walk further up Sundial Hill, just on his own. After all, he had a lot to think about: a lot of good things. With his friend Alex's help he had, that morning, become a successful football scout. From now on, with Hajinder and Warren in their ranks, Darton United would be a very successful Sunday League team. Of that, Damian had no doubt at all.

Eight

Everyone was listening to Damian, and listening with some attention. Damian himself was feeling nervous, more nervous than he'd ever been in his life he thought, and that was why he was pacing up and down the changing-room as he talked about the game ahead of them. They were playing Ellel Thistle, the Division leaders, and Damian was describing it as the most important match in Darton United's history.

'If we win this one it'll show everybody that we have to be taken seriously as promotion candidates,' he insisted, punching one fist into the palm of his hand in an unconscious imitation of one of Bryn Marsden's mannerisms. 'It'll show that we have *really* arrived.'

'It'll also show Thistle that they aren't as sharp as they think they are!' joked Neil Dallimore, and nearly everyone laughed. And that helped to reduce the tension.

Neil had every reason to feel in good humour because he was one of the players who had benefited most from the arrival of Warren Snowball, the boy with the

unbelievable name and the talent that sometimes had to be seen to be believed. His unselfish play had set up several goal-scoring chances for Neil which even he, in his most erratic form, could hardly miss. Of course, he still had managed to miss a few but he'd put the rest away with deep satisfaction. Warren was inclined to play just behind Neil and Jonathan, the two front-runners, and the opposition hadn't always worked out quickly enough just how dangerous he was as the real creator of chances.

'Well, I'm glad we're all in a good mood,' Damian concluded, 'because if we aren't at our best we won't beat this lot. But if we can get an early goal and really rattle 'em then we'll win. Then we can really start thinking about promotion. So, good luck boys.'

As they ran out on to the pitch Damian had a last word with Warren. 'It'd be nice if you could get a goal yourself today, Warren. Be a good way of breaking your duck with United.'

'Yeah, I suppose so,' Warren replied but without much enthusiasm for the idea. 'But it doesn't matter who scores our goals as long as we win, does it?'

Damian had to agree with that view because it was part of his own football philosophy; nonetheless, he wished that sometimes Warren would add a sharper edge to his skills by displaying a real desire to put the ball in the net himself. For some reason he didn't possess what Damian had heard a famous professional describe as 'the killer touch – the determination to finish off things that you've started'. Warren could hardly be called lazy because he was always willing to work as hard as was necessary to set up incisive attacks; but once the opening had been made he was inclined to let others take over. Since he'd joined them three weeks earlier United hadn't been beaten, though they'd won only one match. It had crossed Damian's mind to ask Warren to play as an out-and-out striker and see what happened then. But so far he'd resisted the temptation, not least because he didn't want to risk upsetting the regular strikers. Warren himself might have turned the idea down flat on the grounds that he regarded himself as a play-maker, not a centre-forward.

Thistle, too, possessed a player of star quality in

midfield: a dark-haired, rather plump boy called Ben Shaw who, in addition to carving out openings for their strikers, managed to feature quite regularly on the score sheet. At a team meeting earlier that week Ian had actually volunteered to mark Ben throughout the match. 'I'll cover him like a blanket!' he'd promised. Damian, approving of that determination, had also wondered whether Stevie Pailthorp might provide support, too, but he hadn't liked to suggest it in case Ian felt his marking abilities were being questioned. Yet it was common knowledge in the League that much of Ellel's success could be traced back to Ben's skills and perception of the game.

As usual Thistle, in their dark blue shirts, white shorts and red socks, had attracted a good crowd to their home match and it was rumoured that among the spectators were League officials and at least one talent scout. They didn't have to wait long for something to cheer, for the first goal was scored within sixty seconds of the kick-off. It was, of course, Ben Shaw who set up the chance with a finely-judged pass to the right flank, where the winger eluded a rather careless tackle and then sent in a good cross. There should have been no danger for United because Alex Anson was under no pressure at all and should have been able to head the ball away with ease. Instead, the normally dependable Alex headed it straight to the feet of an in-rushing forward who was alert enough to check his momentum and then hit the ball cleanly and unstoppably past Hajinder's right hand. The goalkeeper hadn't had a chance of making a save as he told everyone within earshot; but he hardly needed to because no one was blaming him.

Alex, naturally, was mortified. 'I can't believe it happened,' he muttered. 'It's a total disaster!'

'No, it isn't!' Damian told him fiercely. 'It could happen to anybody. You've saved dozens of goals in other matches. So just forget it. Alex. *Forget it!*'

Thistle, understandably, now had the idea that they were going to enjoy a goal-rush and their supporters began to applaud every kick and every move. For the next few minutes Ben Shaw was really fizzing, popping up everywhere to take a pass or give one and then, with the goal in his sights, to fire in a bullet of a shot that Hajinder, who only saw it at the last moment, somehow managed to palm over the bar.

Ian, who thought he'd managed to shackle Ben moments earlier, but was defeated by a brilliant 360-degree turn, pulled a face in frustration when Damian gave him a questioning look. The skipper signalled to Stevie Pailthorp to help out as Thistle took what proved to be an unproductive corner.

'You're our fastest runner,' Damian said hurriedly. 'If Shaw gets away from Ian at any point then go after him – pin him down.'

Stevie nodded his understanding. For the next few minutes United's goal was simply under siege as Thistle, determined to get the second goal they believed would clinch the match for them, swarmed all over the penalty area. Warren had dropped back and was doing his best to mark another of Ellel's danger men when the ball, ricocheting from an opponent's knee, struck his hand. Instantaneously, the referee's whistle shrilled.

'Oh no, ref!' Warren protested vigorously, for once losing his icy demeanour. 'It was a pure accident!'

But the referee wouldn't agree and was pointing calmly at the penalty spot as Thistle players told each other jubilantly that it was only what they deserved.

To Damian's surprise, the controversy seemed not to be bothering Hajinder. Rubbing his gloved hands together, he stationed himself on his line, looking quite nerveless. Although he hadn't been aware of it before, Damian sensed now that a crisis simply brought the best out of their new goalkeeper. 'Best of luck, Haji,' he called out as the kicker placed the ball on the spot; but it was doubtful if Hajinder heard him. His concentration on what was happening directly in front of him was total.

The penalty was being taken by Ellel's captain, a centre back with a powerful kick, and he'd selected a spot just inside the right-hand post. By some feat of mind-reading Hajinder guessed exactly where the ball was going and flung himself in that direction as the ball was kicked. He actually managed to get both hands to the ball and though he couldn't hold it he diverted it against the upright. As it spun upwards Haji, scrambling to his feet, dived again to grasp it – and then crashed shoulder-first into the woodwork.

By the time Haji collapsed, prone, on the goal-line

practically all the other players had rushed into the penalty area, those in blue shirts with the faint hope of being able to prod the ball over the line. But it was still firmly in Haji's arms in spite of the pain from his injured shoulder. The referee and Warren's father, who brought several of the boys to the match in his car, were the first to go to the goalkeeper's assistance and discover how bad the injury was.

'Well, I'm sure there's nothing broken, son, but I think we'd better take you off to the hospital for them to have a look at it,' said Mr Snowball, who admired the goalkeeper's determination not to give up the ball until he had to; there were tears in Haji's eyes but he was really being very brave.

'That really was a terrific save – the best I've ever seen,' Damian told him as Hajinder was helped out of his scarlet jersey. 'You've kept us in the game.'

'I'll be back, Damian,' Hajinder promised as he was led away to Mr Snowball's car, a jacket wrapped round his thin shoulders.

'Oh, good grief!' Damian exclaimed, using an expression his mother favoured when she lost a vital point at badminton or a crisis occurred in her household. He had suddenly realised what Hajinder's departure meant. 'I suppose *I'll* have to take over in goal now.'

'No, it's *my* job,' Jonathan put in unexpectedly, holding out his hand for the red jersey. 'I'm the stand-in goalkeeper, remember? We need you in midfield, Damian.'

Damian did his best to conceal his astonishment. 'Oh, thanks, Jon. I'm glad you're taking over.'

These days United could enjoy the luxury of a substitute and Damian now waved to Billy Sandford, who had the role for this match, to come on to the field and give his name to the referee. He was going to give Billy his old place back in midfield and ask Warren to move up to partner Neil Dallimore as a striker.

'OK, I'll try it, but don't expect a net-full of goals from me,' Warren replied.

'Just two will do,' Damian grinned.

But it was some minutes before United even got into the other half of the field. Ellel seemed desperate to make up for the goal they'd missed when Hajinder saved the penalty and their strikers, prompted by the still effervescent Ben Shaw, bombarded Jonathan with shots from all distances. Jonathan, though, was giving the impression that he'd spent his entire life between the posts. His agility and his handling were faultless.

Yet, in spite of their dominance, Thistle couldn't get the second goal they knew they needed. As half-time approached it was obvious that Ben Shaw was becoming less effective at setting up attacks; at last, Ian Venn was getting the upper hand in their personal battle. Ben, tired of being marked out of the game by someone he regarded as an inferior player, rashly kicked out and caught Ian on the knee. Ian, inevitably, made the most of it with a pantomime of pain and passion as he writhed on the ground. Of course he wasn't seriously hurt but he won a free kick, a sympathetic pat from the referee and, in effect, a booking for the offender.

It was from that kick just inside the United half that the visitors produced their best attacking move so far. Damian sent the ball curling towards the edge of the box where Neil out-jumped all the opposition to nod the ball down to Warren who immediately flicked it on to Billy Sandford. Delighted to be in the action at last, Billy had the good sense to return the compliment and Warren, cutting inside the challenging full-back, drove the ball towards the top of the net with his left foot. Unfortunately for United, Thistle's goalkeeper proved to be every bit as competent as Hajinder and Jonathan. Although he'd started to advance as danger threatened he recovered fast enough to fist the ball just as it was passing over his head and send it to safety high over the bar.

Ian, who'd swiftly got over his knock on the knee, took the corner kick and played it short to Stevie. Jinking one way and then the other, the winger beat two defenders and then hammered the ball into the middle. Neil wasn't so much the target as in the way because the ball was intended for Warren. Instead of jumping over the ball, which would have completely fooled the opposition, Neil swung heartily at it – and fairly predictably sent it on an apparent mission to the moon.

Damian raised his eyes skywards, too, but didn't utter a word of criticism. He knew that Neil didn't respond to hard words but only to praise.

During the interval the United players drank tea

from vacuum jugs and ate sugary biscuits kindly provided by Ellel supporters; and talked non-stop about their prospects of getting some League points from this match. Ian even apologised to his skipper for getting booked but promised that he'd be just as determined in the second half to subdue Ben Shaw. Warren Snowball was really the only one who had nothing to say and Damian suspected he might be brooding – either about giving away the penalty or being asked to play as a striker. So he asked what was troubling him.

'Just trying to work out how we're going to win, that's all,' was the grey-eyed boy's response. 'You know, I think there's not much between us. I think the main difference is that they expect to win every game and we don't. Maybe that's why they are top of the division.'

That wasn't at all the insight Damian had expected. 'I reckon you could be right,' he agreed. 'So we'll just have to prove we can be winners, too. Are you happy about playing up-front?'

Warren nodded. 'Sure. It's a new challenge. And I like challenges.'

Thistle, however, were the first to attack in the second half. In spite of the close attentions of Ian, Ben Shaw managed to send a superlative pass to his right-winger and he, in turn, supplied the centre-forward with exactly the kind of ball he liked: one that he could pounce on as he accelerated. His pace took him past two defenders with ease. Jonathan, sensing what could happen, didn't hesitate for even a second.

He charged from his goal, arms spread wide, determined to smother any attempted shot or as least put the striker under pressure so that he made a fatal mistake. Thistle's centre-forward, however, was cool enough to drag the ball to one side, out of the goalie's reach he hoped, before trying to hook it into the net with his left foot. He might have succeeded if Jonathan hadn't caught his ankle with the very tips of his fingers, a contact that sent him rolling over and over. It was the goalie who was first on his feet to grab the loose ball, but by then the referee's whistle had shrilled. And the official was again pointing to the penalty spot.

'Oh no, not *again*!' Damian groaned. 'It was just an accident, like the last time.'

Predictably, the referee would listen to no protests and so Jonathan, shaking his head in disbelief, returned to his goal-line. Once again the kick was to be taken by Ellel's captain. 'Go on, son,' the team's manager urged. 'You can do it this time. Hit it with everything you've got!'

The question in everyone's mind, of course, was where he'd aim for: would he go for the same spot as last time or look for a new target? The boy himself was in some doubt until he ran towards the ball: and then he decided he couldn't be so unlucky a second time. But it wasn't bad luck that kept the ball out of the net, it was the brilliance of Jonathan's full-length dive. He had gambled on the shot going in the same direction and his reward was not only to save his side from going two goals down, but to inspire them to play their best football of the season in the remaining minutes of the game.

Any team that fails to score from two penalties is bound to be dispirited and for the next couple of minutes Thistle resembled a boxer who'd taken a near-knock-out punch and couldn't remember how to get back to his own corner when the bell went.

Damian, convinced now that fate was wearing a green shirt and yellow shorts, set the example of renewed endeavour when he kept possession after picking up a misplaced pass. Evading a couple of ill-timed tackles, he headed for the right wing, always one of his favourite ploys. Ian, of course, was expecting a pass; but Damian was simply using him as a decoy. The Ellel defence, now riddled with uncertainty, either backed away or just stood-off. Damian made as if to accelerate – and instead hit a crossfield pass with all the strength he could command.

Warren, at that moment in complete isolation, moved to meet the ball as if he'd known it was going to be sent to him even before Damian released it. Pulling it down with his usual economy of effort he took it, equally effortlessly, past the one defender stationed on the route to goal. Like Jonathan, minutes before him, the Ellel goalkeeper knew he had to come out to narrow the angle of any shot. But that was simply his undoing as Warren, with rare accuracy and stunning skill, used his left foot to send the ball looping over the goalie's head and into the net.

'Oh, great goal, GREAT goal!' Damian said, over and over again, as he hugged the scorer.

'No, great pass from you, skipper,' Warren replied, still as cool as ever in spite of all the acclaim he was receiving from team-mates and spectators alike.

It was the sort of goal that ought to have won a match; but it didn't. In spite of Darton's almost incessant attacks until the final whistle, Ellel didn't concede another score. They were a resilient unit and they displayed all the considerable defensive qualities that had helped them to the top of the division. But it was an epic struggle because several times United were within centimetres of putting the ball in the net.

'Well, I reckon that's as good as a win for United – drawing away with the top team,' Damian said to Warren as they shook hands with various opponents. 'But now I really fancy our chances of beating them hollow when we get them back at our place.'

Warren was nodding his agreement when Alex came dashing up with a piece of startling news. 'Hey, you see that chap talking to Jonathan? Well he's a selector for the area football association and he wants to know if Jonathan's interested in a trial for the Redbourne Boys' team! Oh yes, and he wants to see Hajinder in action again, too, because he thinks he's a pretty good goalie as well. Fantastic!'

At that moment they saw Jonathan shake hands with the man and then he came running towards them,his eyes alight with pleasure. They all congratulated him but none could suppress a pang of envy.

'Lucky for me I went back in goal when I did,' Jonathan chortled. 'Just at the right moment to be spotted as a future star!'

'Is it only goalkeepers he's looking for?' Warren asked.

'Shouldn't think so,' Jonathan replied. 'He said he wanted the strongest squad he could find. So he's definitely coming to see our next couple of matches. You three will have to shine then, won't you?'

'Oh, we will,' said Damian fervently. 'We will!'

SOCCER SPECIAL

One

Miles Hansen remembered how the ball had bounced right in front of the centre-forward. It was just outside the penalty area. Geoff Leyland had trapped it, dummied past an opponent and then pushed the ball to his inside-right. When the return pass came Geoff hit the ball first time – and it went into the net off the upright. It really was a very good goal.

Miles nodded to himself. That was exactly how it had been scored. He had a good memory and he also had the notes he'd scribbled down at the match itself. Now he was going to write about the game and describe Geoff Leyland's goal.

The story would appear in his own newspaper, *Soccer Special*, along with reports of other matches and items of football news that he'd collected during the week. It would be printed the following day and Miles would sell all the copies himself at 2p a copy. Geoff would probably buy two copies – maybe even three –

because his name appeared several times. Geoff liked to read about himself.

Every word in the newspaper was written by Miles himself, without help from anyone, and so it took quite a long time to produce. But he enjoyed the work. He could write about whatever he liked. There was nobody to tell him what to do or how to do it. If he thought that someone had played badly he could say so; if a centre-forward missed an absolute sitter he could put it in the paper like that: 'the centre-forward missed an absolute sitter'.

Miles believed that a newspaper reporter should be completely honest and accurate in everything he wrote. His readers wanted facts, not fantasy. Miles always gave them the facts in *Soccer Special*. That was one of the reasons why his newspaper was so popular. Readers knew that they were getting the truth.

The paper wasn't only about football, however; it also contained news about his friends and family and neighbours. It was those items which helped to sell the paper. Geoff Leyland wasn't the only one who liked to read about himself. Miles' parents and his sister and the people who lived in the same street all wanted to see what he'd written about them. Every time a new edition of the paper came out they were all willing to pay 2p for a copy.

Miles called his newspaper *Soccer Special* because he liked the title – and because he liked football more than anything else in the world. He wished he could play in a football team and score lots of goals. He'd rather play centre-forward for England than become Editor of the *Daily Express*. But there was no chance of that happening. For Miles didn't play football.

When he was younger he'd had many illnesses, some of them very severe ones, including rheumatic fever. Twice he'd been in hospital and on the second occasion, when he'd had his tonsils removed, he was kept in even over the Christmas holiday. While he was recovering from his last illness he'd actually made a list of all the diseases and infections he'd suffered from in recent years. His sister, peering over his shoulder as he completed it, remarked in a horrified tone, 'Goodness, what a list! It frightens me to death just to read it.'

During his attack of rheumatic fever the family's doctor had said that it might be best if Miles didn't play any really energetic sports until he was older. Miles' mother had never forgotten that. Even though the doctor had sent an official note to the school she sometimes sent notes to the sports master to remind him that Miles was not well enough to play football or other games. So, when the other boys went off to play soccer or cricket, Miles could only watch them. That made him very unhappy. But there was nothing he could do to change the situation.

Sometimes, though, he joined in the games they played in Ransome Park after school. The sports master wasn't present then to tell him he wasn't allowed to take part. Miles just had to take care that his mother didn't get to know what he was doing.

Miles was already the tallest boy in his class. And that was one of his big problems because his mother kept saying, 'You've outgrown your strength, Miles'. He was so tall and thin that some of his school mates had a nickname for him: they called him 'Miles High'. They seemed to think it was a terrific joke. Miles didn't mind too much; some boys had worse nicknames than that. Jackie Barber was known as 'Skinhead' and Ray Gallop was always called 'Horsey'.

As he wasn't able to play very often Miles naturally wasn't much good at football. He knew that – and so did his school mates. All the same, he knew a great deal about soccer. He watched games at all levels as often as possible. On Saturday afternoons he attended matches at the local Second Division ground and he never failed to support the School team when they were playing at home. On Sunday mornings he went to see the Junior League games in

Ransome Park and he never missed any match on television if he could help it. Usually he had to go to bed fairly early because his mother repeatedly pointed out that a growing boy needed plenty of sleep. Fortunately he managed to conceal from her that he often read football magazines under the bedclothes with the help of a pocket torch.

The match which Miles was reporting at that moment and in which Geoff Leyland scored the winning goal had been played that morning. It was one of the Sunday League matches in the park. Geoff played for Wakeley Wanderers, a team Miles wrote about regularly in his newspaper. Several of the players attended his school and they all bought copies of the paper. The team was having a good run and winning most of their matches.

A year ago the team had been so bad they had hardly won a corner kick. Spectators used to yell at them: 'Wake up, Wakeley! You're supposed to go to sleep at night, not during a football match.' All that had changed. Nowadays their supporters roared them on with cries of, 'Whack 'em, Wakeley! You can beat this lot by ten goals.' And sometimes Wakeley actually did score ten goals in a match.

Wanderers had begun to improve from the time Geoff Leyland and another goal-scorer,

Johnnie Evett, had joined the team. At present Wakeley were near the top of their League and had set their hearts on becoming champions.

Miles nibbled at his pencil. He had to make sure the match report was correct in every detail. The Wakeley players would soon tell him if he made a mistake.

Then he began to write: 'Geoff Leyland scored the winning goal for Wanderers in their match against Belville United. It was a brilliant effort. Leyland got the ball just outside the penalty area. He beat one man and then passed to Johnnie Evett. The ball came back to Leyland and he smashed it into the net. It was one of his best goals of the season and it deserved to win any match.'

Miles added some more details about the rest of the game, mentioning as many players by name as possible. Each one referred to in the story was a likely customer when it came to selling the next edition of the paper. With a bit of luck, he might sell as many as sixty copies this time.

After reading through the report Miles thought about the headline. He liked writing headlines, though they weren't always easy to think up – and he could only fit so many words into the available space at the top of the story. After some consideration he pencilled in:

'Wanderers win again'. Then he remembered he'd used that one on another occasion.

He thought again – and had a bright idea. He wrote: 'Leyland hits the winner'. Geoff would be delighted with that, and this time he might buy as many as five copies.

Miles gathered up all his reports and stories and then meticulously checked through every one of them for the last time. If they contained any factual errors they would have to be rooted out now; there wouldn't be another opportunity to spot them before the paper was printed.

When he was satisfied that all was well he gathered the stories together and put them in his school case. When he came down from his bedroom there was no one about to ask him where he was going. In any case, his family knew very well that on Sunday afternoons he always went to see Mrs Jenks, who lived in the next street.

During the week Mrs Jenks worked as a secretary with a big engineering company. Miles liked to imagine that on Sundays she worked as his secretary. For it was she who printed the copies of *Soccer Special* for him. She typed the two pages of the newspaper at home and then took them to her office on Monday. There she used a photo-copying machine and ran off as many copies as Miles wanted. He collected them from her on Monday evening and sold them the next day.

Miles liked Mrs Jenks very much. She was interested in football – which his mother certainly wasn't – and she often called him 'my favourite reporter and budding journalist'. She said she was sure that one day he would become the editor of a big daily newspaper.

Miles had met her one day in the supermarket. She'd knocked down a pile of cans and he helped her to pick them up. After that, he'd offered to carry her shopping for her whenever she needed him. She said she'd be glad of his help. They'd become quite friendly and regularly she supplied him with items of local news for the paper.

It had been a great surprise to him when she'd mentioned that she was a widow. Miles had always supposed that widows were old ladies, and Mrs Jenks was anything but old – and she was very pretty. He hadn't liked, though, to ask what had happened to her husband.

Most weeks he did her shopping for her because, by the time she returned home from work in the evening, the shops were closed; and he also helped her in the garden, though he didn't much enjoy that. Still, it was what Mrs Jenks called a very fair arrangement. 'You help me with the shopping and the garden,' she had said, 'and I help you with your newspaper.' So, instead of paying Miles for his help, Mrs Jenks paid for the photo-copies of *Soccer Special*. He knew that without such an arrangement it would be almost impossible for him to produce the kind of newspaper that people would buy.

When he rang the bell at her home that afternoon he was still trying to work out how many copies he should ask her to print. He wondered whether he dare ask her to do sixty. She had told him that photo-copies were expensive to produce, so he didn't want to waste any. In any case, he liked telling people that he had sold out of the latest edition. He couldn't do that if he had any copies left over at the end of the week.

Mrs Jenks seemed in a very good mood. She gave him some ginger beer and while he drank it she read every story in the paper. He enjoyed watching her reaction. A nod indicated approval, a smile that she had particularly liked a story. Best of all was when she laughed out loud because she'd found a joke or an amusing description of something or somebody. Just occasionally she frowned. That meant she wasn't entirely happy about a phrase he'd used or that he'd failed to express himself clearly. Then they'd discuss ways of improving that story. Not once, though, had she ever suggested that an item should be excluded from the paper because it might offend the person concerned. In fact, she'd once remarked that he had very good taste. Miles wasn't absolutely sure what that meant.

'Very good, Miles,' she smiled. 'It's really full of news this week. You'll sell every copy in no time at all. Will fifty copies be enough, do you think?'

'Well, I was wondering if you could do sixty this week, Mrs Jenks,' he said. 'Sales seem to be going up at the moment, you see.'

To his relief, she agreed without any hesitation.

As he was leaving she gave him a shopping list and some money. He would get the things for her on his way home from school the following evening. Then, just as she was closing the door, he remembered something.

'Oh, Mrs Jenks,' he said hurriedly. 'Could you please add a line after the Wakeley match report? They've got a special challenge match on Friday evening at Ransome Park. It starts at five o'clock. I think we should say, "All spectators welcome". Then, you see, they might get some more supporters. It's a vital match for Wakeley.'

She laughed. 'Okay, Mr Editor. Anything you say!'

Two

The challenge match was against Westhill Albion. Earlier in the season Wakeley had beaten them in a League match by a single goal – a goal scored from the penalty spot. The Westhill players claimed they'd been robbed; it should never have been a penalty in the first place, they insisted. Wanderers, however, had collected the two points and that win had helped them climb up the League table.

In spite of the fact that they, too, were now doing well in the League, Albion hadn't forgotten that controversial defeat. Every time players from the two teams met at school or anywhere else they still argued about the result. Geoff Leyland, now Wanderers' captain, always replied, 'We can beat your lot any time, anywhere. Next time we play you we'll score six.'

'Okay,' replied the Albion captain one day. 'Prove it! We'll play you again in a friendly match. Only it won't be very friendly. We'll squash you into the ground and trample all over you!'

So the challenge match was arranged for a Friday evening in the park. An older boy had been persuaded to referee the game and both teams were absolutely determined this time to win so convincingly that their superiority could never be doubted.

Miles Hansen was just as keen to be at the match – and to write about it in *Soccer Special*. He'd bought a new notebook and wanted to start filling it. He knew some of the Albion players and he hoped that when the next edition of his newspaper was printed they might buy copies. His reputation for writing an honest report was well known by now.

When he arrived at the park a couple of minutes before five o'clock he was glad to see that the match hadn't started. In fact, the teams were still huddled together in two groups on either side of the halfway line. So far there was no sign of any spectators, which was disappointing in view of the publicity he'd given to the match in the paper.

Miles opened his notebook and was just about to start jotting down some details of weather, ground conditions and background to the match when he heard his name being called. He looked up, surprised. Geoff Leyland was coming towards him, holding out a goalkeeper's green jersey.

'Look, Miles,' he said, 'we need a goalie. Colin Ayrton has got measles, the stupid idiot. We didn't know until after school. We haven't had time to find anybody else, so you'll have to play for us. Okay?'

'Me!' Miles swallowed hard. He couldn't believe that Geoff meant it. 'But I can't play in goal! I've never played in goal in my life.'

'That doesn't matter,' replied Geoff, dismissing the objection with a shrug of his shoulders. 'Any fool can play in goal – there's nothing to it. Anyway, all the action will be down at the other end. We're going to hit Albion for six, and I'll probably score all of 'em. So you won't have anything to do in goal for us.'

Miles wished he could believe him. But he remembered the previous match between the two sides when, for several minutes, Albion had attacked continuously and forced a succession of corner kicks.

'Isn't there anyone else, Geoff?' he asked anxiously. 'I mean, couldn't one of the regular supporters help out? Or what about the substitute? Surely he—'

'We didn't bother picking a substitute.

Didn't think we'd need one for this match. And the supporters haven't arrived yet, lazy devils!'

'But—'

'No more buts!' Geoff said curtly. He was beginning to get impatient. 'Look, if you don't play we're down to ten men, and that's no good. You'll be better in goal than anywhere else. Franny Weir will take the dead-ball kicks for you, if there are any. Here's the jersey, and you can borrow my tracksuit trousers if you want. We haven't got a spare pair of shorts.'

Without waiting for any reply he draped the jersey over Miles' head and ran back to the middle to talk to his team about tactics. Numbly, Miles slipped his notebook back into his pocket. He didn't know what he ought to do. He could imagine all too vividly what his mother would say if she could see him with a football jersey in his hands. Yet this really was a marvellous opportunity to play in a real match for a team like Wanderers.

What began to worry him most, however, was the thought of going in goal. If he made a mess of things his team-mates would never forgive him. And, of course, a goalkeeper could never conceal his mistakes. If he let in a soft goal . . .

On the other hand, he told himself, if he

refused to play at all then Geoff and the other boys wouldn't buy any more copies of *Soccer Special*. That would be a complete disaster.

Really, he had no choice in the matter.

Slowly he made his way towards the net. There he took off his jacket and tie and pulled the green jersey over his head. Franny Weir, the right full-back, dashed up and handed him a pair of tracksuit trousers. Miles changed into them while Franny, grinningly, provided him with some cover – though he was aware that no one was watching him.

Somehow, changing into real football gear made him feel a lot better. He jumped up and down on the goal-line and tried to touch the crossbar. His one worry now was his footwear. Naturally, no one had a spare pair of boots to lend him and so he would have to play in his shoes. Fortunately, the ground was quite dry and therefore the absence of studs shouldn't make too great a difference. Inevitably, though, his shoes would suffer when he had to kick the ball.

Geoff, now standing in the centre-circle with the ball at his feet, turned and waved encouragingly to him. Miles waved back. He just hoped that Geoff would keep his promise and score a bagful of goals. It wouldn't matter so much, then, if Miles let in one or two . . .

The referee blew his whistle to start the match – and Miles immediately began to feel terribly nervous. His heart was thumping and his stomach churning madly. From all the football books he'd read he knew very well that even top players confessed to having butterflies in their stomachs before a vital match, so such a reaction was really quite normal. None the less, Miles found himself wishing that he, too, had measles like Colin Ayrton and could go straight home.

Luckily, it was Wanderers who launched the first attack. Geoff Leyland was intent on keeping his promise before half-time! He and Johnnie Evett, an extremely clever ball-player, combined brilliantly to cut deep into the Albion defence. In the first minute of the game they won a corner.

Albion were unable to clear the ball and it bobbed about dangerously in their penalty area. Miles began to sympathize with the plight of his fellow goalkeeper as it seemed that Wanderers must score. Yet, somehow, Albion kept them out. Wanderers piled on more and more pressure and even their full-backs moved up to join in the stream of attacks.

That simply increased Miles' worries. Now there was no one in front of him, no one to give him any cover. He yelled to Franny to drop back but if Franny heard the call he ignored it.

Then, after five minutes, Wakeley at last managed to get the ball into the net. And, of course, it was Geoff Leyland who put it there – from a pass by Evett. Together they returned to the centre circle in jubilant fashion with Geoff still punching his fist into the air to signal his success. Miles felt relief rather than anything else: at least things were going in Wakeley's favour so far. Albion would have to score twice to win.

When Albion kicked off they showed they weren't going to waste any time in scoring the equaliser. The ball was hammered upfield and three of their forwards raced towards the penalty area.

It seemed to Miles that his co-defenders were slow to fall back. But there was no time to point that out to them. He himself had to make an instant decision: whether to move out to challenge the man in possession or to stay on his line. Desperately he tried to remember what top goalkeepers did in such a situation.

He hesitated – and suddenly the ball was swept out to the left-wing. Franny Weir tried a sliding tackle, and missed completely as the winger jinked round him. Without even looking up the Albion player belted the ball into the middle. It bounced just inside the box.

'Come out, goalie!' Geoff yelled frantically as his centre-half failed to get the ball away.

Miles dashed forth, his arms spread wide. But he hadn't moved quickly enough. Albion's centre-forward reached the ball first and, very skilfully, hooked it over Miles' head.

It was the sort of shot that a boy of his limited experience would probably miss nine times out of ten. But this was the tenth time. For the ball dropped just under the crossbar and rolled into the net.

So, before Miles had even touched the ball in

the match, Albion had scored. Wakeley's one goal advantage had been wiped out almost immediately. The teams were level again.

Geoff himself marched up the pitch to pick the ball out of the net. He looked thoroughly disgusted.

'Stop dreaming,' he said cuttingly to Miles. 'Concentrate on what you're supposed to be doing. It's no good me scoring at the other end if you're going to let 'em in at this end. Waste of time, that is.'

'Sorry, Geoff,' Miles muttered. He felt terrible and just as upset as Geoff. He was as keen as any of the other Wanderers to win this challenge match. There was no point in trying to make excuses for his failure to prevent Albion's goal. He had, as Geoff had told him, to concentrate on his particular job throughout the game.

That goal had a wonderful effect on the Albion players. Any sense of inferiority they had when playing Wanderers had vanished. They felt they were as good as their opponents, and their goal had proved it. Their confidence soared, especially as they believed that Wanderers' goalkeeper was useless. So they should be able to score again. That thought made all the difference to their attitude to the rest of the match.

When one of their half-backs won a tussle for the ball in the centre-circle Albion were on the attack once more. Inspired by his goal, their chief striker dribbled towards the penalty area before passing to a colleague.

Wakeley tried to marshal their defence but couldn't prevent one attacker from breaking through.

The Albion player was a strong runner with an equally strong shot. As soon as he had clear sight of the net he hit the ball for all he was worth.

Miles had little enough time to see the ball but he flung himself at it. Luck was on his side this time. The ball struck his arm and bounced over the top for a corner kick. As Miles picked himself up Johnnie Evett ran in to pat him on the shoulder.

'Great save, Miles, great save,' he said. 'Keep it up, goalie!'

Miles knew he'd been lucky but that save gave him confidence. He had at least kept the ball out of the net. Then, when the corner kick came over, he used his height to jump and catch the ball. Bouncing it a couple of times in a professional manner, he then carried it for three steps before carefully kicking upfield.

It was amazing. That save had made him feel like a real goalkeeper!

It had also amazed the Albion forwards. In their next attack they attempted to get closer to the goal-line before trying a shot. Again, Miles didn't hesitate. Hurling himself at the inside-right's feet, he grabbed the ball and pulled it into his chest. In the process he took a knock on the shoulder but he hardly felt it as he cleared his line with a kick. This time the praise came from Geoff Leyland himself.

From then on Miles was without fear when the Albion forwards came storming towards him. His height was a great advantage when the ball was in the air; and when it was on the ground he was prepared to dive full-length.

As their attacks broke down and they failed to score a second goal Albion seemed to lose some of their fire. When the half-time whistle sounded it was Wanderers who were clearly on top again and pressing for the lead.

During a spell of inactivity Miles had been thinking that he should use some of the interval to make notes for his newspaper report on the match. He would have no difficulty in describing Geoff's goal but he knew it wasn't going to be easy to write about Albion's equaliser without saying something about Wakeley's goalkeeper. That was going to be the really tricky bit.

As it turned out, however, there was no time to jot down even one word. For Geoff wanted to talk to him on the subject of goalkeeping. As a leading goal-scorer, Wakeley's captain thought he knew a lot about goalkeepers, so he passed on a few tips.

'Just keep your eye on the ball all the time. Don't look at the players or anything else,' was one bit of advice. 'Don't worry about getting hurt, either. You'll soon get over it if you do get a knock. Nobody gets killed in a soccer match.'

Had Miles been thinking clearly, that reference to injuries might have worried him a lot. But he was simply accepting everything that Geoff told him. After all, Geoff Leyland was the captain, the chief goal-scorer and the side's tactician. He was also the fittest boy Miles had ever seen, with tremendously powerful calf and thigh muscles. He looked every centimetre the complete footballer.

When the second half began Miles soon found himself in action again. Albion were awarded a free kick just outside the box. Wanderers formed the usual defensive wall. Miles couldn't see anything of the ball or the player who was about to take the kick. So he yelled frantically to his own defenders to let him see what was happening. He'd remembered that all League goalkeepers did that when a free kick was being taken from close range.

Rather grudgingly, the defenders responded by shuffling fractionally to one side.

The Albion half-back who took the kick produced an astonishingly powerful shot. Had it been straight it might have gone into the roof of the net. But the ball just flicked against one of the defenders. That took some of the pace off it – and the ball swerved away to the right. Miles hadn't lost sight of it for an instant.

He threw himself across the goal and with his fingertips just managed to push the ball round the post. It was the sort of save a Wembley crowd would have greeted with a roar of cheering. His colleagues did their best to match that sort of applause.

After that superb effort, Miles had a fairly easy time for the remainder of the match. Wanderers, combining well in mid-field, set up a series of attacks whereas Albion seemed dispirited following their failure to beat Miles again. Then, two minutes from the end,

Johnnie Evett scored the winner in a goal-mouth scramble.

Wakeley had beaten off Albion's challenge.

As they left the field Geoff put his arm round Miles' shoulders.

'Great goalkeeping, kid, great goalkeeping,' he said with evident sincerity. 'That save from the free kick was out of this world. As far as I'm concerned Colin Ayrton can have measles and chickenpox and swamp fever and anything else he likes for the rest of the season. You'll take over from him in goal on Sunday when we play Sellerby Rangers.'

Three

The following morning Miles was sitting at his desk in his bedroom trying to write a report on the challenge match. It was what to say about the goalkeeper, himself, that was troubling him. For a newcomer the goalie had played – there was no other word for it – brilliantly (apart from that first mistake, of course). But Miles didn't think it would be right to describe his performance in that way. The rest of the Wakeley players would think he was simply being big-headed. On the other hand, though, he had to keep up his reputation for honest and impartial reporting.

Then, of course, there was the matter of naming Wanderers' goalkeeper. If he used his own name his parents would soon know that he had been playing football. Usually, his mother skipped some of the details of the soccer reports but his father read every line. Vividly, he could imagine his parents' combined reaction.

Miles considered the idea of making up a name. That would certainly solve the problem as far as he himself was concerned in spite of the fact that he would like to be seen to have shared the glory of Wakeley's great victory. Yet, he feared that his team-mates would treat such a stratagem with suspicion. They might think it was just another way of showing-off.

He was still wrestling with the problem when, without even knocking, his sister burst into the room. She was flourishing a copy of the latest issue of *Soccer Special* and plainly she was very angry.

'Miles, you've been spying on me! And I don't like it. I don't want my private life written up in your silly newspaper every week for everyone to read about and joke about!'

'I haven't been spying on you, Rosemary,' Miles protested. He didn't even know what she was talking about.

She thrust the paper in front of his face and pointed with one finger at a story in the Personal Column. It read: 'Rosemary Hansen seems to have a new boyfriend. They were seen talking together for a long time by the Park gates. They were holding hands. Martin, her old boyfriend, hasn't been to visit her for some days. More news about this later.'

'Look, it's nothing to do with you who I meet,' she went on bitingly. 'It just causes trouble when you write things like that.'

'Oh, why?' Miles asked innocently.

'You know very well why! I know you sell copies to Martin when he comes here. So you can just keep quiet about me, understand?'

'It's my job to report the news, *all* the news,' Miles pointed out.

'Sometimes there are things that people don't want put in the paper – things about themselves. Probably one day you'll want to keep something out of the paper about yourself. Some things are *private*, Miles.'

Miles didn't make any reply to that. He knew how true it was. So he simply nodded.

'Good,' said Rosemary, smiling for the first time since she'd entered the Editor's office. 'I'm glad you understand, Miles. So just remember to keep me out of your paper in future.'

She seemed to be on the point of departing when she added, 'By the way, how's your typewriter fund coming along?'

She was referring to the money he was trying to save to buy his own typewriter. And he knew very well why she had mentioned it at this moment.

'Sorry, Rosemary, but that's no good,' he

said bluntly. 'You can't *pay* me to keep news out of the paper. That would be dishonest!'

She spun round and went out of the room without another word, slamming the door behind her. Miles winced at the noise. But he wasn't worried by her remarks. In any case, he was sure she would continue to buy copies of the paper. She'd be even keener in future to see if he had written anything about her.

One minor point did trouble him, however. If Martin had ceased to be her boyfriend Miles would have lost a customer. Miles quite liked him, though they were never able to discuss soccer together for Martin was a rugby player.

Suddenly, Miles remembered that when rugby teams included a new player, and they didn't want other teams to know his identity, they often gave him a special name: A.N. Other. And that, Miles decided, was the perfect answer to his own problem. Wakeley Wanderers' new goalkeeper could be described as A.N. Other.

He had written the first two paragraphs of his report. Now he started on the third: 'Wanderers brought in a new goalkeeper, A.N. Other. He made a bad mistake and let Albion score their only goal, the equalizer. But after that he played quite well and made some good stops. Colin Ayrton couldn't play because he has measles. His team-mates hope he'll soon be better.'

After that, the rest of the report was easy to write. Miles, too, hoped that Colin would soon be well again; but he also secretly hoped that Colin wouldn't be fit enough to play again just yet.

For Miles was greatly looking forward to keeping his place in goal for Wanderers. It had been a marvellous experience to turn out for a *real* football team in a Cup-tie atmosphere. It was very much better than just watching a match and writing about it.

At first, he had been scared of two things: first that he might get hurt, for everyone recognized that goalkeeping was a dangerous job. Whenever a goalie dived at a forward's feet there was a risk that the attacker might kick him instead of the ball. Miles had taken such a knock but had hardly felt it. Perhaps, therefore, he was tougher than anybody imagined.

Secondly, he'd been scared that he might let the team down by making stupid mistakes. He had made one big error, when Albion scored, but in the second half he knew he'd done quite well. When he'd made that save from the free kick he'd felt great: it was as good as scoring a goal. For preventing goals was as important as scoring them.

His big worry now about the game on Sunday was not whether he would play well. It was whether he could keep it a secret from his parents that he was taking part in a League match and not simply reporting it.

All he could hope was that none of his family would stroll through Ransome Park the following morning and pause to watch the game between Sellerby Rangers and Wakeley Wanderers.

Four

Sunday was living up to its name; the sun was shining so brilliantly it might have been mid-summer's day. Miles, as he hurried through the Park, was thinking that the pitch was sure to be hard. Goalkeepers preferred softer conditions. There was less risk of getting hurt when it was muddy.

For this match he didn't have to worry about his shoes, however. He had borrowed a pair of boots from a friend who took the same size as himself in footwear. The friend was one of his customers and Miles had promised to let him have the next three issues of *Soccer Special* free of charge in return for the loan of the boots.

Most of the Wakeley players had their own kit and so Geoff Leyland was going to lend Miles a spare pair of shorts. He had also kept the goalkeeper's green jersey for him.

'Hi, Miles High,' Geoff grinned when he saw him. It was a joke he liked to crack as often as possible. 'Are you in good form today? We don't want to let in any goals against this lot, you know.'

'I feel great,' Miles told him. And he did. He was also feeling just a little nervous but he wasn't going to admit that. He wanted Geoff to think that the Wanderers' goalkeeper was capable of stopping anything.

Geoff began to tell him about the Sellerby forwards and Miles listened carefully to every word. It was very useful to know what sort of players he would be facing. For instance, Rowlandson, their centre-forward, was well-built and almost as tall as Miles. He used his weight a lot and was very dangerous in the penalty area.

Rowlandson liked to think he was a good header of the ball but, Geoff continued, *he* didn't think much of Rowlandson's ability in that direction. In his opinion, Sellerby's best player was the inside-left, a small ginger-haired boy called Reed. Unusually for a schoolboy, Ginger Reed could hit the ball well with either foot. In spite of his size, he possessed a hard shot.

'You have to know about these things when you're the captain,' Geoff added. 'You've got to think about this game of football – use your brains all the time. If you know a player can use only one foot then you know how to tackle him.'

Miles nodded. He was very impressed with Geoff's knowledge and he appreciated being given such information. But more than that he was grateful for the sense of confidence Geoff had given him. Already he had been made to feel part of the team, part of Wakeley Wanderers. It was obvious now that Leyland regarded him as a capable goalkeeper. So Miles was determined not to let him down. The best way of doing that was by not letting in any goals.

As usual, the players went into the bushes to change before going out on to the pitch. Miles couldn't help thinking that it would be marvellous one day to put on his football kit in a real dressing-room at the ground of a Football League club. Pegs to hang clothes on, bench seats round the walls, oranges and cool drinks at half-time, hot showers after the match – fantastic!

When the referee arrived he called the captains together to toss for choice of ends. It was Geoff who called correctly and he decided to play with the sun behind him.

Sellerby, wearing an all-blue strip and clearly eager to make a good start, forced a corner with their first attack. Ginger Reed, showing good ball control, cut in from the left, beating two defenders on the way. To keep him out of the box Franny Weir turned the ball over the line.

Miles didn't feel at all nervous. He was glad of the chance of being in action right from the start. He knew that top goalkeepers liked to 'get a feel of the ball as soon as possible' (as television commentators were always saying). But the kick was not a good one: the ball didn't even reach the edge of the penalty area.

Yet Miles couldn't relax his concentration. For Ginger Reed had dropped back intelligently and when the ball came towards him he deliberately punted it high into the air. It was going to land close to the penalty spot.

Miles judged that it was a goalkeeper's ball. So he didn't hesitate. Moving swiftly off his line, he jumped high to catch the ball. He hadn't taken his eye off it, and so he didn't notice that Rowlandson was also determined to reach the ball.

They collided in mid-air. Miles had just managed to grab hold of the ball in the split-second before they touched and as he fell the big centre-forward came down on top of him. Miles was winded and almost let the ball roll from his grasp. Rowlandson was quickly on his feet and tried to kick the ball out of Miles'

hands. He'd sensed a chance of a goal and he wasn't going to miss it.

The referee blew furiously. Rowlandson, startled, stepped back as the official dashed up to him. He tried to give the impression that he couldn't possibly imagine what was wrong. But the referee left him in no doubt with a severe reprimand for dangerous play.

'You might have caused a serious injury,' he told the subdued Rowlandson. 'If you attempt anything like that again you'll be sent off in double-quick time. Understand?'

Rowlandson nodded and trudged away from the box. Miles was still struggling to his feet. Luckily, he wasn't really injured, although he felt shaken. After all, Rowlandson wasn't exactly a bag of feathers.

Franny Weir took the free kick so that Miles could have more time to recover. For the next few minutes it was Wakeley who set up the attacks and they ought to have scored. Twice Johnnie Evett went close to giving his side the lead but each time he was foiled just when it seemed certain he would get the ball in the net. After the second near-miss Geoff Leyland was seen to be indicating that he himself would have done better in such a situation.

With all the activity concentrated at the other end of the pitch Miles, already feeling perfectly fit again, had time to look round. One or two people walking through the Park had paused to watch the match. But Miles didn't recognize any of them. He was rather hoping that he might spot some of his *Soccer Special* customers. They would surely be impressed to see that the Editor was not only attending the match in his journalistic capacity; he was also playing in it.

He was just turning away to resume his concentration on the game when he saw someone he did know, walking along one of the paths that bordered the pitch. His heart almost stopped.

It was Rosemary!

She was strolling, hand in hand, with her new boyfriend, the one Miles wasn't supposed to mention in his paper. To his dismay, they were heading in his direction.

If she noticed him it could only lead to trouble. There could hardly be any doubt about that. Even if she didn't mention to their mother that she'd seen him playing football she could hold that threat over him for as long as she liked. Moreover, she might let slip the news at home without intending to whenever the subject of football cropped up. And that, he knew, would be the end of his playing career.

Rosemary and her companion were now

close to his end of the pitch. They appeared to be completely absorbed by one another but Miles couldn't afford to take any risks at all. He turned and, as casually as possible, wandered across to the other side of the penalty area. He wanted to put as much distance as possible between himself and his sister. As he heard her laugh at something her new friend had said Miles winced.

If only he could make sure they didn't see his face . . .

He didn't suppose they would recognize him instantly in a goalkeeper's jersey but nothing had to be left to chance. So he lifted his right arm across his face as though he were about to wipe some sweat away. But he kept it there.

Accordingly, Miles wasn't aware of what was happening at that moment in the game. He couldn't see that Rangers had at last broken out of defence, and that some of their forwards were dashing forward in support of a colleague who had the ball. Most of the Wakeley defenders were in the wrong half of the pitch, having gone up to join their forwards. So, when the ball was slipped to Ginger Reed, the Sellerby inside-forward had almost a clear route to goal.

Easily Ginger took the ball round the one defender who was on hand to try and challenge him. Glancing up, he saw that Wakeley's goal-keeper was well off his line and not even watching the play.

From just outside the penalty area Reed took careful aim and hit his shot with as much force as he could muster. The ball bounced before it entered the net but it was a goal all the way. With so much space to shoot at Ginger could hardly have missed.

The ball was just crossing the line when, at last, Miles looked up. He had heard the frantic calls of 'Goalie! Goalie!' from Geoff Leyland. But he didn't immediately realize what they meant.

In any case, his first thought was to find out whether Rosemary had seen him. He needn't have worried. By now Rosemary and her new friend were some distance away and it was obvious that they were still far too interested in each other to notice a game of football.

Miles was horrified to discover that Rangers had scored. As, sad and shaken, he went to retrieve the ball from the net Geoff Leyland rushed up to him. The expression on his face suggested that he would willingly commit murder.

'What on earth were you doing?' he yelled from a distance of less than a metre. 'That was the softest goal anybody ever scored! You just gave it to them, Hansen, just presented it to them on a plate. You must be mad, standing there with your hands over your eyes. What were you thinking about, man?'

'Nothing, Geoff, nothing at all,' Miles mumbled. There was nothing else he could say. Geoff had every right to tear into him. Had their positions been reversed Miles would have done the same.

Leyland had to get back to the centre-circle to kick off again. As he set off he issued a chilling warning.

'Don't do anything so stupid again. *Concentrate* on the game and don't take your eye off the ball *for a second*. Or else . . .'

Miles nodded and edged backwards to his goal-line. In a few moments the disaster began to take second place to a feeling of relief. His secret, he was sure, was safe. No one would be mentioning to his mother that he was playing football in the Sunday League. Rosemary and the mystery man were now out of sight. Miles didn't think there was much likelihood of their returning by the same route.

Wanderers were determined to get the equalizer without delay. Sweeping into the attack, they sent their left-winger off on a strong run down his own flank. As an opponent tried to dispossess him he cut inside and passed to Johnnie Evett. The inside-forward sent a defender the wrong way with a clever dummy and then slipped the ball to Geoff Leyland.

Geoff hit it on the half-volley and deserved a goal for his effort but he was foiled by a fine, diving save by the Rangers goalkeeper. Wanderers' captain flung his arms in the air in despair. Miles could imagine just what his team-mate was thinking at that moment about goalkeepers in general and two of them in particular.

In spite of their furious raids and inventive approach play Wakeley couldn't get the ball into the net. Twice they hit the woodwork and on another occasion a full-back kicked off the line with the goalie beaten.

So, when half-time was signalled, Wanderers were still a goal down – the goal that had been scored because of Miles' mistake. The two teams split up into separate groups to discuss tactics for the second half.

Miles went up to join his team-mates but nobody spoke to him. They seemed to be deliberately ignoring him. Geoff, of course, was talking away, explaining what had to be done to save the match. He felt that at least three goals would be needed.

Then, glancing at Miles, he added, 'Of course, we might need more, if our goalie lets us down again by giving away stupid goals. So we must attack right from the kick-off.'

Miles turned away. He felt dreadful again.

Sellerby Rangers were also determined to attack as soon as the second-half began. They knew that one goal might not be enough to win the match and they thought that Wakeley's goalkeeper could be beaten easily.

The centre-forward, Rowlandson, tore into the defence like a bulldozer. He couldn't control the ball for long but when he lost it Ginger Reed was in attendance to seize on it. He took it forward only a couple of paces before lobbing it high into the goalmouth. He'd sensed the sort of trouble that tactic might cause.

For when Miles looked up to follow the flight of the ball he was at once dazzled by the sun. He couldn't see a thing and he had to close his eyes against the glare. That was just what Ginger had expected to happen. Now, with the sun almost directly behind him, Rowlandson was able to jump for the ball. He headed it well.

Miles, now trying to glimpse something of what was going on in front of him, was still having trouble with the sun but he threw his arms up as some sort of cover. The ball struck his outstretched right hand and then spun high over the crossbar for a corner. It was an exceedingly lucky save, as Miles would later admit, but the ball had been kept out of the net. That was all that mattered.

As Reed dashed away to take the corner kick Miles was startled to hear someone behind him calling his name. He turned to discover that it was Mrs Jenks. Before he could say anything to her she took off the green-and-yellow cap she was wearing and handed it to him. It was a very smart cap with a big peak.

'Put it on, Miles,' she said. 'It'll keep the sun out of your eyes.'

He did so, tugging it well down over his forehead. To his surprise, it fitted him quite well. There was time only to grin his thanks at Mrs Jenks before he turned away to deal with the corner kick.

Ginger put all his strength into the kick and succeeded in floating the ball into the penalty area. A defender managed to get his head to it and tried to clear the danger. He, too, was troubled by the sun and he could only head the ball upwards.

Miles didn't hesitate any longer. 'Mine!' he yelled as he raced forth and, jumping high, he caught the ball cleanly. Then he bounced it a couple of times, dodged round an attacker and cleared upfield. It was a most efficient piece of work. The sun hadn't bothered him at all.

'Well done, Miles,' said Mrs Jenks, still standing behind his net. 'I think you've been keeping secrets from me. Obviously, you've played in goal before today. I must say, I was a bit surprised when I noticed who was wearing that rather nice green jersey. I'd expected to see you standing near the halfway line with notebook and pencil in hand.'

There was no time for Miles to make a reply. Sellerby Rangers were attacking again. Ginger Reed was having a marvellous match and was the inspiration of the latest venture deep into the Wakeley half of the pitch. Keeping the ball right at his toes, he dribbled past two defenders and reached the edge of the penalty area. Momentarily, he slowed up as Franny Weir went in to tackle him; then he darted away again to his right.

Franny was determined not to be beaten again by Rangers' crafty inside-forward. Chasing after him, he lunged at the ball. But he missed it completely and knocked Ginger to the ground.

The little red-haired player wasn't hurt and immediately he leapt to his feet, protesting loudly that he'd been fouled inside the box.

'Penalty, ref! Penalty,' he yelled.

To Ginger's delight, the referee agreed with him. Blowing his whistle, he pointed in dramatic fashion to the spot. Franny Weir started to object in frenzied fashion but it was Geoff Leyland who silenced him. Geoff knew that there was nothing to be gained by arguing with a referee who'd made a firm decision.

For the second time that afternoon Miles was horror-struck. He thought for a moment that his heart had stopped. Then it started to bang away, louder than ever. He swallowed hard. Often he'd wondered, as he watched a match on television, how a goalkeeper felt when he

was about to face a penalty kick. Now he was finding out.

Ginger Reed was taking the kick himself. Miles crouched on his line, trying to guess which way Reed would shoot. Ginger hit the ball with his right foot, though not as hard as he'd planned. The ball kept fairly low and was going to the left of the goalie.

Miles was able to watch it all the way but he had to dive to reach it. His height enabled him to get his hands to the ball and he managed to push it out. He was getting to his knees as the ball, having bounced against the upright, rolled back towards him. Gratefully, Miles scooped it up as Ginger rushed towards him.

He could hardly believe that he'd made such an excellent save but the yells of delight from his team-mates confirmed his success.

'Great save, Miles, great save!' Geoff sang

out to him. Miles jogged forward a couple of paces and then confidently booted the ball upfield.

'My goodness, that was really something!' Mrs Jenks exclaimed. Miles had almost forgotten that she was there. 'After that, I can see I'm watching a future England goalkeeper!'

He grinned at that. Yet, he admitted to himself, it would make a nice story for his paper – if he dare be so immodest as to use it. No, on second thoughts, he couldn't possibly quote that remark.

His penalty save seemed to have put fresh heart into Wanderers as well as shaken their opponents. For, within two minutes, Wakeley had netted the equalizer.

Once again, it was Johnnie Evett who was responsible for much of the build-up to the goal. He was given good support by the left-winger but when the ball was forced into the penalty area Geoff Leyland it was who crashed the ball into the net.

Rangers were badly rattled. Until Miles' penalty save they had felt to be on top. Now nothing would go right for them. Miles himself was just a spectator as the Wakeley forwards pounded away at the opposite end of the pitch. Another goal just had to come and it arrived with only five minutes left to play.

Geoff was making one of his characteristic storming runs through the middle when a Rangers full-back charged into him just inside the box. Wakeley's captain crashed to the ground and the referee, up with play as usual, had no hesitation in awarding the second penalty kick of the afternoon. Normally, Geoff would have taken the kick himself but he had hurt his knee in the fall. He tried to hobble about for a moment or two and then had to sit down.

Miles knew that Geoff really must be in pain and unable to kick the ball. Not for any other reason would he have surrendered his chance of scoring another goal.

So Johnnie Evett was entrusted with the responsibility of taking the kick. Miles closed his eyes and crossed his fingers. If Wanderers scored they would surely win the match and collect two vital points to help them up the League table.

Johnnie took a very long run and then slid the ball very calmly into the bottom right-hand corner of the net. The goalie had been given no chance at all of matching Miles' save.

That was the final score: 2–1 to Wakeley Wanderers. Miles joined in the whoops of delight as the referee signalled the end of the game. He raced across the pitch to join his team-mates and everyone congratulated everyone else.

In spite of the fact that his knee was still worrying him Geoff Leyland was in high spirits.

'Well done, Miles High,' he grinned. 'That save of yours kept us in the match. It was crucial. If Rangers had scored then we'd have been in dead trouble. Dead trouble. So keep up the good work in the next match.'

Somebody pointed to the cap Miles was wearing. 'I think that brought us a bit of luck,' he remarked. 'You'd better wear it next week as well.'

Until that moment Miles had completely forgotten he was wearing it. Guiltily, he thought he should return it right away. Fortunately, Mrs Jenks was still in sight, strolling along the path beside the pitch on her way home. He ran across to hand it over to her.

'Well, I'm glad I was able to help,' she said as she put it back on her own head. 'But in future, young Miles, you'd better have a cap of your own to keep the sun out of your eyes. Tell you what, I'll buy you one for Christmas – a real goalkeeper's hat. I think you deserve one. Then everyone—'

Miles gulped as he struggled to speak. 'Thanks a lot, Mrs Jenks. But I don't think I'll be playing again. You see, my mother says—'

'Oh, I know what you've always told me about your mother,' said Mrs Jenks, cutting him off. 'But I expect she was thinking about you dashing all over the place in the middle of the field and getting over-tired. It's different when you play in goal. You don't use up so much energy, for one thing. Instead you use skill and judgement.'

Miles didn't know what to say. But Mrs Jenks hadn't finished yet.

'Anyway,' she added, 'I think you're a lot fitter than she imagines. And I'm going to tell her so.'

Miles hardly knew what to say but his hopes suddenly began to rise.

'Do you mean that, Mrs Jenks? You'll ask her if I can continue playing for Wakeley?'

'Of course I will, Miles. I'll also tell her how much hard work you do for me in the garden and carrying those heavy shopping bags. That *proves* you're very fit. She might as well know, too, what a very fine goalkeeper you are and that your team needs you.

'So, nip off and get changed quickly and I'll walk home with you. Your mother's in for a bit of a surprise, I reckon.'

Five

Horrified was the word Mrs Hansen used to describe her reaction to the news. Judging by the expression on her face, Miles was well aware that she meant it, too. He knew that there was no hope of her rescinding her decision to ban him from playing football.

'It's your treachery that horrifies me as much as anything, Miles,' she said as soon as Mrs Jenks had left. 'You've been so very, very underhand in what you've done.'

'But, Mum, it was the only way I could *prove* I was fit,' Miles pointed out. 'The one sure way to prove you're fit to play football is actually to play in a game, a real, hard, competitive game with boys who're playing all the time. And I didn't come to any harm – you can see that for yourself, Mum. I mean, look at me. I look perfectly healthy, don't I? And I feel great, just great. Physically, I mean.'

'I've told you before, Miles, appearances

aren't everything,' she replied with no hint of any sympathy for his point of view in her voice. 'A person can feel perfectly well one minute and quite wretched the next. It's happened with you before. A boy of your age is no judge of what's best for him in health matters, especially when you're so tall for your age. As Dr Moray said, you've simply outgrown—'

'—my strength,' Miles muttered wearily. He really was sick to death of hearing that phrase. 'But, Mum, he said that *ages* ago! I haven't been ill for years. So Dr Moray doesn't know how fit I've become. I'm sure he wouldn't say that if he'd seen me playing for Wanderers today.'

Suddenly, he remembered something he'd heard his parents discussing over lunch. 'Hey, it's tomorrow night, isn't it, that Dr Moray's coming round to play cards with you and Dad? Well, then, you could ask him to give me a check-up before you start. I mean, I'm sure he wouldn't mind if *you* asked him, even if it is his night off.'

'Oh no, Miles,' his mother said firmly, shaking her head with great solemnity. 'I wouldn't dream of imposing on Dr Moray in that way. When he comes here for an evening of cards it's a relaxation for him – and a doctor needs complete relaxation like everyone else. Dr Moray is a friend of the family, a very good friend, and one doesn't make use of friends for that sort of purpose except in an extreme emergency.'

'He may be your friend, and Dad's, but he's no friend of mine,' Miles murmured truculently. 'Last time he was here he wouldn't even buy a copy of *Soccer Special*. Said he ought to get a free one for services rendered, whatever that means.'

'That's quite enough, Miles!' his mother said sharply. 'I won't have you insulting Dr Moray after all he's done for you. He's a very fine medical man and I trust him implicitly. Now, you can get off upstairs and have a proper lie down. Rest is more important than ever after what you've been up to. Go on now, off you go.'

He was halfway up the stairs when she called out with fresh instructions. 'On second thoughts, you'd better have a hot bath immediately. After all the running about you've been doing there's bound to be the risk of a chill. So you must have a bath. And, Miles, that means you're not to go out of the house again today.'

At the top of the stairs Miles uttered the worst curses he could think of as loudly as he dared. Then, after slamming home the bolt on the bathroom door, he turned both taps full on.

As the water gushed into the bath he slowly stripped off his clothes and tried to think constructively about the latest disaster in his life.

He realized now that it would have been better if he hadn't accepted Mrs Jenks' offer to speak on his behalf to his mother. It was obvious that his mother resented what she said was Mrs Jenks' interference in the matter of his health, something she claimed to understand better than any outsider possibly could. Miles didn't believe that was true but he was hardly in a position to dispute it; when his mother made a pronouncement like that there was simply no arguing with her.

No, what he should have done was just to mention casually at home, when he was sure no one was really listening properly, that he'd given Wanderers a bit of a hand when they had a problem to sort out. That was the truth. It was unlikely that anyone would have asked for further details or suspected that Miles' hands had been sticking out of the sleeves of a goal-keeper's jersey. Then, if the subject had ever cropped up again, he could have protested, with absolute sincerity, that he'd told them he was helping the team. It might have been weeks before any member of his family learned that he was playing football regularly and, by then, he would have had real proof that it was doing him no harm at all.

He hated being accused of treachery and he supposed that was why he had retaliated with his remark about Dr Moray. That, he recognized, had probably done him a lot of harm. On the other hand, he wasn't sorry he'd criticized the man. He didn't like him and he had a feeling it was mutual.

As he stretched full-length in the bath and allowed his chin to sink to the level of the water, Miles switched his thoughts to the team, *his* team as he'd begun to think of Wakeley Wanderers. By not playing for them again he would be letting them down. Geoff Leyland and the other players had never really understood why he wasn't allowed to play soccer; so now, when he told them he'd played his last game for them, they'd be even more puzzled. Geoff himself was a fitness fanatic, always had been, and it was his opinion that everyone could be as fit as he was (well, *nearly* as fit) if they took the trouble, as he did, to go through a regular routine of strength-building exercises. He'd tried to impress that on his teammates but only a couple of them followed his example.

Of course, with luck Wanderers should have their regular goalkeeper back for the next match. By then Colin Ayrton should have recovered from his bout of measles and be ready to return to the team. Whether he'd really be match-fit was another matter. Miles allowed himself a rueful grin as he reflected on that situation; for in his own mind he had no doubt at all that he himself was completely match-fit. On top of that Geoff made it plain that he regarded Miles as the better goalkeeper; so if both players were available for the next match Miles would be the one selected to play. In those circumstances, poor Colin might just as well have remained on the sick list!

Miles tugged the plug fiercely from the bath, stepped out and slowly began to dry himself. There was one consoling thought: he still had *Soccer Special*. No one was going to take that away from him. Writing about football wasn't the same as playing football but it was the next best thing. His newspaper gave him the freedom to say whatever he wanted about any person and any team.

It occurred to him as he went into his bedroom that in the next issue he could write about his own performance in the Sellerby match. Now that his parents knew what he'd been up to there was no longer any need to conceal his identity. He could discard 'A.N.

Other' and give the credit for that penalty save to the player who'd made it: Miles Hansen. His team-mates would think it strange if he didn't. They expected the editor to highlight brilliant saves as well as brilliant goals. He wouldn't, however, mention that it was Hansen's last appearance in Wanderers' colours. That would only look as though he was pleading for sympathy. His brief career as a goalkeeper was over; but his editorship would continue. From now on it was his job to build up circulation and make *Soccer Special* required reading for everyone he knew. Success as an editor would help make up for all the disappointments he'd suffered in his efforts to become a footballer.

After making some notes for the Sellerby match report he put down his pencil and started to think about the sort of features his readers might like to find in the paper. Naturally, the subject of soccer came first. But what could he write about that was original and newsworthy and that everyone would want to read? It was no good picking one of the teams he normally wrote about or even one of their star players. That would arouse only limited interest. No, it had to be a team everyone knew even if they didn't support it . . .

Got it! Athletic, the town's Second Division

club, now in a mid-table position. Miles grinned with delight at the idea of writing about a professional team: it was an inspiration. So far as he could tell, the boys at his school were completely divided on the subject of Athletic. Half of them believed that the team had a real chance of promotion that season, the other half were convinced they were certainties for relegation.

So it was obvious that both halves would be interested to know what actually went on at Highdale, Athletic's famous ground on the outskirts of the town. If he could arrange to interview Dave Rosborough, the team's Manager, and get his personal views on the club's prospects for the season it would be a marvellous story. Best of all, it would be an 'exclusive' story, and that was something he'd always wanted to write in *Soccer Special*. An exclusive about Athletic ought to guarantee that the next edition of the paper would be a sell-out even after printing extra copies.

Miles had never been behind the scenes, as he thought of it, at a professional football club, though often enough he'd wondered what real dressing-rooms would be like, and the Manager's office, and the treatment room, and the huge bath into which, so he'd heard, all the players dived after a match. Now, if Athletic agreed to allow him to visit their ground, he could describe everything he saw in great detail. With luck, he might even get a chance to talk to some of the players. Maybe one of them would even be willing to write a special article for the paper – and autograph it so that every reader would recognize that it was yet another *Soccer Special* exclusive.

There wasn't a moment to be wasted. Miles turned to a fresh page on his notepad and began to draft the vital letter.

Dear Mr Rosborough,

I would very much like to interview you for my newspaper, *Soccer Special*. It would be an 'exclusive' article and I know it would interest all my readers. Many of them attend the same school as I do and they all take a great interest in Athletic. So they would be fascinated by any news I could give them of the team and of yourself.

I know that you are very busy every day but if you could spare me about half-an-hour of your time one day very soon I would be very grateful. School finishes at 3.30 p.m. and I could be at Highdale within twenty minutes.

I do hope you will agree to be interviewed by me. I look forward to meeting you very much.

All best wishes to Athletic.

Yours sincerely,
Miles Hansen

Word by word he went over what he'd written and decided he really couldn't improve on it. His English teacher, had he seen the letter, would have disapproved, no doubt, of the excessive use of the word 'very' but Miles himself wasn't worried about that; he preferred to let his enthusiasm show through. According to Press reports that Miles had read, 'enthusiasm' was one of the chief attributes Dave Rosborough expected to find in his players and staff so he would certainly look for it in a newspaper reporter who wanted to interview him.

Miles hurried along to his sister's bedroom to persuade her to let him have a sheet of writing-paper, envelope and stamp. Rosemary, who was doing something to her hair, handed them over without any inquiry at all about why he wanted them (he'd been sure she'd ask who on earth he was writing to). She seemed to be in a blissful mood and Miles correctly concluded it was entirely due to the effect her new boyfriend was having on her.

After writing the letter, and signing it with a flourish, he propped it against his school case to be posted the following morning. If all went well it would be delivered on Tuesday and thus there was a distinct chance he might receive a reply on Wednesday. He crossed his fingers on both hands.

Dave Rosborough didn't let him down. His letter arrived second post on Wednesday and was handed to Miles by his mother when he returned home from school. Although she didn't say anything she appeared to be expecting him to tell her what it contained. He tried to look nonchalant as he opened it but his heart was thudding with excited anticipation.

Dear Miles,

Thanks for your letter. Yes, I'll be pleased to give you an interview for your newspaper. Let's make it Friday of this week. I'll expect you about four o'clock.

If you'd like to bring a pal with you (your Assistant Editor perhaps) that'll be okay. But only one, please – not the whole class!

Also, perhaps you'd bring a copy of *Soccer Special*. I'd very much like to see it.

Looking forward to meeting you on Friday,

Yours in sport,
Dave Rosborough
Manager

When Miles glanced at his mother he saw that her eyebrows were raised.

'Oh, it's nothing much,' he explained, folding the letter and putting it back in its envelope. 'Just something about my newspaper.'

It was only when he reached the privacy of his own bedroom that he let his feelings explode in a whoop of joy.

Six

Geoff Leyland really did look as delighted as he said he felt. He and Miles had dashed headlong to the bus stop as soon as school was over on Friday afternoon and now they were trying to get their breath back as, impatiently, they waited for the Highdale bus to arrive. Several times already he had said what a great, fantastic, brilliant, super-splendid idea it was to fix up an interview with Athletic's Manager. Miles glowed with satisfaction as well as with his exertions on the way to the bus stop. He would always be grateful to Geoff for allowing him to play those couple of matches for Wakeley Wanderers; now, by taking Geoff with him to Highdale, he was repaying some of that debt of gratitude.

Almost literally, Geoff had jumped at the chance of meeting Dave Rosborough when Miles had shown him the letter. Although he himself was hardly one of Athletic's most faithful supporters, Geoff was quick to point out that he'd always admired their Manager because, 'when he was a player with Arsenal and Northampton he was one of the fittest men that ever kicked a ball – that's what my Dad says, anyway.' Miles hadn't questioned that judgement. It was a well known fact that Geoff's father, a county squash player, was the ultimate authority on the subject of physical fitness. Geoff made sure that every acquaintance of his was aware of it.

'Anything he tells us when he shows us round the place will be useful and probably we can include some of their ideas in our own training routines,' Geoff had added confidently as he accepted Miles' invitation. 'So I'll make a note of what he says about getting really fit for a big match. I'll remember to take my own notebook with me.'

'Well, that'll certainly make you look just like an assistant editor. Dave Rosborough will be impressed when we both take notes,' grinned Miles.

'Hey, don't tell him that's what I'm supposed to be!' Geoff protested. 'I mean, English isn't exactly my best subject, you know. I like to do things, not just write about 'em.'

Then, realizing what he'd said, he hastily added, 'Oh, sorry, Miles. I wasn't getting at you personally. Anyway, you do both, don't you – write about the team as well as play for it.'

Miles had made no reply to that. So far he hadn't been able to bring himself to the point of mentioning the ban on playing for Wakeley Wanderers or any other team. He was well aware that there wasn't one chance in a hundred that he'd be granted a reprieve but he sensed that by telling Geoff what had happened he'd be admitting total defeat. In any case, Mrs Jenks had advised him not to give up hope, 'Because *something* – I don't know what, but something – could turn up and cause your mother to change her mind at the last minute. We ladies have a habit of changing our minds, you know!' Mrs Jenks was full of sympathy for his plight and said that she was responsible for it. So, in compensation, as she put it, she'd produced an extra twenty copies of the paper that week and Miles had managed to sell every one of them.

However, he'd kept two copies to give to Athletic's Manager and, as he and Geoff hurried to the ground after dropping off the bus, he checked that they were still safe in his pocket.

When they reached the 'Players' and Officials' Entrance' Geoff stood aside for Miles to enter first – and Miles couldn't help grinning to himself at that because it was probably the first time in his life that Geoff Leyland had deferred to a team-mate.

To the right of the entrance hall was a high glass-topped counter and behind it was an elderly man apparently totting up some figures in a thick black ledger. After giving them a quick glance he continued with his counting until he'd reached the bottom of the page. Then, with a look of irritation, he slid back a glass shutter and brusquely asked them what they wanted.

'We've come to see the Manager, Mr Rosborough,' Miles explained. 'He's expecting us.'

'Oh, is he?' said the man in obvious disbelief. 'I doubt that. If it's one of those schoolboy trials you're after then you've come on the wrong day at the wrong time. They're on Wednesdays. And you've got to write in and ask for one. You can't just turn up here without warning and expect us to fit you in at your convenience. So you're wasting your time turning up here like this. Best be off and apply through the proper channels.'

Miles was thoroughly dismayed. 'But, you see—'

The glass shutter was being thrust back into

the closed position when a door opened at the far end of the room behind the old man and Dave Rosborough came into view.

'Thank goodness for that!' Geoff muttered. 'Another half-minute and we'd've been thrown out of the place.'

The Manager caught sight of them, smiled broadly and indicated that they should go through the swing doors to their left. This time it was Geoff Leyland who led the way.

They were in a corridor that stretched as far as they could see in both directions. A moment later Dave Rosborough emerged from the reception area and shook hands warmly with each of them.

'Don't let old Jack put you off,' he said breezily, jerking his thumb towards the room he'd just left. 'He's getting on a bit and when we're short-staffed he's not exactly the sweetest-tempered chap you've ever met. But he's been a loyal supporter of Athletic for over fifty years and that's what counts.'

Still chatting affably about the club and its staff, he led the way along the corridor to a door which bore the word 'Manager' in white lettering on a transparent plastic plate. Ushering them into the office, he told them to make themselves at home and ask any questions they liked.

'I meet the Press boys regularly and sometimes they give me a hard time after we've had a bad result,' Mr Rosborough added. 'So I've had to learn to cope with tough grillings from sports writers like yourselves!'

Miles decided that this was the right moment to hand over the copies of *Soccer Special* and they were received with evident interest. While the Manager scanned them Miles glanced round

the office. It was much smaller than he'd imagined and contained only a plain desk, three chairs, a metal filing cabinet, a small cupboard and, the only surprise, a pile of yellow-and-green football shirts that obviously were brand new. Yet Athletic's normal colours were red-and-white. Miles had also expected that their host would be attired in a red tracksuit for he'd often been described in the local paper as 'a typical tracksuit manager, one who always takes part in training sessions with his players.' On this Friday afternoon, however, the former Arsenal and Northampton winger was casually dressed in a polo neck sweater and a sports jacket in broad checks.

'Well, this is a very professional effort,' said the Manager, laying the copies of the newspaper on his desk. 'I'm really very impressed. What made you start it up, Miles?'

'Well, I had a lot of illnesses when I was younger and I used to get bored with nothing to do when I was getting better. I liked writing about real things – in English lessons at school, you know – so that's why I began to make up a newspaper. I like thinking up headlines as well.'

'You look pretty fit to me now, Miles,' Mr Rosborough remarked.

'He plays football for my team now,' put in Geoff Leyland. He felt he was in danger of being left out of the conversation altogether. 'That's Wakeley Wanderers and we're in the Sunday League. Miles is the goalie.'

'Good,' said the Manager approvingly. 'You've certainly got the right build for a goalkeeper. To my mind, he has one of the most important jobs in the team.'

He paused, and then went on, 'Look, boys, how would you like it if I showed you round now? You can ask your questions while we're on the move; some of the things you see just might give you some fresh ideas. Anyway, I think better when I'm on my feet instead of being stuck behind a desk. So maybe you'll get some smarter answers that way!'

Eagerly they followed him into the corridor which, he explained, ran the full length of the main grandstand. 'Right above our heads are the posh seats, the most expensive ones, and the directors' box – oh, and next to that is the Press box. I must remember to show that to you, Miles. You might have a seat there yourself one day.'

Further along the marathon corridor they came to the players' dressing-room – but Miles' attention had been caught by a football, suspended by a long cord from the ceiling, just above an adult's head height. Spotting the boy's interest Dave Rosborough jumped from a standing position and neatly headed the ball forward and upwards.

'Just a fun thing really,' the Manager

grinned. 'But it helps to keep the players on their toes. Few of them can resist practising a header when they're walking down this corridor. Plenty of visitors like to have a bash at it, too.'

The home team's dressing-room wasn't as interesting as they'd hoped it would be. It was unoccupied and there wasn't so much as a single shirt hanging up on any of the pegs round the walls and the benches were just as bare of boots and football gear. What it did possess, though, was a faint odour of ointment and antiseptics, a smell which Miles remembered vividly from times when he'd received medical treatment. He was glad to move into a connecting room – only to be confronted by what he recognized as an operating table!

'Don't look so aghast, we don't cut anybody up on that!' Mr Rosborough said cheerfully, correctly interpreting Miles' thoughts. 'It's just an ordinary treatment table such as you'll find in every football club today. This gleaming equipment over here is for providing special heat rays. They're marvellous for clearing up bruises and deep-seated strains in muscles. We have a physiotherapist who comes in when we need him and he's the expert on all the stuff we've got in here for dealing with sprains and knocks.'

He opened a tall white-painted cupboard and the boys stared in awe at the contents: bandages, tubular sleeving ('a special kind of bandage to give extra protection to ankles – a very vulnerable spot for footballers, as you'll know'), jars of oils and Vaseline, sticking plasters, tapes, cans of antibiotic sprays and pain-killing sprays, and even boxes of chewing gum.

'Here, catch!' Dave Rosborough called, tossing each of them a packet of chewing gum. Automatically, they both pocketed them, not to be eaten later but kept as souvenirs of their visit to Highdale.

'You wouldn't think we'd need all that medical stuff when you see what we do to get the players fit in the first place,' the Manager remarked as they accompanied him further along the corridor and into a large gymnasium. With its wall-bars and pile of mats to land on it greatly reminded Miles of the one at his school but some of the equipment he'd never seen before anywhere.

'That's the thing that really pinpoints any player's strengths and weaknesses,' said Rosborough, nodding towards a device that appeared to consist of gleaming metal bars and levers, pulleys and iron weights and leather support straps and harness. In height it was taller than the Manager and to Geoff it resembled a rather crazy geometrical design. He voiced that thought.

'Maybe so,' Dave Rosborough laughed, 'but it does a great job in testing a man's physical resources and co-ordination. Or a boy's, for that matter. Want to have a go and see for yourself?'

'Sure thing,' said Geoff, stepping forward eagerly and slipping off his jacket. The Manager showed him how to lie at the foot of the machine, his feet slightly higher than his head on a narrow board that would pivot when the correct pressure was applied. After checking that Geoff's ankles were comfortably positioned in leather slings the Manager made some adjustments to the balanced weights and then told him to start pressing down.

Within seconds the strain of Geoff's efforts to lift the weights began to show on his face. Soon he was sweating quite freely and he looked to be in anguish.

'I don't think – I've quite got the – the hang of this,' he gasped. And Miles laughed. He knew the pun hadn't been intended but he couldn't help being amused by it. Geoff tried to glare at him but succeeded only in making his grimaces look even more grotesque.

'Don't overdo it,' Dave Rosborough said warningly. 'Better relax now, Geoff.'

Wakeley Wanderers' captain relaxed so quickly that the weights clanged against each other noisily. After being released from the slings it was a moment or two before he staggered to his feet.

'It's my knee, you see, Dave,' he mumbled. 'I hurt it in the last match and perhaps it's not quite right yet. In fact, I'm still getting a bit of pain in it.'

'Yes, well, it's just been confirmed that you aren't one hundred per cent yet in your leg muscles,' the Manager told him. 'This machine is designed to find out exactly those sort of weaknesses. For any player, the one certain cure is rest – and you shouldn't need much of that at your age.'

He turned to Miles. 'Do you want to have a go, Mr Editor?'

Miles was no less enthusiastic than Geoff had been and promptly settled himself into position to be tested in the identical exercise. After pausing for a few moments to relax himself completely, he began to exert the necessary pressure with his thighs and legs. To his delight, the weights moved appreciably and he had by no means exhausted himself.

'Well done, Miles!' Dave Rosborough called. 'Didn't take you long to learn proper coordination. But that's far enough, I think.'

Geoff was scowling at him as Miles stood up and when the Manager asked if they'd like to have a go at anything else it was Geoff who responded first. The next exercise was aimed at developing strength and suppleness of shoulder and arm muscles. 'Because a footballer,' they were told, 'has to be healthy in every part of his body, not just in his legs and feet. In soccer all the body comes into play during a true, competitive game.'

Again it was Geoff who went into the harness first, determined to prove his superiority over Miles. But the performances, which this time were actually recorded on a dial by electronic digits, were practically identical. If anything, Miles, much to his surprise and delight, had the slightly better score.

'Well, that really proves how fit you are, Miles,' Dave Rosborough said admiringly. 'And it's just as well because a goalie has got to be tough, really tough. But I can see you'll make the grade all right if you keep up the good work.'

Miles grinned his appreciation of the compliments but he daren't look at Geoff. He could sense his friend's reaction to such praise after he himself had been told he lacked complete fitness. To Geoff, that really was a case of adding insult to injury.

After a quick glance at the players' lounge ('this is where they can relax both before and after a game') and the boardroom, where the directors of the club met to discuss business matters and the team's performances, the boys were taken up into the main stand and shown the Press box. Miles was fascinated to learn that some of the reporters had their own private telephones so that they could ring through reports to their offices during the game or immediately it was over. The phones were kept on a shelf under the sloping wooden ledge, rather like an old fashioned school desk, that served as a writing table.

'So this is where you may sit one day, Miles, when your own playing career is over and you're working as the sports editor of a big national paper,' the Manager smiled. 'I just hope that you'll be reporting that we went to the top of the League after thrashing Manchester United, or Liverpool, or Spurs by six goals to nil!'

Miles thought he detected a hint in all that and so, at last, he started to ask the questions he'd prepared the previous evening. Dave Rosborough, perching on the edge of the box, took care to give a precise answer to each one – and Miles, having no knowledge of shorthand, was thankful that he didn't speak too quickly.

He'd been worrying that he wouldn't be able to get down half of what he was told.

Once or twice it seemed to Miles that Geoff was on the point of interrupting with a question of his own so each time he shot him a warning glance. He guessed that the Manager, who'd so far been very generous with his time, had other things to do that afternoon and Miles didn't want to outstay his welcome.

Eventually, however, Geoff had to say something. He felt he'd been left out of the conversation long enough.

'I thought we might be meeting one or two of the first-teamers, Dave. I mean, I wouldn't have minded a chat with a couple of the strikers. We could've discussed ways of getting through tight defences.'

The Manager smiled sympathetically. 'Not on a Friday afternoon, young man. All the first team squad go home early on a Friday in readiness for tomorrow's match. Gives me a chance to catch up with paperwork and so on. You wouldn't believe how many forms and things I have to sign in a week.

'No, the only players who come in at this time are those who need special treatment for injuries and so on. Luckily, everyone's fit at the moment. Which is a happy, if rare, state of affairs. Injuries, especially those that don't quickly respond to treatment, are really what play havoc with a manager's plans.'

'Yeah, I know. I mean, it's the same with us—'

'Look, I think we'd better be off,' said Miles hurriedly, cutting off Geoff's meanders. 'We're very grateful to you, Mr Rosborough, for giving us so much of your time. It's been great seeing round a club like Athletic. And I know my readers will be fascinated to hear about your views on the team's prospects.'

'Delighted to have you,' replied the Manager, keeping in step with his visitors but leading them towards the exit. 'And don't forget, Miles, I shall be looking forward to seeing the article in your newspaper.'

'Oh, I won't forget, Mr Rosborough. I'll send you two copies as soon as they're printed. You should get them on Tuesday – or Wednesday at the latest.'

The Manager accompanied them to the players' entrance, shook hands with them and wished their team luck in its next match.

Geoff had little to say until they reached the bus stop. It was unusual for him to be so subdued but Miles didn't comment on it. He was already thinking about the article he was going to write. He would enjoy underlining the exclusiveness of it by reporting that: 'The Manager himself told me . . .'

'You know something?' Geoff said suddenly. 'I don't believe Dave Rosborough knows what he's talking about.'

'Eh?' Miles was thoroughly startled.

'Not about injuries, anyway,' Geoff continued as though Miles hadn't uttered a sound. 'It's crazy to say that you're fitter than I am – crazy! I've always been the fittest player in the team by miles – and that's not a joke, Hansen. You aren't in the same street as me when it comes to *real* fitness.'

'But, Geoff, I've just proved it – you saw what happened on that machine . . .'

'Rubbish! That wasn't working properly. Or probably Dave didn't know how to set the balances and things. I'm not having it said that I'm not fit. So I'm going to prove, *really prove*, that you don't stand a chance with me in a *genuine* fitness contest.'

'But how? How?'

Geoff, eyes narrowing, gave him a hard look.

'Now, just listen to this . . .'

Seven

It was even colder – much colder – than Miles had feared it would be. Under his borrowed tracksuit he was wearing a long-sleeved sweater as well as a woollen shirt but somehow the wind was still getting right through to his bones. Or, at least, that was what it felt like. He shivered and told himself he was crazy. When he found that he was nodding in agreement with himself he shook his head angrily. For the umpteenth time he wished he'd been bold enough to resist Geoff Leyland's challenge.

He had actually been on the point of laughing off the whole idea when Geoff had suggested he didn't have the nerve for it. That was the word that had really stuck in Miles' throat.

'Nerve!' he'd protested. 'Of course I've got the nerve to try it. The one thing goalkeepers must have is strong nerves. It's the most – the most *dangerous* job in football.'

'Maybe, but having the nerve for tackling a

real Army assault course in the dark from start to finish is different,' Geoff had continued relentlessly. 'That takes real courage, real guts – not your sort of quick grab in the penalty area. You've got to be dead cool with nerves of steel to do what I'm going to do on Sunday night. If you chicken-out, Miles, it'll prove for ever that you can't match me in fitness or in mental toughness!'

'Right then, Leyland, I'll do it!'

As soon as the words were out of his mouth Miles wished he could have swallowed them. But then he'd seen the expression on Geoff's face: a mixture of triumph and wariness. So, after all, perhaps the great fitness fanatic wasn't absolutely confident of success.

Now, as he tried to keep warm at the bus stop while waiting for his rival to join him, Miles took comfort from one stroke of luck. It was a night of the full moon. So at least they should be able to see where they were going; and that was of vital importance if they were going to come through this venture unscathed.

He had only a rough idea of what was involved in competing over the abandoned assault course at Daleside. Like many boys at his school he had taken a brief interest in the Army camp on the edge of the moors above the town. When a party of them had gone up there one summer afternoon they'd hoped to catch a glimpse of tanks and armoured cars and perhaps even rocket-launchers. But apart from Land-Rovers fitted with signalling equipment and a few heavy trucks they'd seen very little of real interest. There'd been rumours in the town that before long the Army would be moving out altogether and already some parts of the camp had been closed down.

The main section of the assault course had been constructed in a wood that clung to an unexpectedly steep hillside. It was some distance from the camp itself and that, of course, was why it was accessible to the public nowadays. According to Geoff, who had reconnoitred it on several occasions, some parts of it were almost hidden by undergrowth but he insisted that it was still in a fit state to be used. He had listed some of the obstacles: a tunnel made of barbed wire which had to be crawled through at speed (and speed, he pointed out, was what it was all about anyway); a deep pit that had to be crossed by poles made out of saplings; wide, water-filled trenches which you swung yourself across on ropes suspended from tree branches; a maze of sharp stakes, all placed very close to each other; and a high thorn fence similar to those found on steeplechase circuits.

'It's really quite formidable,' Geoff had warned him delightedly.

Miles didn't doubt that. But he doubted his ability to complete the course. All he could hope was that Geoff would have problems, too, in spite of his belief that he could overcome any obstacle.

There was confidence in Geoff's very stride, however, as he marched up to the bus stop and then, slipping the pack from his back, wriggled his shoulders. After swinging it freely a couple of times to demonstrate its quite obvious weight he tugged the harness over his shoulders again before leaning, with studied nonchalance, against the signpost.

'Feeling on top form, then?' he inquired.

'Oh, sure, just great,' Miles told him flatly. 'Just great. Ready for anything, you might say.'

'No trouble in getting away? I mean, we don't want a hue and cry like those times when your Ma suspected you might be playing football after school. Had everybody going round in circles when that happened.'

'No worries,' said Miles, annoyed that those embarrassing days should still be remembered. 'I told 'em I had to go and see a pal to compare notes on that farming project we're doing. Said I'd probably be late because it involves masses of research.'

Geoff nodded his approval and started to whistle rather tunelessly. Miles couldn't bring himself to ask whether Geoff had difficulties in disappearing in the evening when he wanted to. He knew that his rival would instantly produce some utterly plausible story.

His curiosity had been aroused, though, by the size of that pack. He asked what it contained.

'Oh, various useful things for an expedition like this. Torch, groundsheet (got that from my brother who had it when he was in the Army), vacuum flask of drinking chocolate and, er, running shoes. Spiked running shoes.'

'Hey, that's not fair!' Miles protested. 'Spikes'll give you an advantage. I haven't got any.'

'It's perfectly fair,' Geoff assured him coldly. 'You could've used 'em if you'd thought about it. I'm a good planner, that's all. Pay attention to planning and the battle's half won – that's what my brother learned in the Army and it makes fairly good sense.'

Before Miles could argue the point further the bus arrived. Geoff athletically leapt aboard first, paid the fares for both of them and refused to accept any contribution to the cost from Miles.

'It was my idea and so I'm quite willing to pay the expenses,' he explained. 'It wouldn't be right for you to pay to be beaten.' He paused, then added, 'But you can pay on the way back, if you like. The winner ought not to have to cough up for everything!'

The journey should have taken no more than half-an-hour but the driver seemed to be conducting a private go-slow campaign so it was almost forty-five minutes before they reached their destination. Miles, beginning to worry about how late it was going to be before he got home, wanted to push on with all speed as they began to climb the deeply rutted track to the moor. Geoff, however, refused to be hurried. It was essential, he pointed out, to conserve their energy because they were going to need all they possessed for the assault course itself.

'Your knee's not still bothering you, is it?' asked Miles, undecided whether he wanted the answer to be yes or no.

'Of course not!' was the spirited reply, accompanied by a vigorous flexing of the joint. 'I've told you, this mustn't be rushed, Miles. Honestly, I don't think you've any idea what you're committed to.'

Another twenty minutes passed before Miles saw for himself what was in store for them. When they entered the wood it was so dark that progress would have been practically impossible without the aid of Geoff's torchlight. But soon the trees began to thin out and it was just possible to see by the light of the moon.

'Lots of the trees were chopped down to make way for the assault course,' Geoff explained. 'There has to be room, you see, for several men to have a go at the same time. With us it'll just be a case of follow-my-leader. That's *you* following *me*, I mean!'

'That's what you think,' Miles told him with a sudden surge of determination. 'I'll just overtake you when I feel like it.'

Not deigning to answer that, Geoff led the way to the first obstacle on the horseshoe-shaped circuit. It wasn't easy to see just what had to be attempted for, to Miles, it seemed to consist of a shapeless mass of barbed wire, much of it inextricably entangled with ferns and bracken and even exposed roots of trees.

Geoff, poking around with a stick he'd picked up, said it was all perfectly clear even though it was in bad shape. He shone his torch to show what he meant.

'It's a series of tunnels, each one made out of the wire. Look, they're in parallel lines. I think those two side-by-side in the middle are the best. All we've got to do is crawl through from one end to the other as fast as possible. Then—'

'But one of those tunnels as you call them seems to have caved-in in the middle. Whoever goes through that one will get stuck in all that wire. I bet it's as sharp as a razor, too. And it seems very narrow.'

'It's wide enough to take a soldier in full battle-gear – you know, automatic rifle, helmet, back-pack. So it's bound to be big enough for us – and especially you, thin as a walking-stick!'

'Thank you very much, *captain*!' Miles answered with all the sarcasm he could muster. He thought of reminding Leyland that it was only a few days ago that his slimness and height had proved rather useful to Wakeley Wanderers; but he realized there was nothing to be gained by that when Geoff was in such an overbearing mood.

'Right, I'll show you what's in store for us next,' continued Geoff, marching off briskly towards the second obstacle.

It consisted of four saplings, each completely stripped of any branches and foliage, laid across an open (and, as far as Miles could tell, bottomless) pit. He guessed that it wouldn't be easy to cross from one side to the other in daylight, let alone in semi-darkness. One false step and you'd be a gonner . . .

'This one should be right up your street,' Geoff was telling him blithely. 'You weigh so little that the pole won't bend much in the middle when you cross. With a heavier, better-muscled bloke like me it's bound to give a bit in the middle.' He paused and then added, 'I'll have further to go, you see, if it bends – so you'll have an advantage on this obstacle. Still, you're going to need some advantages when you're up against me!'

'Weight won't come into it when you're going at speed,' Miles pointed out mildly. 'I mean, balance will be the important thing. One false step and, well . . .'

'Oh no!' Geoff yelled. Then, very theatrically, he groaned. 'You don't *walk* across it, or *run* across it, you idiot! You swing yourself along with your *hands*, like a monkey on the top bar of its cage. It's a long way down to the bottom and I reckon it'll be pretty muddy down there as well. So it would be fatal to try and cross any other way. The whole idea of this obstacle is to test the strength of your arms, of your grip. Get it?'

'Oh,' murmured Miles. He should have thought of that.

'What comes next?' he inquired, anxious to put that blunder out of his mind.

'Oh, just the wall jump. But it's not worth looking at now. There's nothing to it because it's not even very high. You're supposed to take it in your stride. Come on, we'll go on to the fourth.'

Geoff was still chortling about Miles' mistake when they reached the next obstruction: the fearsomely-sharp mass of stakes that appeared to have been planted in haphazard fashion but which, on closer examination, proved to have been placed with quite fiendish ingenuity. For it was just impossible to pass through them in anything like a straight line. To make any progress at all a competitor had to duck and weave from side to side while finding the easiest, and shortest, route. To add to the difficulties, the stakes were of different heights.

'It'll be a bit like playing touch-rugby and trying to swerve past every opponent on the way to scoring a try,' Geoff said complacently. 'Should be fun. You'll also have an advantage in this one as well, Miles High. Being so thin, you should be able to avoid every single stake. Actually, come to think of it, you're almost *thinner* than some of those stakes!'

'If that's what you think – that I have all these advantages – then I can't understand how you expect to win the race.'

'Well, I just want you to have a fair chance. I mean, it should be a handicap really, with you getting some start. But I'll win all right because I'm stronger and fitter. And that's what it's all about, Mr Editor. You'd wish you'd stuck to writing your little paper instead of taking me on over a real, tough, Army assault course.'

By now, Miles was only half-listening. He had been worrying about the time the preliminary survey was taking. They hadn't even started on the race yet and already it was quite late. At this rate, they were going to be out most of the night.

'Look, I think it's time we got started,' he said decisively. 'Let's forget about checking over the course first. I don't think that's necessary. I mean, you've already told me all about it, and the order the obstacles come in. Now I've seen some of them let's get on with the race. Okay?'

'Well, if you want to,' replied Geoff, sounding very doubtful. 'I just don't want you to think you didn't have a fair chance because you hadn't seen the entire course in advance. But if you really want to get cracking . . .'

'Yes! Right away.'

Still Geoff was hesitating. 'Er, but, how about a drink first? I could open that flask of hot chocolate just to—'

'No! Save it till after it's all over. You're going to need it then, *Captain* Leyland.'

It still rankled with Miles that his friend had referred to *Soccer Special* as 'your little paper'. That wasn't Geoff's description when he himself was featured in it. And, doubtless, if he did win the race he would want the full story to be written up, complete with banner headline. Well, Miles was determined Geoff Leyland wasn't going to win; the great fitness fanatic would finish a bad second.

Resignedly now, Geoff was taking off his shoes to replace them with his spiked footwear. As he watched him, Miles' impatience began to ebb. He had a sudden recollection of his mother's expression when she learned that he had been playing football on Sunday morning. Now he could imagine how she would look, and, worse, what she would say if she could see him at that moment. He dreaded the thought that she might, within a matter of hours, discover what he had been doing on the moors. He would be lucky to get back into the house without arousing his parents.

Desperately, he wanted to get the whole thing over with as quickly as possible. It had struck him that this race was both stupid and pointless. Even if he did win he couldn't publicly boast about his success. If he came second he would be a loser twice over because Geoff Leyland certainly wouldn't be inhibited about relating his triumph to everyone who listened to him – in addition, of course, to having the full story published in the paper.

'Come on, come on!' Miles muttered fiercely, clenching his fists.

Startled, Geoff hurriedly got to his feet and didn't even attempt to try out the effectiveness of his spikes. Together they made their way back to the starting point where Wanderers' skipper placed his torch and discarded shoes beside his rucksack. He couldn't, however, resist carrying out a couple of knees-bend exercises and flexing other muscles, just as he did before kicking off in a soccer match.

'Okay,' he said softly. 'I'll give the signal, counting down to zero – and on zero we go, flat out.'

Miles just nodded that he understood. Momentarily, he shivered. It could have been caused by the increasing coldness of the night or by apprehension. It didn't matter which it was. The time for thinking about anything except the race itself had gone.

'Three – two – one – ZERO!'

Geoff shot away even as he was uttering the last syllable.

Miles didn't grudge his rival his start. He was content that Geoff should lead the way over the first few obstacles; but Miles planned to stay on his heels so that Geoff would be aware all the time that he couldn't relax. Then, when the moment seemed right, Miles would overtake him. A race between two people was always a matter of tactics.

Even after choosing the widest tunnel through the barbed wire Geoff wasn't finding it easy to get through to the other side. Twice he snagged his tracksuit top on spikes and there was the sound of ripping cloth as he wrenched himself away from the second one. Miles could hear him cursing his luck.

Not that it was any easier for Miles. At just about the narrowest point of his tunnel he encountered a tangle of brambles wrapped round the wire itself and, as he struggled to make a passage, he wished he'd thought to wear goalkeeper's gloves. His hands were going to be in a terrible state by the time he completed the course.

Using his elbows and knees to push himself along, he was conscious that he was ahead of his rival. Geoff was alternately grunting and muttering and Miles sensed that he had the edge on him when it came to stamina. But that gave him little satisfaction. If the first obstacle was a true indication of what lay ahead of them then it was going to be a punishing course. Physically, they were going to suffer appallingly.

The friction caused by squirming along on his stomach was making him feel sore already and more than once he had to slow up to ease his discomfort.

'I must have been mad, stark raving mad, to have agreed to this,' he told himself.

Then, with a gasp of relief, he was clear of the savage wire. Staggering to his feet, he turned to glance at Geoff.

'Don't blame you for taking – taking that pack off,' he commented as he tried to get his breath back. 'You'd never – never have made it – wearing that.'

Geoff, kicking himself free of the last coil, gave him a look of sheer malice but made no reply. Then, taking a lung-stretching breath, he sprinted towards the poles that spanned the pit. For a moment Miles thought that his challenger was going to attempt the crossing on foot; but, preferring reason to rashness, he sank to his knees and then, taking a firm grip on the pole with both hands, began to work himself across, centimetre by centimetre.

Miles, following his example, soon began to feel that his arms were going to be pulled from their sockets. He'd thought this obstacle would be easier to overcome than the first. It wasn't. All the weight of his body was straining against his shoulder muscles and every fibre of them was signalling its protest at such treatment.

One thing only kept Miles going: the fear of what would happen to him if he relaxed his grip for even a split-second.

At one stage he tried to rest from his exertions. But as soon as he stopped moving the pain in his shoulders became worse. Yet it was just as great an effort to start moving again. The agony was almost unbearable.

He sensed that he needed to concentrate his mind on something else, however momentarily. He and Geoff were back to back as they edged towards their objective; but, by craning his head over his right shoulder, Miles was just able to catch a glimpse of his rival. He saw that Geoff, in spite of starting first, was about a metre behind him. Now grunting, now gasping, Geoff was struggling to keep up.

Miles' elation at being in the lead was short-lived. Even though he had managed to force his body into movement again he was sure he wasn't going to get to the other side of the pit. His muscles were going to collapse under the strain.

'Think ahead ... think ahead ... think ahead,' he kept telling himself. Into his mind

came a picture of a notice he had once seen on someone's desk, a jokey reminder of the need for good planning. The words 'Think Ahead' were printed in large type . . . except for the last three letters which were very small indeed because there wasn't enough space left on the card for them to be printed the same size as the others!

Somehow that silly notice helped him to keep going. For a few moments his mind had ruled his muscles: for those few precious moments the pain had been suppressed. And now he was within a couple of metres of the end of the pole. The torture and the torment were nearly over.

Seconds later, as he slid his right hand along the pole, his hand came into contact with good, moist, black earth. He had made it! Now he needed the strength to heave himself upwards and then claw his way forward until he was again on solid ground. Where he found that strength he never knew. But, at last, the fearful pit was no longer beneath him but behind him.

Still trembling, he turned to see where Geoff was. Although still making a lot of noise, the Wanderers captain seemed to have found his second wind and was swinging towards him at a surprisingly good speed. As he touched the side of the pit Miles tentatively made a move to help his friend up on to firm ground. Then he realized that assistance was the last thing Geoff would want or allow.

Geoff, too, appeared to be shaking as he got to his feet. He also seemed to be struggling to say something. Miles waited to hear what it was. He just hoped that Geoff was going to suggest that they called the whole thing off, that they should settle for an honourable draw or dead-heat or whatever he wanted to call it. After all, they'd both surely proved already that they possessed strength and fitness in abundance.

'Go on, then, go – on,' Geoff gasped. 'I don't need you to – to wait for me. Get on to the next – it's the wall jump.'

Miles' heart plummeted again. He should have known better. Geoff wasn't a boy who would capitulate while there was still a chance of winning.

As Miles hesitated it was Geoff who led the way towards the next obstacle. It was one which Miles hadn't seen but which had been described by Geoff as, 'Dead easy – you just run up a grassy slope, a bit like a ramp, on to the top of a brick wall, then jump off into a sandy trench. Easy, 'cos it's such a soft landing.'

Staggered by his friend's show of renewed energy, Miles followed him at a slower pace. Geoff reached the top of the slope almost before Miles was at the foot.

The leader paused, yelled, 'Here we go!' – then vanished.

Miles was still struggling up the incline when he heard a terrible cry of pain.

Eight

Miles stood on the parapet, peering down into the dark. Vaguely, he could make out something white but couldn't tell what it was. After that one anguished cry, there was no sound from Geoff.

'Geoff, are you down there? Geoff, what's happened? Geoff?'

'Of course I'm here! God, the pain's awful. I've smashed my leg up.'

Geoff's voice was surprisingly close at hand and, after the silence, it startled Miles. His first thought was to jump down beside Geoff.

'Some stupid idiot's filled the trench up with rubbish,' Geoff was calling. It's all over the place. God, I really think I've broken it. Get down here quick, Miles, but watch out where you're going.'

Hurriedly, Miles retreated down the slope and went round the side of the wall. As far as he could tell the trench was full of tree branches, some of them very solid indeed. Gingerly, he made his way to where Geoff was lying.

'Don't move!' he said warningly as Geoff struggled into a sitting position, still clutching his leg just below the knee. He was biting his lip hard and for a moment didn't answer when Miles asked where the pain was.

The question had hardly been necessary. There was a long, jagged rip in the trouser leg of the track suit and blood was oozing from a gash just under the knee. But, to Miles, it didn't look as though the bone was broken.

'We've got to stop the bleeding, that's the first thing,' said Miles, kneeling beside him and reaching into his pocket for a handkerchief. 'I'll tie—'

'Go and get my pack,' Geoff interrupted him. 'I've got a medical kit in there.'

Miles was astonished, and his reaction was visible.

'I brought it for you. I thought you'd be sure to need it,' muttered Geoff. 'Now, go and get it before I bleed to death!'

Skirting the two obstacles on which they'd expended so much time and energy, Miles dashed back to their starting point and grabbed Geoff's pack and the torch which lay beside it. In his experience Geoff had always told the truth and so he really must have carried the first aid kit for Miles' benefit. Yet, in spite of his careful planning, Geoff had failed to check whether the landing zone under the wall was free of danger. Miles knew that, for once, he himself had been very lucky. If he'd jumped first . . .

'It's still bleeding,' the victim greeted him on his return. 'So do something quick.'

Miles cleaned the wound with cotton-wool and then smeared it liberally with antiseptic cream. Apart from wincing and biting his lip Geoff bore the treatment stoically. In such poor light it was hard to tell how shocked he was by the incident but Miles thought he looked whiter than usual. He was thankful his friend hadn't fainted. He'd known other boys do that when they'd seen the extent of their injuries.

'You'd have no trouble getting a job as a medical orderly,' Geoff murmured as Miles started to apply a dressing.

'Oh no, I'd be a top surgeon at least!' Miles grinned.

He was aware that Geoff had started to shiver again, quite fiercely this time, and he knew it was essential to get him into a warm atmosphere as soon as possible.

'Hey, how about some of that hot chocolate?' he suggested. 'We could both do with a drink.'

As he rummaged in the pack he came across something that felt like a pocket watch. But when he drew it out he saw that it was a compass. Well, at least that was one thing they didn't need.

Gratefully they both sipped at the chocolate and presently Geoff admitted that he was beginning to feel a little warmer. But, he added, the pain was still as bad.

'Do you think you'll be able to walk – with my help, I mean?' Miles inquired.

'I'll have to, won't I?' was Geoff's grim reply. 'There's no phone for miles so we can't ring for help. This would happen just when I was winning the race. I'd've won by a street.'

Miles ignored that. He recognized that his rival now needed some consolation.

'Well, we'd better get started, Geoff. Otherwise if your leg starts to stiffen up you may not be able to use it at all. Come on, I'll help you up.'

'Ouch!' yelled Geoff when he made his first attempt to put weight on his injured leg. But for Miles' supporting arm he'd have slumped to the ground again. 'Oh God, it's worse than I thought. I'll have to lie down again.'

'No you won't,' Miles told him sharply. 'That's no good. We've got to start moving.

You can't stay here much longer. It's getting colder for one thing.'

He didn't mention it but it seemed to him that it was also getting darker by the minute. The moon was disappearing behind a cloud formation – or was that mist coming down? Suddenly, Miles began to feel very alarmed; but it was important not to communicate that to his friend.

With one shoulder supporting Geoff's rucksack and the other Geoff himself, Miles only managed to stagger for the first few steps. Geoff was a complete dead weight but, of course, he could do little to help himself. Eventually, Miles adjusted his stride to cope with the situation.

There was no longer any doubt about it. A mist was descending on the moors and accounting for some of the chill in the air. So they might need that compass after all.

'How's it feel now?' he asked so that he could think of something else.

'Rotten. No better at all. I feel a bit sick as well.'

'Well, don't be sick down me if you can help it – I've got enough to support as it is,' Miles joked.

Luckily, they were going downhill in the direction of the lane that would eventually lead them back to the bus stop. Though, Miles feared, it was hardly likely that buses were still running past that spot.

The journey to the lane was a nightmare. Several times they both stumbled and each time, as his foot touched the ground, Geoff let out a yelp of pain.

'I can't go on, I can't,' he cried. 'It's sheer agony, Miles.'

'We've got to keep going,' was the determined answer. 'We've had it if we don't. This mist's getting thicker.'

They staggered on. Miles, crushed by Geoff's weight and thoughts of what might happen to them, often felt like giving up, too. Never had he felt so exhausted; not even in some of his worst illnesses. Every part of him was aching. But he wouldn't relent. His will-power didn't weaken. Even his mother had more than once told him that he possessed real determination to see things through. He kept thinking, too, of what Dave Rosborough had told him about his physical fitness. That was like a bright light that led him on irresistibly.

At last, after what seemed like hours, they entered the lane. Geoff suddenly sagged against him and muttered, 'Let's have a rest now. I must sit down for a bit.'

Miles thought it could be fatal to stop now

but he, too, needed a breather. He refused, though, to allow Geoff to lie on the ground, which was bound to be damp. Instead, he propped him against the drystone wall.

'Look,' Geoff said a few moments later, 'we just can't go on like this. You must be shattered – and my leg's just about killing me. We've got to get help, fast. It'll take ages for both of us to get down to the road. So you go ahead and get somebody to rescue us. Stop the first car you see. Or, better still, find a phone box. Ring somebody to come and fetch us.'

'I'm not leaving you, Geoff!' Miles was appalled by that idea.

'You must! Get to a phone quick, that's the best thing.'

'You mean the police – ambulance . . .'

'No, not them! My folks'll murder me if I get involved with the police, or get them involved rather. Don't ring my home, either. They mustn't know I've been up here. I've been warned off this place umpteen times. When we get home we can say the accident happened somewhere else. What about your parents? Your Dad'd fetch us, wouldn't he?'

'No, not them either!' That suggestion was even more appalling. 'But I'll have to get somebody who'll come quickly. But – but who?'

For a moment or two there was silence.

Then, exasperatedly, Geoff snapped, 'Look, you're supposed to be a newspaper editor. So you should have a load of ideas.'

'Oh! Oh, yes, *of course*. She'll help, I know she will. Oh God, I just hope she's in when I ring.'

'Who d'you mean?'

'Mrs Jenks! My – er – you know, that secretary girl who types the stories for me.'

'Good. Well, go on, go and get her, Miles.'

Still Miles hesitated. 'Okay, but look, Geoff, don't move from here for heaven's sake. If you got lost in this mist we might never find you. So—'

'I won't move because I can't. So get going. And leave the pack with me. I think there's still some chocolate in that flask.'

Miles began to run down the lane. It didn't occur to him that it was almost a miracle that he had energy enough to walk let alone run after what he'd just endured. He was thinking about Mrs Jenks, praying that she wouldn't let him down. She never had, and that was everything. All the same, everything now depended on her being at home. If she wasn't he would simply have to phone his parents and tell them where he was. There'd be no alternative.

Once, on the way down, he stumbled and banged his knee. That made him think of

Geoff and his plight and so resolve to take more care. It would be utter disaster if both of them were injured and unable to walk.

When, with heart-thumping relief, he reached the main road it seemed to him that the mist had lifted a little. But it was eerily quiet. Not a sound of any kind. He paused, wondering which direction to take for he'd no idea where he might find the nearest phone box. Up here on the moors, call boxes would be well spaced out. That seemed crazy to him. There should be *more* telephones in isolated places because that's where they were vital.

He turned left, the direction from which they'd come on the bus – a million years ago that seemed now. He alternated his pace between a fast walk and jogging, continually glancing over his shoulder in hope of seeing the lights of a vehicle.

Then, distantly, he heard the noise of a car engine somewhere behind him. Miles stepped into the middle of the road. It didn't matter how fast it was going, he had to stop it.

The blur of yellow lights came nearer and grew brighter. Miles held his arms wide and, to his intense relief, the car slowed and pulled sharply into the side of the road. Miles dashed forward as, cranking down the window, the driver called, 'What's up?'

When he learned that Miles was asking for a lift to the nearest phone box the driver, a middle-aged man wearing a tweed cap and a scowl, looked even more dubious. He wanted to know who was to be telephoned and why and what Miles was doing out on his own at this time of night in the middle of nowhere; he kept glancing over his shoulder as if expecting someone else suddenly to appear at one of the car's windows. Despairingly, Miles tried to explain that his friend had injured a leg, was immobilized and that they needed to summon a friend, a lady who would know how to cope with the situation.

'Is this lady a nurse?' asked the driver, beginning to sound helpful.

'Oh no!' Miles said, and immediately wished he'd answered differently.

The driver gave him a long look and then, grudgingly, said that Miles could get into the front seat. 'But behave yourself or you won't get very far,' he added to Miles' amazement.

As it was, they'd travelled only a few hundred metres when the headlights picked out a very modern-looking telephone box. At once, the driver braked hard to a halt.

'There you are then,' he said in a tone of triumph mixed with assumed cordiality. 'Hop out. Goodnight.'

Miles barely had time to close the door before the car was speeding away again. He didn't dwell on the strangeness of the driver's attitude; he was just thankful that he wouldn't have far to walk back to where Geoff was lying when he'd made the call to Mrs Jenks. All he could hope now was that she was at home. What he'd do if she wasn't he dare not think.

'Please answer, oh please answer,' he prayed as he listened to the dialling tone. He was so apprehensive he almost dropped the coin he was waiting to push into the slot. It wasn't the cold that was causing him to shiver.

And then he heard her voice. He rammed in the money.

'Mrs Jenks? This is Miles Hansen. I'm at Daleside with Geoff Leyland and he's had an accident and we need your help right away and . . .'

She was marvellous, not interrupting once until he'd completed his story. As always she was the perfect editor's secretary. Afterwards Miles thought it was wonderful that she hadn't suggested (as surely anyone else would have done) that his and Geoff's parents be contacted immediately. But then she was well aware of what Mrs Hansen's reaction would be. Instead, she said it was lucky that she had a friend visiting her and so they could come straight away in his car. All she asked for were precise details of where the boys were so that no time should be lost in locating them.

'Go back to Geoff and help to keep him as warm as possible, Miles. And yourself, too. Don't worry about anything. We'll be there in a flash.'

It took a little longer than that and Geoff, who had found that his leg wouldn't bend at all, had begun to complain bitterly that Miles had done the wrong thing: he should have rung for an ambulance. By now Geoff had forgotten that he'd vetoed that course of action. Miles had insisted that they should try to get closer to the main road to save time. In reality, he feared that Geoff's condition would be aggravated by his remaining motionless in the cold of the lane. So, for some distance, Miles struggled along, supporting Geoff almost to the extent of carrying him. He didn't think about the effort involved; he knew that, very soon, they would be on their way home by car.

Distantly, they heard it arriving. 'Thanks for what you've done, Miles,' Geoff murmured. 'You've been great. I'll never forget it.'

'This is Brian Alton,' was how Mrs Jenks introduced the man with her and he looked rather amused by something until he saw the exhaustion on Geoff's face. Then, without another moment's delay, he gently hoisted Geoff on to his shoulder and assured him that the worst was over.

After that, it seemed to Miles that everything happened with astonishing speed. Mr Alton, it turned out, was an occasional rally driver and he now drove like one. Miles heard him whisper something to Mrs Jenks about the risk of suffering from exposure and he gathered that they were heading straight for hospital.

'But we didn't want to go *there*,' he tried to

protest. 'They'll find out about what we've been doing and we'll be in real trouble, with everybody. That's why I rang you, because you could handle everything on your own and keep it secret!'

'Miles, that's very sweet and flattering of you,' Mrs Jenks smiled. 'But you know – *you*, especially, must know – that health comes first. We've got to check that Geoff doesn't need any further medical help. You've obviously performed miracles but . . .'

It occurred to Miles that he could have asked the man in the tweed cap to take Geoff to hospital. He supposed that would have been the sensible thing to do. So, if Geoff was worse because of the delay, he, Miles, would be the one to blame. And then . . .

The heater was on in the car and Miles was just too drowsy to think about any more implications of their visit to the Army assault course. He was too weary even to keep his eyes open.

Someone was shaking him gently but persistently by the shoulder. He murmured crossly, 'Stop it. I'm asleep.'

'I know, old son, but if you'll just wake up for a minute or two you can then go back to sleep for as long as you like,' a friendly male voice was telling him.

He opened his eyes and saw a man in a white coat. Miles sat up at once. He knew exactly where he was. He was in hospital again. Then he caught sight of someone else: Mrs Jenks. She was smiling warmly at him.

'Miles,' she said softly, 'you're a hero. Dr Grant here has just said so. He just wants to tell you that himself.'

Miles blinked disbelievingly. But the man in the white coat was nodding genially.

'You've been fantastic, old son, fantastic. And the amazing thing is, it doesn't seem to have taken much out of you. Miles, my boy, you're not only tall for your age, you're strong for your age as well. And that's rare, believe me. So you're very, very lucky.'

'And we've got that in writing, Miles,' Mrs Jenks said with a laugh. 'While you were having a nap Dr Grant examined you pretty thoroughly and when I told him about – well, told him about your mother's views – he said he'd be happy to put his findings on paper. So you've got an A1 fitness certificate to prove it!'

'Can I go home now, then?' Miles asked.

'Just as soon as I've finished my check-up now that you're awake,' replied Dr Grant; and willingly Miles submitted himself to the stethoscope and tappings and gentle pressures. The doctor's radiant approval wasn't dimmed by anything.

'What about Geoff?' Miles asked diffidently. Were they saying nothing about him because . . .

'Ah, well, he's been lucky, too – thanks to you,' said Dr Grant. 'But we're keeping him in here for a day or so, just as a precaution, you understand. After all, he did get knocked about a bit and we want to make sure he really is quite sound. You can pop in and see him tomorrow, if you like. I'll be glad to have a chat with you myself. But now I think it's time you went off home to bed. Mr Alton here is going to be your chauffeur again.'

'It's my privilege,' Brian Alton added.

They were almost at the door when suddenly Miles remembered something.

'You've got that note, haven't you?' he asked Mrs Jenks anxiously.

'Certainly have, Miles!' she replied, and held up a white envelope.

'Great,' he said happily.

Nine

One week later Miles was sitting at his desk in his bedroom checking through the news items and stories that would appear in the next edition of *Soccer Special*. One particular article was worrying him. He wished that he could leave it out but he'd given the writer a firm promise that it would appear, and Miles didn't go back on his promises. A responsible Editor always kept his word.

The story was to be date-lined 'Moorlands Hospital, Monday' and was scheduled to appear under the by-line of Geoff Leyland.

It began: 'Miles Hansen saved my life last night. We were having a race over the old Army assault course at Daleside in the dark. When I fell into some junk after jumping . . .'

Miles shook his head. That wouldn't do at all. The story was melodramatic; worse still, it wasn't factually accurate. So it would have to be corrected *and* toned down. Very firmly, he crossed out the first sentence.

Geoff had remained in hospital for twenty-four hours and, apart from his injured leg, had emerged from their escapade without ill-effects. He had written the article while still in bed and pleaded for it to be published. 'After all,' he'd pointed out, 'it *is* news. There must be a lot of rumours flying about and this article will give the facts about what really happened.' So Miles, determined as ever to present the truth about everything, consented to print it; though, of course, as Editor, he had the right to revise any contribution to the paper.

After making one or two further amendments to the article Miles put it on the pile of material that was ready for the printer. He was looking forward to visiting Mrs Jenks later that afternoon, not least because she'd invited him to stay for tea. Brian Alton would be there too, and, Mrs Jenks had hinted, there was every likelihood that he would become a regular customer of *Soccer Special*.

Miles turned his thoughts to that morning's match and the report he was about to write. It had attracted a larger crowd than usual and, to his joyous amazement, among the spectators had been his parents. For his mother was now quite reconciled to the idea of his playing soccer regularly. It was, of course, that medical report from Dr Grant that had done the trick. Dr Grant, too, was going to become a regular reader of *Soccer Special* because he would receive complimentary copies from the grateful Editor.

The fans had enjoyed a brilliant match with plenty of goals to cheer, though Miles himself hadn't let in even one. He'd enjoyed that success almost as much as the other gift from Geoff, which, in the interests of sheer accuracy, simply had to be mentioned.

Miles took a clean sheet of paper and began

to write the match report: 'Wakeley Wanderers had a brilliant 5–0 victory over Craydon Juniors in their vital Sunday League match. Johnnie Evett scored a hat-trick. In the absence of the injured Geoff Leyland, Wanderers were captained for the first time by Miles Hansen.'